#HOTANDHANDY

LYNNE HANCOCK PEARSON

ISBN: 979-8-9853527-6-4

Published by All That Editing LLC

This story takes place on the ancestral lands of the Coast Salish. I honor, with gratitude, the land, and its people.

Editing by: wordsmithalchemy.weebly.com

Proofreading & formatting by: TAFKAM

Cover art by: Designwheelgraphics.com

Visit the author at www.lynnehancockpearson.com

PREFACE

I wrote *#HotAndHandy* to determine whether I could write a novel from start to finish. It went through the complete editing process before I stuffed it in a drawer and wrote another book.

I dusted it off in the spring of 2024, realizing it was time for Vincent and Hilary to have their time in the sun. I hope you think so too.

Lynne

CHAPTER 1

*V*incent watched the thin, gray-haired woman climb into her car. His landlady, Iris, waved as the small, red Prius backed down the driveway. When the car was out of sight, Iris danced her way into the house. With someone else close by, someone close to her own age, hopefully Iris would leave him alone. He loved the support she and his mom gave him, but God, it was frustrating being unable to support himself.

His phone rang. This was the call he'd been waiting for. Heart racing, he wiped his hands on his jeans and let out a breath before answering, "Vincent here."

Twenty seconds later, it was all he could do not to throw the phone against the wall. There was no money to replace it.

He took three deep breaths. Each breath was accompanied by a positive thought. He had a family. He had somewhere to live. He was out of jail. He just wanted to add a fourth positive: having a job.

This wasn't how it was supposed to be. He was thirty. At this point, he should have his own construction business and a string of successful projects behind him. Not a prison record. Not a history of temporary jobs that barely paid minimum wage. Not living in his mother's best friend's garden shed. Shit. How would he earn the money to pay for his contractor's insurance? The worst part was telling his mom he had been turned down again. Wanting to put things off for a bit, he headed over to see Iris.

After two quick knocks, he entered the lower half of Iris's house.

Beaming, she scurried toward him.

He stuffed his hands in his pockets and propped a hip against the side of the kitchen counter. "Things go well?"

She hugged him, then twirled away. "Yes! She didn't question the cost. Doesn't have pets or stipulations and is ready to move in next week."

"Sounds too good to be true. She must be an axe murderer." Vincent hid a smile behind his frown.

Whirling back, Iris pushed against his shoulder. "Oh, God, I hope not! I don't want to interview another prospective tenant." A year after being widowed, she'd decided her split-level home was too big for her but didn't want to move away. She and Vincent collaborated on a renovation design to create an apartment on each level. He did the construction work, and Iris now lived in the lower level.

Laughing, he turned to make his exit.

"Have you heard back from the contractor?"

His back stiffened. "Yeah. They have all the help they need right now. They'll, um, call if there's an opening."

"Their loss." Iris laid a tentative hand on his shoulder.

Shrugging, he pushed open the door.

"Oh!" she called. "The new tenant asked if I knew anyone who could help her move in. She'll pay them, of course."

Vincent sighed, though not loud enough for Iris to hear. He tossed a smile over his shoulder. "Sure. Let me know where and when. I'll pencil her into my schedule." With a wave, he headed across the backyard to his refuge: the garden shed.

*D*etermined to be pleasant to a mousy old lady, he approached the driveway where Iris and the new tenant stood watching the moving pod being delivered. "Good morning."

The two gray-haired women turned his way...and there the similarity ended. Tongue-tied, he stood and stared as introductions were made. The too-slim woman named Hilary surprised him. Devoid of makeup and jewelry, the gray hair was the only thing that made her look older. Dark slashes of eyebrows above green eyes added color to her smooth, pale complexion. She stood tall with the erect posture of a dancer and a smile that didn't quite meet her eyes. He took her outstretched hand, aware of his calluses against the cool smoothness of her slender fingers. Of its own accord, his hand squeezed hers, then he dropped it like a hot potato. Cheeks heating up with mortification, he caught her wide-eyed gaze and the slight flare of her nostrils before she turned away, stammering out a quiet hello. They watched the pod being unloaded while Iris nattered away.

When the truck left, she turned to them. "Well, you two have fun unloading this." Iris disappeared into her house.

"Where do you—"

"I think we should—"

Vincent dipped his chin toward Hilary. "You go first."

Cheeks slightly reddening, she tucked a curl behind her ear. "I think we should start with the big stuff."

Two hours later, one-third of the meticulously packed storage pod had been emptied of the labeled, neatly stacked, organized-by-room boxes. As well as the larger pieces of furniture. She was stronger than she appeared. It wasn't like he had gone all he-man, but she easily kept up with his pace and muscled around the bigger pieces requiring two people without complaint, without dropping anything, or without calling attention to his clumsiness.

Because, for the third time, Vincent dropped his end of the hutch. Hilary arched an eyebrow but didn't say a thing. In fact, she'd barely spoken since Iris introduced them. What the hell was wrong with him? He was years younger, four inches taller, and at least fifty pounds heavier. Yet he was the one bobbling, jockeying, and fumbling like a middle school boy with a crush. So much for looking cool. This quiet woman in baggy clothes was his undoing. So far, he'd broken a lamp and dropped a suitcase on the stairs, which then popped open, spilling brightly colored panties and camisoles all over.

Pulling her ringing phone from her back pocket, Hilary looked at him in silent question. She moved to the back lawn at his nod to take the call. Thank Christ. Vincent wiped his sweaty hands down the front of his jeans. He thought about his least favorite prison guard to distract himself from catching her scent on the breeze sifting through her curls. The one who ate onions with every meal and apparently didn't own a toothbrush. The memory worked. *Until* he looked at Hilary, wondering what color lingerie she wore under the shapeless jeans and sweatshirt.

"Fine. I'll be there in half an hour." Ending the call and stuffing her phone into the back pocket of her jeans, she returned quickly, huffing as she lifted her end of the heavy furniture. Vincent picked up his end, and they carried it up the stairs leading to the back deck and into the dining area.

Hilary stood and stretched, one hand on the small of her back. "I have to take off. The sprinkler system went off in my office, and I need to assess the damage." She walked to the sink and bent over to drink from the tap as the glassware had yet to be unpacked. "I don't know how long I'll be. Will you be available this afternoon?" She took another drink.

"Yeah. I'm around." Standing with his hands propped on

his hips, he stared at the roundness of her pert backside until she stood and pivoted toward him. He could practically hear the gears grinding. She leaned against the sink, drumming her fingers on the countertop as she stared into space, paying no attention to him at all.

She pulled her hoodie over her head, revealing a baggy, faded, long-sleeved T-shirt, and ran her hands through curls that sprang up around her face. "Good. I'll lock up the pod, and we'll finish when I get back."

"I can unload as much as I can while you're gone, if you want." The words emerged without thought. What was it about this woman that compelled him to help her? She certainly wasn't helpless; she'd proven that this morning.

He didn't have much to offer but was certainly built for heavy lifting. He watched her gaze as it traveled over him, taking in the clean, white, well-worn T-shirt covering his broad shoulders. He knew what he looked like, wasn't self-conscious, but didn't preen. Her gaze traveled down his firm chest and flat stomach. Hoping to disguise the impact she made on him, he shoved his hands in his front pockets. Her glance skittered away when it hit the buttons of his jeans, and she moved quickly to the sliding glass door.

"If you don't mind, that would be great," she said over her shoulder as she started down the stairs. "Just put the boxes in the appropriate room, and I'll take care of unpacking."

She stopped on the bottom step and turned back, unaware he was right behind her. Caught off balance, she gasped and reached for the railing. He was quicker and grabbed her by the shoulders. They froze, Hilary's wary green eyes colliding with his own. Once she had a firm grasp on the railing, Vincent smiled crookedly and released her. She continued to stare at him, so he took the time to take in her features, the dimple in her chin, the faint lines around her eyes, the full, soft lips on a wide mouth. They were still gazing at each other when Iris interrupted.

"How's it going?" She kept talking as Hilary stepped away from Vincent and moved to stand beside the open pod. "I've made a pot of coffee. Help yourselves, and there are cookies on the counter." She walked over to the pod and peered into the container as if eager for a glimpse into Hilary's life. "My, aren't you organized. Writing the contents on each box would never have occurred to me. That will make unpacking so much easier for you."

"The unpacking will have to wait for a while. I have to head over to the college to clean up a mess." Hilary stepped around Iris and squeezed past Vincent, unaware that he leaned forward to take in the scent of lemon and lavender following her.

"Is there something I can do?" Iris called after her, but Hilary had already carried a lamp into the house. So Iris followed Vincent into the pod, where he stooped to pick up a heavy box. "What happened at the college?"

He shrugged. "Something about the sprinklers going off in her office."

"I wonder if there was a fire." Iris's eyes went round. "I'll check the Keeney community Facebook page." She bustled off into her part of the house.

Alone with his thoughts, Vincent continued to haul boxes up the stairs, stacking them in the living room. He had to get it together. He would be seeing the woman often, maybe on a daily basis. It wouldn't do for her to think he wanted to get into her pants. He rounded a corner and bumped into Hilary again. This time *he* was startled and swore softly as he bobbled the box he was carrying.

"Sorry about that," she murmured, avoiding his eyes.

He gave her a lopsided smile and placed the box on top of the others. She'd changed into black yoga pants and an over-sized loose gray V-neck sweater and was fastening a gold hoop earring to her right ear. He looked from her to her belongings. What a contrast. Why would a woman who bought her furniture in bright, bold colors dress as if she were trying to disappear? But it wasn't his business. She was a successful professional, and he was an ex-con. They just happened to be neighbors.

"Can I get your number?"

Hilary cocked her head to the side.

Vincent rolled his lips between his teeth. "So I can contact you in case I have a question about your stuff." He looked at her in expectation.

"Oh, right." A soft pink stained her cheeks as she reeled off her number, and he tapped it into his phone.

"Thanks. Umm…do you want mine?" He didn't realize he was holding his breath until she pulled out her own phone and nodded.

After unloading more of the pod, he knew a little more about the careful, quiet woman who would be his neighbor. Delivery labels on new kitchen appliances had an Olympia address, and when a lid came off a banker's box, he saw files marked MEDICAL EXPENSES and DIVORCE. They were none of his damn business, so he replaced the lid and put the box in its designated location.

So far, he'd carried ten boxes of books into one of the smaller bedrooms. Three were non-fiction. He longed to open the seven boxes of fiction. What was she into? Historical? Political thrillers? Maybe romance novels featuring half-naked men on the front. Those were the books his mother read. As if conjuring her out of thin air, he heard his mother's voice.

"Vincent? Where are you?" Marcia Ortiz nosily peeked into each room she passed.

"Ma, what are you doing here? You can't just walk in; this isn't Iris's house anymore. It belongs to her tenant."

She waved away her son's protests. "I brought you some lunch. I didn't want to yell because that would be impolite."

As if *trespassing* was polite. "Thanks, Ma." He bent to kiss the tiny woman on the cheek.

She gave him a quick, fierce hug and backed off. "Come, I've only got an hour. It's downstairs. We'll eat with Iris."

His mother worked from home, handling the billing for a number of doctors. She set her own hours and did fairly well for herself. She and Vincent shared a meal at least once a week. The cost of meatloaf sandwiches and lasagna was filling his mother in on the details of his life. Rather intrusive to a man of thirty, but he didn't feel like he had a choice. Without her help, he'd still be in jail.

"Where did you apply this week?"

Holding up a finger, Vincent chewed a delicious piece of homemade calzone and swallowed it before answering. "I applied online to Starbucks, Home Depot, and the Garden Center."

Like she was following a tennis match, Iris moved her head back and forth, watching Marcia grill him. He stayed with his mother when he was first released from prison, but her hovering nature wore thin. Fortunately, Iris stepped in to save him. In exchange for doing yard work and converting the garden shed into a tiny house, she offered him a clean, quiet place to stay and all the food he could eat without charge.

Her husband, Darryl, died when Vincent had been in prison and was unable to attend the funeral. To make up for Iris's generosity, Vincent happily took care of the little repairs that accumulated in the year since Darryl's death. The washing machine no longer vibrated in the spin cycle, the bathroom door opened without squeaking, and the dead flies had been cleaned out of the light fixtures.

When Iris decided to renovate her home to take in a tenant, the tiny house plans were put on hold in favor of the renovation plans. Asking Vincent to do the work was a huge leap of faith for which he would be forever grateful.

Iris was loading the dishwasher when she spoke, "Vincent, can you fix dishwashers?"

He nodded.

"Garage door openers?"

He nodded again.

"What about door locks?"

Vincent nodded again. "Why?"

Marcia shot a quizzical look at Iris. "What are you thinking about?"

"I'm thinking about Lois Johnson, Char Floyd, and Virginia Smith." Closing the dishwasher, she leaned back against the counter.

"What about them?" Marcia asked.

"Lois's dishwasher hasn't worked in six months. Char's garage door opener turns on the television, and Virginia has to use her back door because there's a key broken off in her front door." Iris gazed at Vincent, a small smile on her face. She sat back down at the table, folding her hands before her. "They need work done. Vincent is looking for work."

Marcia shook her head. "The reason they haven't had the work completed is because they're too cheap to pay someone to do it. And Vincent can't work for free."

"True, but he could certainly work for good reviews posted on social media."

"Huh," his mom responded, sitting back and crossing her arms.

He took his dirty dishes to the sink, rinsed them, and added them to the dishwasher. Both women were eyeing him with matching smiles when he turned back. "What?"

"How do you feel about going into the handyman business?" Iris asked.

"Setting up my own business? I don't know if I can do that with a record. Besides, who'd hire me?" Turned down by every contractor he'd applied to, the dream of starting his own business was beginning to seem like that—a dream.

"I would, or more precisely, Keeney Building Supply would." A gleam entered her eye, and she waggled her eyebrows.

Iris and Darryl started a small building supplies store shortly after marrying thirty-five years ago. Darryl took care of the day-to-day running while Iris did the bookkeeping in a tiny office in the back of the store. Something she continued to do after their son Eddie was born. The business succeeded, but Darryl's ambitions were not big, so he and Iris never expanded beyond the one store in downtown Keeney. They made enough money to support themselves, put Eddie through college, and build a nice retirement fund for when the time was right. But fate stepped in, and Darryl developed colon cancer. While he went through treatments, Eddie took over the business. After Darryl's death, Iris retreated from KBS; too much of her life centered around it.

Vincent could see she was ready to get back to work. She missed her small office, she missed working with numbers, and she missed feeling useful. She was beaming. He was frowning.

What would it be like to work at KBS? For a time, his mother worked there, and Vincent spent countless hours roaming the store, hunting down supplies, ogling the power tools, and developing a love for building things. He'd liked the purpose of the place. Closing his eyes, he could smell the combination of lumber, oil, and burnt popcorn. But to work there? Without Darryl and *with* Eddie? Somehow, he didn't think it would be smooth sailing. Eddie had made life difficult for Vincent while growing up. And while he had not seen him in almost four years, he doubted Eddie had changed.

CHAPTER 2

*H*ilary pulled into the driveway with a sigh. The water damage in her office hadn't been too bad, but assessing the property for damage and getting a crew to do cleanup took two hours. What saved her from a tension headache were the texts from Vincent. He'd moved the desk into the apartment and placed it under a bedroom window. Then he took a photo of it and sent it to her with a question mark. She'd texted back a happy face. This was the routine for any piece of furniture that did not have an obvious location. The photo of her printer in the bathtub made her smile. And the last picture of an empty pod made her respond with an applause GIF. She hadn't known what to expect when Iris suggested he help her and went into the day hoping they'd complete the job with minimum fuss. His sense of humor was a nice bonus.

Yanking down the visor to access the mirror on the back, she applied lipstick and fluffed her hair, grimacing at her reflection. Makeup wasn't going to help; she still looked like a forty-year-old woman. A forty-year-old woman who was about to spend time with a much younger, hot guy. A much younger, hot guy who made her heart go pitter-pat. She and

David had been together for twelve years. When he left her, she thought she'd never feel this awkward, tongue-tied sensation again.

It had been so long since she had chatted with an attractive man. Did she still know how to do it? She hadn't spoken to Vincent for fear of saying something stupid like offering to wipe his sweat off with her tongue. Perhaps they should just send GIFs to each other.

Grimacing again, she shoved the car door open. She had one hundred dollars in her back pocket and carried two six-packs—one of Pepsi and the other of a local microbrew—which she had every intention of sharing.

Music played in the apartment. Closing the door, she looked around with a satisfied smile. The furniture was exactly where she wanted it. Small appliances were lined up on the counter, and boxes of kitchen goods stood on the peninsula separating the kitchen from the dining area. She placed the six-packs in the fridge and followed the music to her bedroom.

Vincent was muscling the mattress into place and singing along to Bon Jovi. If you could call it that. It wasn't the worst she'd ever heard, but she hoped karaoke wasn't his favorite pastime. That would be painful. Leaning against the door frame, she took a moment to admire the way his butt filled out his jeans. Two perfect globes begging to be squeezed. Her divorce was finalized more than a year ago, and the last time she'd had sex was…she could not count that high.

She took in the boxes stacked against the walls, labels facing outward, just the way she had organized them in the pod. Clasping her hands so they wouldn't go wandering uninvited, she cleared her throat. "You've gotten so much done."

Vincent jumped. "God, woman! I'm gonna have to put a bell on you."

"Sorry about that." She grinned. "I'll be sure to stomp next time."

"Do that!" he replied with a scowl that was chased away by a twitch of his lips.

With a slight bounce and a quick nod, she said, "Thanks for assembling the bed."

He stretched, loosening the muscles in his back. "Not a problem. Do you want help unpacking? I can do the books for you."

"Are you a reader?"

"I am. I'll read just about anything, but I prefer historical fiction when I have a choice." He stood with his hands on his hips, smiling easily.

"That's an odd way to put it."

"I assume Iris told you I'd been in prison?" He continued at her nod, "We didn't have the greatest library, and the pickings were sometimes slim. I was like a kid in a candy store when I walked into the Keeney Library."

"I can see that." Look at her, talking to the hot guy without drooling all over him. Inwardly, she gave herself a high five. "I have some Mary Stewart and Ivan Doig. Have you read any Dick Francis? I have all of his books."

Vincent's eyebrows came together. "Horse racing mysteries, right?"

Unpacking the books was way down on her priority list, but she'd move it to the top if it meant spending more time with him.

"There's some drinks..." Hilary stopped speaking when she spotted the trunk. The lid was ajar, and the corner of a quilt peeked out. With three quick steps, she crossed the room and snapped open the lid, stiffening when she saw the photo album. Her heart sank, and she whirled around to glare at Vincent.

"You went through my things? Is this why you were so eager to help when I was gone? So you could pry?" She yanked the money out of her pocket and thrust it at him. "Here. You're done for the day."

Wide-eyed, Vincent opened his mouth. Then closed it and shook his head. Dropping tools into the metal box on the floor, he slammed the lid shut with a clang. With quick, jerky movements, he shut down his cellphone and shoved it in his pocket. It was a moment before he reached out to take the money. He returned her glare and made his way out of the silent apartment.

She moved to the trunk and retrieved the photo album when she heard the door close. It opened to a page of vacation photos of her younger self with David. On a beach, holding up tropical drinks and smiling at the camera from lounge chairs. She was pressed against David, breasts practically falling out of the bright yellow bikini. She slammed the album shut and buried it beneath the quilt.

With a jagged exhale, she studied the boxes neatly stacked against the walls. She could pick them up, stuff them back into the pod and leave. And go…where? Back to Olympia? Back to familiar faces and places, for sure. But also back to loss and pain and sadness. Olympia was where cancer had caused the loss of her breasts, her inability to bear children, and eventually, her marriage. No, Olympia was not an option. Her parents had passed, and her only sibling, a brother, lived in Maryland, so she didn't have any close connections anywhere.

She slumped onto the trunk and rubbed a hand across her chest, feeling the mastectomy scars through the fabric of her shirt and staring at the bed. The mattress was stacked neatly atop the box spring. The nightstands were nestled against each side. Her eyes drifted toward the boxes once more. The box on top of one stack was labeled BEDDING. The one next to it said BEDROOM LAMPS. She snorted. Vincent might be nosy, but he was organized. She pushed herself up and set about making her bed.

Throwing a ball of wadded-up newspaper against the wall wasn't satisfying, so she tried slamming a cupboard door. But her nosy handyman neighbor had installed cupboard doors with hinges that refused to slam. Sighing, Hilary pulled out a glass and filled it with water from the kitchen sink. Big mistake. Through the window, she could see Vincent stomping back and forth across the yard from the garden shed to the garage. He looked pissed. He should look guilty. He should be in hiding.

Righteous anger had fueled her drive to unpack the boxes in the kitchen. Dishes, pots, pans, and cooking supplies were now stored in their new homes. The only thing left was to flatten the boxes and take them to the recycle container beside Iris's garage. She checked the window again. Vincent wasn't in sight, so she gathered up the cardboard and newspaper and headed down the stairs.

Closing the lid to the recycle bin, Hilary looked up at the sound of a car. She wanted to head back into the house but figured ignoring her landlady would be rude, so she waited for Iris. The older woman parked in the garage, taking forever to retrieve her belongings and exit the car. Hilary glanced over her shoulder, hoping Vincent wouldn't appear.

"How's it going?" Iris emerged, squinting against the sunshine, a bright smile on her face.

Hilary gave a one-shouldered shrug and dredged up a smile of her own. "Almost done. A few boxes to unpack still."

Iris peeked into the empty pod and clapped her hands. "It's empty! Isn't Vincent wonderful? He's such a good worker."

Hilary hummed in agreement, not trusting herself to speak.

"Can I give you a hand?" Iris turned for the stairs.

"No!"

Iris started.

Hilary blew out a breath. "Sorry." She sidled around Iris and stopped two steps above her, effectively blocking her path. "It's been a long day, and I want a chance to settle in."

"Okay," Iris said slowly.

A noise caught their attention, and they looked over to see Vincent using a crowbar to take apart an old potting bench. Hilary huffed, then stomped up the stairs and disappeared into the house.

The bathroom was the perfect place for covert observations. Of course, that meant standing in the bathtub in order to peer out the window, but needs must. She wasn't able to hear the conversation, but she watched anyway.

The wood from the potting bench wasn't going to be of any use if Vincent kept up his attack on it. Iris stopped well out of the distance of flying splinters. He tossed the crowbar to the ground, gesturing at the house. Iris covered her mouth with her hand and moved like she was going to the house. He snagged her arm and shook his head. Shoulders slumped, she turned back toward him. Hands on hips, he stared over her head at the garage wall while she spoke. It seemed to work because the rigidity left his posture, and he reached into a pocket to thrust something at Iris. She backed up and shook her head. He tried again, but whatever Iris said had him shoving it back into his pocket. He bent over and retrieved the crowbar. As Iris walked away, he started to pick up the pieces of wood strewn around him and stack them neatly in a pile.

Hilary climbed out of the bathtub and went into the kitchen. She made herself busy filling up the kettle to make tea, expecting to hear a knock from Iris any moment. It never came. She opened the fridge and stared at the beer inside. She didn't like beer. She glanced over her shoulder at the man working in the yard.

What had he seen? What must he think of her? Had she

overreacted? No. He'd invaded her privacy like he had a right to do so. She was definitely not going to lend him any of her books!

The small painting was of a lone gnarled tree on a cliffside with a swirling ocean in the background. She'd forgotten about it. She'd forgotten she once displayed her work proudly. She'd forgotten creating art had once been her passion. About to store it in the back bedroom, a knock sounded. The problem with having French doors as your entrance was that you couldn't hide from unwanted visitors.

Iris stood hunched over a plate of cookies, a sheepish look on her face. "Don't be mad at Vincent," she said, thrusting the cookies at Hilary when she opened the door. "It must have been an accident."

Hilary accepted the plate and set it on the counter. "I know you two are close, but I will not have my privacy intruded upon."

"What do you mean?"

"What do *you* mean?"

Iris shifted from one foot to the other. "Didn't he break something?"

"I don't think so." Hilary crossed her arms over her chest and leaned against the counter. "Did he say that he broke something?"

"Didn't he?"

"Did he?" Hilary shook her head. "I'm confused. Come in."

Closing the door behind her, Iris silently switched her gaze from where Hilary stood in the kitchen plugging in the teakettle to the living area where an open box sat on the coffee table, colorful pillows and a crocheted afghan poking out of it.

"Is it strange seeing someone else's belongings in your

house?" Hilary asked, pulling mismatched mugs out of the cabinet.

Iris looked to be in her late sixties, with soft gray hair, soft features, and a soft belly. She'd told Hilary that she hadn't wanted to leave her house, but it was too big for her, which led to the decision to renovate.

Taking a tentative step forward, Iris agreed, "Yes. But without the wall between the kitchen and the living room, it looks so different. The hardwood flooring and the pale yellow paint, it doesn't look like my house at all. So...it's good."

The kettle boiled, and Hilary set about making the tea. With two steaming mugs in her hand, she froze when she saw Iris holding the painting. She willed herself to relax and put a mug on the table. Iris smiled, placed the painting down before picking up her tea, and followed Hilary to the seating area.

Both women sat, their stiff postures negating the coziness of the scene. Hilary took the initiative in order to forestall questions.

"Why do you think Vincent broke something?"

Iris sipped her tea and threw a tense glance at her. "He didn't say so, but when I asked him how it went, he grunted at me and stomped off. Vincent has been accused of things but is a good, honest boy. He would not have taken anything." When they'd signed the rental agreement, Iris had told Hilary that she believed he'd been wrongfully accused.

Her concern for Vincent was palpable. But Hilary was too tired to care what was at the root of it. She shook her head dismissively. "Nothing is missing, and nothing is broken. He did go snooping, though, and I snapped at him."

"Snooping?" Iris frowned, and then her face cleared, "Oh! The photo album."

"What do you know about the photo album? Did he show it to you?" Hilary left Olympia to make a new start. To get away from gossip and false concern. Was Keeney going to be the same thing?

Shaking her head vehemently, Iris spoke in a rush, "Don't blame Vincent, it was my fault. It was…there was a quilt sticking out of the trunk, and I opened the trunk to tuck it back in." She leaned forward to touch Hilary's hand. "The photo album caught my eye, but I never opened it."

Was she telling the truth, or was she covering for Vincent?

Hilary didn't know Iris well enough to answer the question. However, her distress was obvious and Hilary wanted to believe her. Which meant Hilary had snapped at Vincent without reason. Dismissing that uncomfortable thought for the moment, she said, "I haven't been a tenant in a long time and have never been in a place where I lived so close to the owner. And I know this is new to you."

Iris nodded.

"Can we agree that no one will enter my home without my approval? You won't let anyone in here without my say-so?" She softened her request with a slight smile.

Iris nodded again with big, serious eyes.

"Good," Hilary said, rising from the couch. Iris rose as well and took her half-finished tea to the counter. "Thanks for stopping by and clearing things up."

Iris moved to open the door, looking both relaxed and tense at the same time. "Do you want me to talk to Vincent?"

"No, that's fine, thank you though. Good night," she replied and watched Iris walk down the stairs. Blowing out her breath in a big gust, she dumped the two mugs of tea in the sink and stared broodily out the window at the yard slowly coming alive after a long winter.

April was not a kind month in Western Washington. Days were normally wet, soggy, and uninviting. The backyard of Iris's home was no exception. Tall evergreens ringed the property, sagging under the weight of wet branches. There were bare deciduous trees that would be lovely in a few weeks' time but now looked sad and lonely. A vegetable garden in the right-hand corner was awaiting preparation for planting. The only evidence that rebirth was coming was the smell of sawdust emanating from the old garden shed.

The four places she'd looked at before finding Iris's were cramped and dark. None with access to the outdoors. Living above the landlady wasn't ideal, but the trees and back deck sold her. She figured she could get outside, and if the garden shed dweller wasn't too much of a troll, the place might be quite peaceful. Then she'd spotted Vincent hauling something from the garden shed.

She had no idea what he was carrying because she was fixed on him from the top of his head, covered in curly, blue-black hair, over bunched tan biceps, and corded forearms, past washboard abs and narrow hips peeking over low-slung jeans which clung to muscular thighs. When he turned and bent to drop his load, his perfect butt came into view, and her knees gave out. Seeing him every day would not be a hardship.

Working with him today hadn't been a hardship, either. It was enjoyable until she assumed the worst, jumped to conclusions, and didn't bother to hear his side of the story. Seeing a light come on in the little house on the other side of the yard, an unpleasant tingle that felt suspiciously like guilt assailed her, and she kicked herself for misjudging him.

CHAPTER 3

Vincent stepped inside Keeney Building Supply after taking a fortifying breath. It had only taken Iris a couple weeks to follow through on her idea. Now, for the first time since returning from jail, he entered KBS by the front doors. While working on Iris's house, he'd used the loading dock to pick up supplies. The place still smelled the same, a combination of fresh lumber, a sharp metallic tang, and burnt popcorn. A smile pulled at the corner of his mouth when he spotted the old popcorn machine beside the customer service desk. A small bagful was handed out to customers, free for the asking. He couldn't wait to help himself to a bag.

Angling toward the back of the store, he eyed the changes that had occurred over the years. The paint section was gone, replaced by a large selection of indoor and outdoor lighting. One aisle contained samples of doors, and another was dedicated to toilets and bidets. He snorted. Bidets in Keeney, go figure.

This early in the morning, the place was quiet. A couple of employees stocking shelves looked up at him as he passed, and he was glad to be wearing the T-shirt Iris had given him.

It was gray, with Keeney Building Supply in large red letters on the back and KBS on the upper left side of the front. Beneath the letters, in smaller font, was his name—Vincent. He lifted his chin at the employees without speaking and moved confidently to the stairs centered in the rear wall.

Four doors opened off the small landing at the top of the stairs. The employee breakroom contained a utilitarian table and eight folding chairs and smelled like stale coffee. One wall was taken up by a small kitchen, complete with a dishwasher, sink, refrigerator, and microwave. A heavy-duty coffee maker sat on the counter, and KBS mugs were hung on hooks under the upper cupboards. Two rows of five small lockers covered another wall. Each had a combination lock and was labeled with an employee's name. The one on the far-left side had his name. He walked over to the coffeemaker, found a mug labeled Vincent, and poured himself a cup. Taking it with him, he checked out the other rooms.

Next door to the breakroom was the restroom.

The third door opened to a small office, but it was empty. It held filing cabinets, a desk, and a desktop computer. Like the breakroom, the far wall was an expanse of windows overlooking the floor of the store.

The last door stood open. Unlike the other rooms, it was far from utilitarian. The floor was carpeted in a deep pile, the dark green color matching the drapes framing the windows. The desk was big, dark, and obviously expensive. Facing it were two club chairs upholstered in burgundy leather. Framed prints of local landmarks hung on the walls. He took everything in before locating Iris, dwarfed by the imposing office chair she occupied.

"Dammit!" She smacked her hand on the desk.

"Trouble?" he asked from the doorway.

She looked up, her frown disappearing as she stood.

"Look at you! Do you like the shirt?" She came around the

desk to admire him. The soft cotton molded to his form, the sleeves clinging to his biceps.

"It beats the hell out of an orange jumpsuit. And I like the mug." He held it up in a salute.

Laughing, Iris patted him on the arm. "What do you know about computer passwords?"

He pushed off from the door jamb and followed her behind the desk. "Some. What's the problem?"

"Eddie was supposed to leave the new password for me before he went on vacation and forgot."

Vincent managed to stop himself from rolling his eyes or snorting. Like Eddie forgot. "Did he leave it on a piece of paper somewhere?" he asked instead, eyes scanning the huge expanse of desk. "Maybe in his planner?"

"I didn't look." She picked up the leather portfolio sitting on the corner and turned to the first page. "Here it is. Can you read it out to me? His writing is tiny."

He read out the password, then closed the book and placed it back on the desk.

"In. Thanks." Iris smiled up at him. "I'm surprised it was that easy."

"Most people have too many passwords to memorize, so they write them down."

"I get that," Iris said. "I'm surprised he left his planner here. It normally goes with him everywhere. He keeps track of everything in there."

He made a noncommittal sound. Eddie McLeod had never been his favorite person. While their mothers were the best of friends, he and Eddie barely got along. They didn't fight, but he felt Eddie looked down on him. After high school, he'd gone off to college and completed an MBA in California. It seemed he stayed away as long as possible, finally returning to Keeney when Darryl got sick. KBS became his domain, and he was quick to put his stamp on it, including an office that rivaled any hotshot CEO.

"Are you ready for your first solo job?" Iris asked from her perch on the imposing office chair.

With a quick nod, he pulled some papers from his back pocket and spread them on the desk. Iris and Marcia had accompanied him to each of the repair jobs. All three clients were reluctant at first but thrilled in the end, insisting that Marcia take a photo of them with him, which they posted on their Facebook pages.

Today's client was a member of Iris's church. Fiercely independent, Judy Crawford wanted modifications made to her home so she would not need to move into senior housing. She wanted drawers installed in her lower cabinets.

Kneeling to save Iris from craning her neck to look at him, he replied, "It shouldn't take long. I took the measurements yesterday and will do the install today."

"Oh, good. Bless her heart, she can barely bend with those arthritic knees of hers. Are the cabinets the same as the ones you did for me?" She followed the design with a finger.

"Yeah. I showed her the video Mom took, and she was excited."

Iris nudged his arm. "Your mom is a marketing genius. I'm glad she took all those pictures and videos."

He rolled his eyes but smiled all the same. "Don't tell her that, her head is big enough already."

Iris laughed and led the way out of the office.

"Do you want me to lock the door?"

She stopped and glanced over her shoulder. "Just log me out of the computer."

"Got it." He did as requested, then clomped down the stairs after her, his heavy work boots loud in the narrow space.

"Do you have a shopping list?" she asked, heading for the front of the store.

With two long strides, he caught up with her before she reached the first aisle and gave her a handwritten list. "On the bottom are the tools I'm going to need, and I don't already own myself."

Stepping behind the customer service desk, she stopped next to a balding, pot-bellied man with Ali printed on his shirt. Ali smiled down at Iris and acknowledged Vincent's presence with a nod. A KBS employee for more than twenty years, Ali worked his way up from stocking shelves to store manager. He thumped Vincent on the shoulder. "I knew you'd be working here eventually. You're a builder with talent. Iris hiring you will be good for KBS and give you great experience."

The praise from Ali felt good. He and Darryl were father figures when Vincent was younger. From them, he learned how to handle power tools, how to select wood for a project, and to never cut corners. Thrilled to work with the older man, he tipped his head in acknowledgment.

"From now on, I want you to email Ali your list in advance." Iris switched her gaze between the two men. She was in her natural element, clearly pleased to have a new purpose at KBS. "He'll enter it into the store's computer, and when you get here, the items will be waiting for you on the loading dock as well as an invoice for you to give to the client. Soon, I'll get you set up to access the store computer so you can enter the order yourself."

Clearing his throat, Ali shot Vincent an apologetic look, pulled Iris aside, and spoke in a whisper still loud enough for him to hear. "Eddie didn't tell me to give Vincent access to the computer."

Tensing, Vincent turned and busied himself with his phone. He glanced up when Iris harrumphed.

She glared at Ali over her glasses and didn't bother to lower her voice when she replied, "Vincent is a KBS employee. He will have the same access and privileges as *all* our employees. Do you have a problem with that?"

Ali shook his head. "No, ma'am, I'm just repeating

instructions." He cleared his throat again. "How 'bout I show Vincent how to enter an order?"

The ringtone from a cellphone came from Ali's shirt pocket. Ali grabbed the phone and frowned. "It's Eddie." He turned away to take the call.

Iris motioned Vincent over and started to explain the computer program. Ali thrust the phone at her. "Eddie wants to talk to you."

Stepping away from the computer, Iris took the proffered phone. "Hi Honey, how's Vegas? Have a good flight? I can barely hear you; I'm putting you on speaker." She fiddled with the phone and then laid it on the counter.

For the first time in four years, Vincent heard Eddie's voice.

"Mom, you can't send an ex-con to a client's house. They'll freak out."

Vincent went stiff. He clenched his fists at his sides and stared at the floor.

Iris gasped. "How can you say that? You know Vincent didn't—"

"He has a record for a reason! He'll probably make off with the supplies and sell them."

Glancing up, Vincent saw the look of horror on Iris's face. Ali wasn't as easy to read. His lips thinned, eyes narrowing, as they moved between Vincent and the phone.

"That is nonsense! Vincent is an honest man and a great employee." Iris's face was red when she glanced at Vincent.

"Please tell me you haven't made him a full-time employee. We talked about this. I know Marcia has been crying on your shoulder, and your heart is in the right place. But he's stringing you along. That greasy wetback will ruin KBS."

At this point, Iris took the phone off speaker, pressed it against her ear, and scuttled away from the counter. Vincent's shoulders slumped as he watched her. His father,

Ray Ortiz, was the only child of apple farmers in eastern Washington. He'd fallen for the raven-haired Marcia Fraser, a member of the Chelan tribe, when they were college seniors, and they'd married shortly after graduation.

"I always knew Eddie was an entitled asshole, but I didn't think he was a *racist* asshole." Ali stepped closer, bumping Vincent's elbow with his own.

Vincent looked at the older man in surprise.

Ali continued to watch Iris. "How the hell that piece of shit came from Iris and Darryl is beyond me."

Vincent remained silent. If he trash-talked with Ali, would it get back to Eddie? He and the older man had had many conversations but never about the McLeod family.

"I'm glad Iris is back. I hope she can rein in Eddie 'cause God knows he needs it."

Vincent frowned and turned toward Ali. "Why do you say that?"

"I can't quite put my finger on it, but things aren't quite right." It was Ali's turn to frown as he looked up at Vincent. "When Iris quit working to look after Darryl, Eddie changed the payroll system. Iris and I used to do payroll together, but Eddie's taken me completely out of the loop. And you've seen the office, right? God, it's like he thinks he's the CEO of Home Depot or something. He also insisted on having his own parking space with a sign that says, Reserved for E. McLeod in big letters. What an ass." Ali shook his head.

Iris's return put an end to the conversation. Red-faced, her lips had all but disappeared. Her former confident demeanor had all but disappeared as well. She moved behind the counter and busied herself at the computer, not looking at Vincent.

"Eddie and I decided we would hire an assistant for you. The assistant will take care of materials and equipment so you can concentrate on the design and build."

Eyebrows drawing together, Vincent said, "I don't need an assistant. They'll just get in the way."

"No, no," Iris cut him off. "It will be better this way. Ali, there's that new kid working part-time, see if he wants to work with Vincent." Iris grabbed a bunch of papers, calling over her shoulder as she hurried to the back of the store, "I'll call today's client and reschedule for later this week."

Vincent balled up a fist and banged it on the counter, swearing at Eddie under his breath.

Stepping forward, Ali grabbed his hand and squeezed. "It sucks that Eddie is in charge, but this is a golden opportunity for you. Don't blow it. You need KBS, and KBS could use you." He flicked his glance at Iris's departing back.

Pulling back, he ran a hand through his hair and glowered at the older man. Ali was right, Vincent couldn't afford to lose his temper. He saw concern and care in Ali's eyes. Gusting out a sigh, he nodded. "Right. I'll see you soon."

"What are you doing?"

Vincent answered his mother without looking up from the lawn mower, "I'm fixing the choke."

"Why? And why aren't you over at Judy Crawford's house?"

Not getting an answer, she marched down the stairs from the back door of her house and pulled the screwdriver out of his hand.

"Hey, I need that." He scowled up at her.

"And I need an answer," she said, glaring at him.

He rose slowly from where he crouched beside the lawn mower and made to wipe his hands down the front of his jeans. She swatted them out of the way and handed him the tea towel from over her shoulder.

"Iris rescheduled it for later in the week," he responded, concentrating on wiping his hands.

"Did something happen to Judy?" Marcia asked, crossing her arms and planting her feet wide as if preparing for a long conversation.

He regretted showing up at her house. He was too old to go crying to his mother, and wasn't that exactly what he was doing? Shuffling his feet in the wet grass and knowing she would not let it go, he heaved a sigh and looked straight at her. "Eddie convinced Iris I can't be trusted. Someone has to go with me so I don't rob the client or steal supplies." When would his time in jail no longer haunt him? When would he be seen for who he was, not where he'd been?

"Seriously?"

"Iris called it an assistant, but I know what a guard looks like." Humiliation hummed through his being.

Marcia blew out a breath. They rarely talked about his time behind bars. She'd traveled two hours each way every Sunday to see him for three years, always cheerful, always optimistic. When he found out she had taken out a loan to finance his legal appeal, he was both thankful for her faith in him and furious she'd needed to do it in the first place. Her generosity and dogged determination meant an early release for him but a delayed retirement for her. Paying her back was his number one priority despite her insistence that it wasn't necessary. To Vincent, it was. He'd do just about anything for her.

"Asshole."

His mouth quirked up. His mother never swore.

Marcia took the towel out of his hand and replaced it with the screwdriver. "Come in and eat. We need to talk."

Vincent trudged after her, not sure he liked the sounds of that.

When he returned from washing his hands, a plate heaped with empanadas sat on the table with a glass of milk beside it. His mouth quirked up again. God, he loved his mother. She busied herself at the sink as he made quick work of the first empanada.

"It's no secret Eddie is Iris's weak spot. The scrapes she's bailed him out of..."

"What scrapes?" Eddie had always been a shit, but as far as Vincent knew, he'd never gotten into serious trouble.

Marcia glanced at him. "Don't you remember the time he got arrested for possession of marijuana?"

Vincent's eyes bugged out. "Seriously?"

Shaking her head, she explained, "That must have been when you were in Australia. The amount he had was just enough for him to be charged with intent to sell. He claimed he was innocent and that it wasn't his marijuana, but Iris and Darryl had to hire a very expensive lawyer who managed to get him off."

Vincent sat back in the kitchen chair and crossed his arms. "Why don't I know about this?"

Marcia shrugged as she came to get Vincent's empty plate. "It happened down in Portland. Most of Keeney didn't know about it. And those of us who did, didn't talk about it. We didn't want to hurt Iris and Darryl." That made sense. Both Iris and Darryl were loved and well-respected in the community.

Returning to the table, she sat down, running her finger along the table's edge, teasing a small chip in the surface. Her gaze rested on Vincent, but he knew her eyes were really looking beyond him. "When you and Eddie were small, I wanted you to be close. But no matter how many times we got together, you two just didn't click. Did he ever...hurt you?"

Vincent pulled back in surprise. What did that mean? As close as he and Marcia were, they didn't go deep. Instead of giving a quick denial, he leaned forward and stilled his mother's restless hands. "I knew he didn't like me, hated having to share his toys with me, and ignored me at school. But I was okay with that, my world was bigger than Eddie McLeod. I wasn't interested in hanging out with him and his friends in high school, and I think that pissed him off." He stopped abruptly. His mother didn't need to know about Eddie's jeering remarks when Vincent ignored him. She also didn't need to know Vincent threatened to turn Eddie in for shaking down students for their lunch money. There was a lot of history between them neither Marcia nor Iris needed to know.

"I know he taunted you with his toys. I saw the way you looked when he got that BMX bike." She held up a hand when Vincent tried to protest. "I know you didn't want me to see it. You never asked for anything because you knew we didn't have the money. I think you wouldn't give Eddie the satisfaction of being envious. I think *that* pissed him off.

"I believe this business will take off, and when it does, you won't need KBS. You can have your own. But until it does, as much as it pains you, you have to keep your nose clean around Eddie. It will make it easier for Iris as well. Even though KBS is her business, she wants to prove to Eddie she makes valid contributions and is a vital part of its success."

Vincent crossed his arms and glared at Marcia. She was right, but Christ, he hated having his past thrown into his face. He couldn't hide his jail time, not in Keeney. He would just have to prove himself by his craftsmanship and work ethic. Getting up from the table, he kissed Marcia on the forehead and headed back outside. "Fine, I can do that. I sure hope they find me someone who knows their way around a hammer."

CHAPTER 4

Getting into a car using only her left hand wasn't easy. The sound of an engine drew her attention as Vincent pulled into the driveway, which was narrow at the entrance and then widened so that three cars could park abreast in front of the garage. It worked out that he always parked to the right, Hilary to the left, and Iris went straight up the middle and parked in the garage itself. Hilary angled her body so her back was to Vincent as he made his way to the tiny house.

She hadn't spoken to him since the day she'd moved in. After the visit from Iris, she thought about leaving the beer outside his door as a peace offering but hesitated for too long, and the window for the peace offering closed. She'd kicked herself for being stubborn, but speaking to that beautiful young man, let alone apologizing to him, was more than she could handle. It was best she stayed away from him. While she didn't speak to him, she knew his routine. She knew the sound of his vehicle. She knew he looked after Iris. She knew he filled out his jeans better than any man had a right to.

Throwing herself into her new job was a great distraction. Her colleagues at Keeney Community College welcomed her and seemed genuinely pleased to have her there. The job was more creative and less repetitive than managing a dental office. Her evenings she spent organizing her new home. Finding suitable places for her belongings and relishing a space that held no trace of her ex-husband. However, her gaze was repeatedly drawn to the small house across the yard, and she wished she hadn't been so quick to judge. When she'd finally unpacked her books, she'd unintentionally put together a pile for him. Now, they sat on a chair, mocking her every time she passed by. She'd get around to giving them to him one day.

Fortunately, he did not appear to be in the mood for small talk, as a chin lift was all he did to acknowledge her. Something must have caught his attention because he was beside her the next moment.

"What the hell happened?" Vincent stared at her right hand. Wrapped in a blood-soaked towel, Hilary held it upright as if she were pledging allegiance.

"Oh! Hey." She turned to face him. Attempting to shrug, she swayed instead. "It's no big deal. It's just a—"

"Don't you dare say flesh wound!" Vincent said as he clasped her by the right elbow and managed to liberate her car keys and propel her gently toward his truck. "How about I drive you to the urgent care."

"That's where I was going," she grumbled. Her stomach swooped as he helped her into the truck and buckled up the seat belt. She convinced herself it was because of blood loss and not the way he smelled, a combination of wood and leather that was distinctly his, or the look of concern on his handsome face.

"Wait here," he ordered and raced off to his place, leaving the truck door open.

"Do I have any choice?" Wincing, she closed her eyes and laid her head back against the headrest. Her day had started well; she'd finished a project at work, stopped at a produce stand, and was spiralizing a zucchini when her hand slipped, and her thumb made contact with the blade. The damn thing wouldn't stop bleeding. Now, she was being rescued by Vincent. Ugh. The embarrassment was worse than the throbbing pain.

The rustling of plastic made her open her eyes. Vincent was placing a grocery bag over her hand and wrapping it around her forearm. He then secured it with duct tape.

"Seriously?"

His mouth was tucked in at the corners like he was holding back a smile that could escape at any moment. "What? It's good enough for the astronauts, and I can't have you bleeding all over the company truck."

She smiled back at him. He was so close she could see a tiny circular scar above his right eyebrow. Chickenpox, maybe? Hilary ducked her head, knowing he was taking in the myriad of wrinkles on her own face. "I think that's good. Can we go?"

Vincent straightened. "Sure," he answered, his tone clipped.

They made the trip to the urgent care clinic in silence.

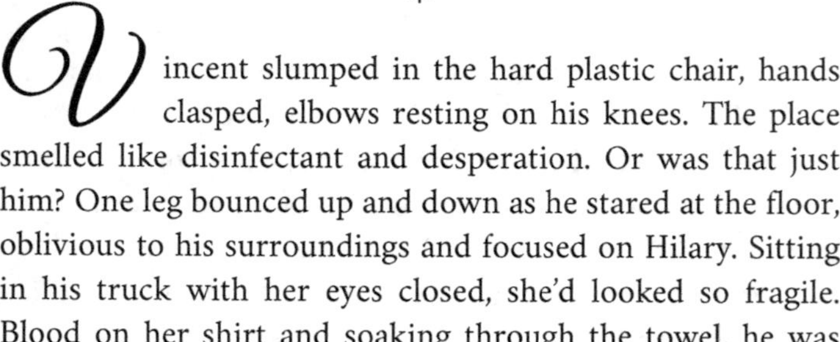

incent slumped in the hard plastic chair, hands clasped, elbows resting on his knees. The place smelled like disinfectant and desperation. Or was that just him? One leg bounced up and down as he stared at the floor, oblivious to his surroundings and focused on Hilary. Sitting in his truck with her eyes closed, she'd looked so fragile. Blood on her shirt and soaking through the towel, he was afraid she'd pass out. He was prepared to carry her into the clinic, but she brushed off his assistance, clearly not wanting him to touch her. But, oh, how he wanted to. Wrap his arms around her and keep her safe from whatever it was that scared her. Because she was scared of something. Why else did she hide in her house? And why else had she reacted so strongly to the photo album?

A pair of pink Crocs entered his line of sight. He looked up. It was the clinic's receptionist, holding a clipboard and smiling politely. "Mr. Banks? Your wife is almost done. I'll take you back to her."

Vincent looked at her in confusion before it dawned on him that she was talking about Hilary. He hadn't known her last name was Banks. He stood and wiped his hands down his pant legs. "She's not my wife. We're umm...neighbors."

"Oh!" The smile on the receptionist's face got bigger. "Well then, Mister...?"

"It's Ortiz. Vincent Ortiz." He met the receptionist's frank perusal as he made his way through the swinging doors leading into the clinic's exam area. Hilary sat on an exam table, cradling her right arm, hair a mass of messy curls, face lined with either exhaustion or pain. She looked up at his approach, the lips of her generous mouth pressed together in a thin line. "Thank you for waiting," she said softly, standing with slow, deliberate movements.

Vincent checked himself from rushing forward to assist her, not knowing how she would react, so he shoved his hands in his back pockets and shrugged. "No problem. Ready to go?"

She nodded and made to grab her purse but hissed when her bandaged hand hit the table. He snagged the purse handle with one hand and Hilary's elbow with the other. A zing went up his arm with the contact. Had she felt it, too? Because her mouth had rounded into an O, and her green eyes were wide as she looked up at him. He stood lost in their depths until the receptionist's voice broke through to him.

"I'll get the door for you," she said, shoulders slumped as she looked back and forth between Hilary and Vincent.

"Thank you," Vincent didn't let go of Hilary until she was safely in his truck.

CHAPTER 5

Vincent turned off the engine, and Hilary opened her eyes to find him watching her, his mouth curved into a one-sided smile. She looked away quickly and fumbled with her seat belt, only to hiss in pain. He reached over to undo the buckle and gently squeezed her right wrist. "You'll get used to it."

"I hope so," she grumbled. "This is frustrating."

"True. But it's a great story, and think of the scar you'll have."

Snorting, she turned entirely to the right to open the door with her left hand, only to find his body draped across hers as he opened the door to the truck. She sucked in a breath at the contact, and he drew back.

"Did I hurt you?" he asked, eyebrows drawn together.

She grimaced. He didn't need to know it was his proximity setting her off.

"Sorry about that. Wait there, and I'll help you out."

"No! Umm. I can do this. Thank you." She pushed the door open with her foot and slid out of the truck to find him there, ready to take her arm and close the door.

Hilary sighed. "Seriously, I'm fine. I appreciate your help, but I'm alright."

"Stop being a martyr, and let me help." He ignored her grunt of displeasure and continued to hold her arm as they ascended the stairs to her apartment. She scowled and grumbled until they made it to the top and were confronted by the open door and the trail of blood on the floor.

"Oh! I always lock the door."

Shaking his head, he led her through the doors, around the drops of blood, past the dining table, and eased her gently down onto the couch. She leaned her head against the cushions and closed her eyes, wanting him to leave her alone but secretly hoping he wouldn't. It was nice having someone take care of her.

Not saying a word, he moved quietly around the place, running water in the sink, opening cupboards. There was the hiss of a spray cleaner and the scent of bleach.

The tantalizing aroma of pizza awoke her. She was lying on her side, head on a pillow, covered by an afghan, shoes removed. Her stomach dipped. She couldn't remember taking off her shoes. A noise caught her attention. Vincent sat in the armchair reading the latest Louise Penny novel. She watched him for a moment. How long had she been out? With his legs stretched out in front of him, he seemed comfortable and relaxed, idly stroking his bottom lip with one long finger wrapped in a Snoopy bandage.

"What did you do to your finger?"

Vincent looked up at her voice. "Jammed it fixing my mom's lawnmower."

"She has Snoopy bandages?"

He chuckled. "She bought them by the caseload when I was a kid. I was an accident waiting to happen."

She should get up but was warm and comfortable, her thumb thrumming with a dull ache. And it was nice to have someone to talk to. Other than work and the grocery store, she rarely talked to anyone.

"There's some Okanagan Porch Banger wine in the fridge. Any chance I can convince you to pour me a glass?"

He raised an eyebrow at her and closed the book. "For medicinal purposes, I suppose?"

Smiling innocently, she pushed herself up, shifting around to prop her feet on the coffee table. "But of course."

As he went into the kitchen, she fluffed her hair as best she could and grimaced at her blood-stained shirt. No point in changing it now. Vincent had seen her at her worst. She hoped she hadn't drooled in her sleep.

A moment later, he returned, handing her a glass of white wine. She raised the glass to take a sip and realized he didn't have any. "Do you not drink wine?"

He stepped back and rubbed the back of his neck. "Didn't know if I was welcome."

"Of course you are," she said, getting up from the couch. She thrust the glass at him and pushed past to the kitchen. She grabbed another glass from the cupboard, the wine from the fridge, and turning, found Vincent leaning against the dining room table, his arms crossed, mouth in a thin line.

"What?"

Straightening up, he replied, "I wasn't sure if you would be able to do that."

Hilary put the wine bottle down and held up her thumb. It was wrapped in a dressing and covered with a rubber sheath. "They used some kind of super glue and then taped it. There aren't any stitches, so it's not too bad." She poured herself some wine and then took a sip. She held up her thumb again and studied it. "I didn't know they made condoms this small."

Vincent snorted and busied himself with the pizza on the table. He opened the lid, releasing a mouthwatering aroma of garlic, cheese, and tomato. "I figured you'd be hungry and not up to cooking. I wasn't sure what you would like, so I played it safe and ordered cheese."

"That was very kind. Thank you so much." About to offer payment, she stopped, somehow knowing that would ruin the evening.

A blush stole up his cheeks as he dipped his chin, not meeting her eyes.

She took a seat at the table, arching a brow in inquiry. He hesitated a moment, then sat across from her, his gaze bouncing around the room before landing on the painting of the tree on the wall behind her. It had initially hung in the dental office, and more than one person had commented on it, with a few asking if they could buy it. The receptionist later told Hilary that David was mad when he discovered she'd taken it. Which pleased her immensely, especially because patients remarked upon its absence.

"The initials HB are in the corner. Did you paint that?" Vincent asked.

"I did."

"Seriously? It's really good."

"Just good?" Angling for compliments wasn't something she usually did. It must be the wine.

"You're right. It's definitely more than good. Where do you paint?" He looked around the apartment. "The back bedroom?"

Her smile faltered. "I hadn't really thought about it. Possibly." It would require buying supplies. They'd been left behind or tossed aside. She couldn't remember because it had been so long since she'd wanted to paint. Maybe now that she was settled, though....

With open admiration on his face, he continued to study the painting. And she studied him. Bronze skin, thick dark hair, thick dark brows, and eyes so dark she couldn't tell if they were brown or black. What colors would she use to paint him?

"Do you only do landscapes?"

"Hmm?" She blinked. "Oh, yes. I know you work with wood. Iris told me you did the work in here and that you're starting your own business."

"That's the goal," he acknowledged with a tight smile. He sat back and indicated the printing on his shirt. "But right now, I'm a KBS employee."

She tore her gaze away from the broad expanse of his chest and caught the scowl on his face. "You don't sound pleased about that."

"Don't get me wrong, Iris is great." He toyed with the base of his wineglass.

"I'm sensing a 'but' there."

He gave her a lopsided smile. "Have you met her son?"

She shook her head. "No, but I've seen the photos, and she's gushed about him a lot."

He focused on the contents of his glass, appearing to be searching for words. Leaning forward, he said, "I'm not going to trash talk Eddie, but be careful around him. He doesn't take 'no' for an answer, especially from attractive women."

"I'll keep that in mind, but I doubt I need to worry." She waved a hand in dismissal.

Hilary's face heated as he continued to look at her with narrowed eyes. She crossed her arms self-consciously and met his gaze. His eyes did not waver. He wasn't assessing her body, which she knew was too thin and lacking in curves, he was seeing *her*. Something in her chest loosened, and a warmth spread through her.

Vincent's gaze softened, and his jaw relaxed. "Yeah, you do."

Not knowing how to respond, she pushed back from the table, forgetting about her injured thumb. "Ouch!"

He winced in sympathy. "I'll clean up." He rose from the table and picked up the plates.

"You've done enough already," she protested. "I'm really thankful for your help."

He reached for the bottle of wine, refilled her glass, and took it over to the coffee table. "Sit," he ordered.

"Fine," she huffed, moving toward the couch. Watching him move back and forth between the kitchen and the table, competent, confident, his big frame filling the small space, she searched for a safe topic of conversation. "Where did you learn your carpentry skills?"

"In prison."

The gulp of wine turned into a cough.

He poked his head from around the kitchen and grinned at her.

"Seriously?" she asked when she could breathe again.

He wiped off the table and nodded. "What do you want to know?"

What did she want to know? She knew the bare bones from Iris but hadn't bothered to dig further. Her heart told her this was a man who had been screwed over. Finally, she responded, "Whatever you want to tell me."

"I heard someone say, 'The road to hell is paved with good intentions.' That's pretty much what happened to me," he said, settling his butt against the counter edge. "I was in Australia on a ski trip and met these girls." He grinned at Hilary's snort. "Yeah. I was thinking with my dick. Ilsa and I hooked up, and I stayed with her and her sister Nadia for a while, then broke it off when I returned to Keeney. A few months later, they came here to ski and stayed with me. They were here for a few weeks, then Ilsa left to ski at Whistler. I'm not sure why Nadia didn't go with her. I was working and getting ready to go to school for a construction management program and didn't see much of her. Anyway, a couple days after she left, the cops were at the door in the middle of the night."

Hilary sat up straight, dropping her feet to the floor and concentrating on the man before her who refused to meet her eyes, staring at his feet instead.

"I had no clue why they were there. I was scared shitless and not cooperative. A cop shoved a search warrant in my face, then pushed me against the wall and held me there while two others tossed the place. The cops found a bunch of stolen shit—cell-phones, tablets—brand new, still in packages, in the bedroom Nadia and Ilsa had used. I just about passed out. I hadn't been in that room for a while and had no idea that stuff was there."

Eyes filled with frustration, bewilderment, and pain, Vincent finally looked at her. "Then the nightmare really started. Even in Keeney, spending a night in jail is scary. I called my mom." The knuckles on his hands whitened as he gripped the lip of the counter. "She bailed me out. A proud parent moment for sure. I was assigned a lawyer who couldn't tell the difference between his ass and a hole in the ground. That and a judge with a hard-on for brown people got me sentenced to seven years."

"Seven years? That's a long time."

He shrugged. "I only served three years. Ma took out a loan and got me a better lawyer who got the sentence reduced."

"Still. Three years."

"Yeah. But I completed the contracting program without having to pay for it."

She stared at the young man in front of her, imagining having three years of her life taken away and being able to look on the bright side. Clearing her throat, she said, "It must have been a good program. The cabinetry work is excellent."

He smiled slightly but stood tall. "Yeah, it is."

Fuzzy-headed but content, she finished her glass of wine

while he finished cleaning up the kitchen. His quiet presence was so calming she didn't feel self-conscious about her appearance or the fact he'd watched her sleep. She blurted out the words she'd held back since moving in. "I owe you an apology."

He turned, one eyebrow raised.

"Iris told me about the quilt and the trunk and the photo album. I should have apologized then, but I didn't know how and..."

"It's okay. You didn't know me, and privacy is important."

"Still..."

He smiled his acceptance and turned back around.

That was it? An unexpected warmth coursed through her at the thought that he wasn't going to hold a grudge. He was a much better person than she was. Sitting back, she shook her head and asked, "What has Eddie done to annoy you?"

Facing the sink and with the water running, it was possible he didn't hear her, but she saw him stiffen and remained silent as he finished the washing. He grabbed a tea towel and dried his hands while walking toward her.

"He thinks I need a watcher. Someone to make the clients feel safe and make sure I don't steal shit." There was more than a trace of bitterness in his voice.

"Does he not trust you, or is he trying to humiliate you?" Feet on the coffee table, the wineglass resting on her stomach, she watched as he all but choked the tea towel, the muscles in his forearms rigid with tension. If she were another woman, a bolder woman, she might lean forward, take his hand, and stroke the tension away. But she wasn't. She was Hilary, so she poked at him.

"Both."

"So, what are you going to do?"

Vincent flicked an irritated glance at her.

She waved her glass at him. "I've had two Tylenol with

codeine and most of a bottle of wine, your frowny face doesn't faze me right now."

Quirking an eyebrow, he sank into the chair. "I'll play nice. I need KBS, and Iris put a lot of effort into hiring me. I don't want to let her down." His attempt at nonchalance wasn't working, though his respect for Iris was clear.

"And you succeeding is the ultimate 'screw you' to Eddie." Hilary's words were beginning to slur.

Vincent's gaze moved over her, then a smile spread slowly. "I think it's time you headed off to bed."

Hilary shook her head, which was more like a sloppy nod. "Nope. I'm fine here."

He stood and took the wineglass from her hand, placing it on the coffee table. With care, he moved her feet to the floor and pulled her up from the couch. She fell against his chest and giggled. "If only I were a wee bit younger," she whispered, nuzzling against the softness of his T-shirt.

She was practically asleep on her feet as Vincent led her down the hallway. When they got to the bedroom, he hesitated before pulling down the covers, wondering if he should undress her. Deciding against it, he guided her into bed. While she nestled down on the pillow, he went to the bathroom, rustled through the medicine cabinet, and returned with a glass of water and a bottle of ibuprofen. He placed these on the bedside table and sat on the edge of the bed. Again, he watched her sleep and marveled at her beauty. Yes, her hair was gray, and there were lines on her face. But those testified to a life lived. Would she be willing to share that testimony with him? He hoped so.

He reached out to stroke her hair but stopped himself. Back in the living room, he folded the afghan, gathered the wineglasses, rinsed them in the sink, and turned out the lights, then stopped by the door. His eyes moved about the apartment, Hilary's space. Full of light and color, but something was missing. He stood still, eyes darting around. It wasn't long before he realized…the walls were covered with artwork, but there were no photographs. No pictures of loved ones. Curiosity and a touch of sadness hit him as he exited, ensuring the door was securely locked behind him.

CHAPTER 6

Finally, Vincent was finally back at the loading dock. He'd followed Ali around the store for three days, learning how the business had changed since he'd been away. Inside the store wasn't where he wanted to be, but the time had not been wasted. He learned that KBS did not have the lowest prices in town but prided itself on customer service. Every employee was expected to know the layout and contents of the store to quickly assist both builders and DIY homeowners. Adding contractors to their staff would enhance KBS's ability to compete against the big box hardware stores.

Many of the older employees were friendly enough, not shunning him, but there were no lingering conversations. Someone glanced up at the windows overlooking the store more than once as if expecting a reprimand for socializing. Iris and Darryl had reputations as generous employers. Things had definitely changed since Eddie came on board.

During those three days, he left early, returned late, and hadn't seen Hilary. However, the day after the trip to urgent care, a six-pack of beer was left on his doorstep. Attached was a sticky note with a bandaged thumbs-up drawn on it.

He happily stuck the note to his fridge, smiling every time he saw it.

With a skinny Black kid in tow, Ali approached the truck. Vincent closed the tailgate with a bang, tempted to pretend he didn't see them, climb into the truck, and take off. But that would get Ali into trouble, and Vincent wasn't one to pass the buck. So, he waited and watched. The kid looked like he was being led to his execution, eyes getting bigger, Adam's apple bobbing repeatedly as he and Ali got closer. Christ, was he *that* intimidating?

"Hey," Ali called out, a huge grin on his face. "I'd like you to meet Carl Gilbert. He's going to be working with you."

Vincent nodded at Carl and hoped he didn't groan out loud. The kid was tall, with big hands and feet. His shoulders held promise but now had all the shape and form of a coat hanger. He wore new, matching Dickies work pants and hoodie. He looked to weigh no more than one of Vincent's thighs. Carl ran a hand through his cropped, curly hair and surreptitiously wiped beads of sweat from his smooth, dark forehead.

"Do you have work gloves?" Vincent removed his own and held them up.

If possible, Carl's eyes got even bigger as he shook his head.

"A spare pair should be in the truck's glove box." He gestured to the front of the vehicle. "Check them out and see if they fit."

Carl nodded mutely and made a beeline to the passenger side door.

Turning to Ali, Vincent cocked his head to the side. "Seriously? This is my assistant? Did I piss you off, too?"

Ali wrapped a meaty arm around Vincent's shoulders, leading him away from the truck. "I seem to recall a pimply-faced, high school kid who made my life miserable, hanging around the store, getting in my way with a thousand questions. I believe this is called karma." He grinned up at Vincent. "Ain't it a bitch."

Vincent snorted and shoved Ali aside. "Asshole."

Ali was right. Vincent had followed him around the store, eager to do small jobs in exchange for scraps of wood and access to the big saws. Ali was patient, took the time to explain the qualities of different woods, and emphasized safety. Perhaps because he knew teenage boys never believed anything bad could happen to them. Vincent fingered a scar on the back of his left hand. A reminder of the need to always wear gloves. The memory made him look at Carl, who stood beside the truck clutching a pair.

"He's here on an internship from the college." Ali went to stand next to him. "He's taking the general contracting course and needs some experience. I figured he would learn a variety of skills from you." Ali stepped back to look at Carl. "Pay attention to Vincent. He's patient and precise. It may seem like he's being picky, but his clients don't complain about shoddy workmanship."

Vincent's face warmed; he knew he was good, but it was validating to hear it from Ali.

Ali clapped Carl on the back, who stumbled forward a few steps before catching himself.

Vincent climbed into the driver's side. Carl hesitated a moment before getting in and buckling himself into the passenger's seat. Ali grabbed the door and leaned in before Carl could close it. "There's a clipboard with a checklist on the dash. Fill it out, and return it to me at the end of the day. It's from Eddie, but don't sweat it." Ali leveled a look at Vincent. "Got me?"

He nodded, his mouth in a tight line, while Carl looked back and forth between the two men, clearly at a loss. Ali closed the door as Vincent started the truck, then he and Carl headed off on the job.

Noon approached, and they were just about finished

installing a retractable awning for a house. The job went both slower and faster than expected. Slower because Vincent explained each step: the choice of tools, the placement of supports, the installation of the electrical outlet. Faster because Carl was eager and attentive, handing tools to Vincent like a surgical nurse in an operating room. Carl barely said a word, but his stomach started talking. He looked away when Vincent glanced at him with a raised eyebrow.

Vincent gave the screwdriver one more twist before dropping it into the toolbox. "Lunchtime," he announced, removing his gloves and going to the truck to haul out a cooler roughly the size of a coffee table. His mother had bought it for him. Each morning, he stopped by her house and found the cooler on the table, filled with enough food to feed a small army. It wasn't his idea; he was quite capable of making his own lunch, but she insisted, and he was no dummy. There was more food than he could possibly eat, but his mom got pissed if he brought food home. So, he distributed leftovers to his coworkers. Perhaps it was his mother's way for him to make friends. Who knew? Each evening, he would drop the cooler off at the house and tell her about the day, sending her photos of the completed work. He dug his heels in at first, but she insisted. She explained that she wanted the pictures for a digital record of his work, a portfolio for when he had his own company. He hadn't thought that far ahead, so was grateful that she did. She joked that she was angling for a corner office. He'd give it to her, custom-making each piece of furniture that went into it.

He headed over to sit beneath a big maple tree and leaned against it. Carl hadn't moved from the deck of the house.

"Didn't you bring anything?"

The younger guy grimaced. "I've got cash. I thought we'd be stopping by a drive-thru or a store."

Flipping up the lid of the cooler, Vincent gestured inside. "Help yourself, there's more than enough."

Hesitating, Carl asked, "You sure?" At Vincent's nod, he quickly made his way over to the cooler and peeked inside. His eyes widened as if he were seeing the contents of Aladdin's cave of wonders.

"What can I say, Ma loves me." Vincent thrust a hoagie roll stuffed with salami and cheese at Carl.

Settling on the ground next to Vincent, Carl unwrapped the sandwich in a businesslike fashion and finished eating in four bites. Vincent reached into the cooler and handed another hoagie to him. Carl took it gratefully, this time taking the time to chew each bite. Vincent smiled to himself, remembering being a gawky, hungry teenager.

"Why do you want to go into construction?"

Carl shrugged and continued eating. After a few minutes of silence, he looked up to find Vincent staring at him. "Huh?"

"That was a question. It requires an answer." Vincent glowered.

Carl chewed more rapidly, then swallowed. "Um…it's good money?"

Vincent rolled his eyes. "Yeah, it is good money. But when someone asks you why you are interested in a job, you need a better answer than that."

Taking another bite, Carl chewed slowly and nodded his thanks as Vincent handed him a can of pop. "I like building things. I like working with wood. And I want to make things that will last a while."

Vincent grunted. "Not bad."

"Can I ask you a question?"

"Yep."

"Did you really go to prison?"

Vincent's hand tightened on his own can of pop, then slowly released. He should have known it was coming. Was it worth saying that his sentence had been reduced? Probably not. People were only interested in the fact that he'd served time, not that he'd had a crap lawyer or a racist judge. He could force a change in subject. Instead, he eyeballed Carl. He didn't look like he thought serving time made you a badass. So, he answered.

"Yep."

The kid slowly rolled the can between his hands. Vincent hated talking about being in jail, but he might as well get it over with. "What do you want to know?" He leveled a look at Carl.

Carl gulped audibly. "Were you scared?"

That wasn't the question he was expecting. Most people wanted to know if he'd seen any fights, if he had a prison tattoo, or what he did during the day. He had answers for those; yes, no, read. Scared? Vincent didn't want to go there, but he sensed there was a reason for Carl's question.

"For the first two months, I barely slept. I kept expecting something to happen. And when it did, I was relieved.

"I made a friend pretty quick by giving the guy the last brownie." He shot a wry grin at Carl. "The guy *was* a badass. I was bigger than him, but he had attitude and the fiercest scowl you've ever seen. He also had a serious sweet tooth. So when my mom would bring me cookies and stuff, I put them aside for Tomas." Vincent stretched his legs out in front of him, settling into his story. "This new kid arrived. A scrawny little thing, scared shitless and too dumb to hide it. He'd been there a day or two when I passed his cell. I looked in and saw an asshole had him backed into a corner while another guy was trashing the place. The kid's stuff had been tossed on the floor and trampled. The goon who was holding him was demanding money and threatening to break his fingers. The other goon was taking photos off the wall and methodically tearing them into little pieces. When the kid saw this, he pissed himself and started crying at the same time. The two assholes were laughing." Vincent shook his head slowly, unconsciously rubbing his left hand with his right.

"The goons were gangbangers and I knew they could make my life miserable. I'd started to walk away when I heard one of them say he was going to get some pliers. When he came out of the cell, I hit him so hard he went flying back into his asshole friend. Their heads banged together like in a Three Stooges movie. Next thing I know, they're out cold, the kid is collapsed in the corner, and my knuckles are bleeding. Then Tomas shows up. Looks around and leaves without saying a word. I figured I was screwed. It would be either solitary or an extended sentence. But before I could really panic, Tomas was back. He pushed me aside, and four guys came into the cell. They dragged out the two assholes, Tomas gave me a shirt to wrap around my hand, and then he started cleaning up the cell, all the while speaking quietly to the kid."

Carl shifted to face him. "So then what happened?"

Vincent shrugged. "Nothing. Someone must have spread the word because guys either gave me a wide berth or a high-five. Two days later, I found out I got into the contracting program. I think Tomas pulled some strings because the waitlist was six months long."

"And the kid?"

"Tomas told us both to eat our meals with him. The kid, I think his name was Kyle, kept his head down, served his time, and was out in six months." Vincent snorted. "Had himself a good lawyer."

Carl's mouth was open, ready to ask another question when Vincent rose and packed away the remainder of his lunch. He'd spent too much time thinking about the unfairness of it all. The difference between a good lawyer and a bad lawyer, and the impact on his life. He didn't want to brood, and he didn't want to take it out on Carl, who was just being curious. "This awning isn't going to hang itself. Let's go." He strode toward the house, wondering where

Tomas was. He should have gotten out by now. Vincent knew Tomas had both his and his mother's addresses and phone numbers.

He and Tomas had a plan. They would put in their time working for others, saving up until they had enough money to open their own home renovation business. Having a record wouldn't make it easy, but they were willing to work hard. With KBS behind them, it should go a little faster. But what was taking Tomas so long to reach out?

Offloading the truck, Vincent called out each item to Carl, who meticulously ticked them off on his clipboard. He then presented the clipboard to Vincent so he could sign on the bottom.

"Don't you need to go through the toolbox to make sure I didn't take a tape measure?" Vincent asked with a scowl on his face as Ali walked toward them.

Carl shook his head, refusing to meet Vincent's eyes, then scurried over to the loading dock desk.

"You requiring a minder won't last long. How'd he do?" Ali asked, nodding at Carl's retreating back.

Vincent drank deeply from his water bottle. "Green, but pays attention. He knows enough to measure twice and cut once. Doesn't know enough not to grab the wood before the saw has stopped moving."

Ali swore softly. "He seems to still have all his fingers."

They watched Carl veer out of the way of a KBS employee pushing a dolly loaded with lumber. Vincent shook his head and sighed. "He's got a lot to learn, but he's a good worker."

Ali scratched the back of his head and spoke over the loud beeping of a forklift backing up. "This may not be the best way to start, but an assistant will come in handy for you. You've got four more jobs lined up this week."

"Yeah? Cool." Vincent gave Ali a small smile and turned to leave.

"Pictures are showing up online of the work you've done for KBS." The older man gave him the side-eye. "Satisfied customers mean Eddie doesn't have a leg to stand on. He won't be able to get rid of you."

Vincent nodded his understanding, inwardly heaving a sigh of relief as he headed up to the breakroom. If things kept up, he'd be able to chip away at the loan his mom had taken out. He'd promised to do so the day he was released, and it bothered him that he'd given her very little so far.

He was sitting at the breakroom table with a fresh cup of coffee and a notebook when Carl joined him.

"What are you doing?" he asked, seemingly unaware of the sawdust clinging to his short, curly hair.

Vincent wrote a few more sentences in his notebook before looking up. "I take notes on each job. What materials were needed, the product brand, tools I used, tools I should have used, the time it took, anything unusual that came up..."

Carl sat down at the table. "Like what?"

Vincent snorted. "Like opening up a wall and finding a snake."

"No shit?" Carl's mouth dropped open.

"Didn't happen to me, but it happened. These notes help me prepare for jobs in the future. Later, I'll enter and save them into the KBS computer." Vincent had picked up the habit from his instructor in prison. A lot of the training consisted of work on the prison grounds itself. The buildings were old and in need of upgrading, but the state did not have the money for new construction materials, so old buildings were torn down and used as material for the new buildings. The general contracting program was put in place to educate the inmates and provide workers for the construction. Thus, Vincent's education had been on-site and varied. The lessons ranged from carefully tearing down walls to reuse the materials, to constructing compost bins from repurposed roofing materials.

Carl watched while Vincent continued to write in the notebook, his handwriting small and precise. "Why not make notes in your phone? Then you could upload them directly."

"I suppose. I didn't have a phone in prison. Now, writing in a notebook keeps me focused. Transferring the notes to the computer is another way to cement my thoughts in place." Vincent finished and looked up at Carl, one eyebrow cocked. "Also, this notebook can take a lot more beating on a job site than a cellphone."

"I'll um…pick one up after work." Carl cleared his throat and picked at a cuticle while he spoke. "Eddie told me I needed to be careful around you. That you'd learned stuff in prison and might try something on me."

Vincent froze while drinking his coffee. He placed the cup down on the table, not speaking as a muscle ticked in his jaw. Great, now he was a predator.

Carl looked up and shrugged. "You might be queer. I don't know. I just know I trust you more than I trust Eddie."

Vincent rubbed his temples and swore softly under his breath. "Eddie and I have history, and he doesn't want me here," he snapped. There was no way Carl was going to hear anything that could be used against Vincent.

"I get that, but I like working with you." One leg bounced up and down as Carl watched Vincent. "I umm…learned a lot today."

With a grunt, Vincent pushed back his chair and stood, placing his notebook and pen in his back pocket. He washed out his mug, hung it to dry, pushed the chair back in, and headed to the door.

"I'll see you in the morning. Remember to bring your gloves."

"Got it!" Carl smiled and slumped back in his chair.

Vincent stopped at the door. The day went a hell of a lot

better than he thought it would. Explaining things to the kid made him consider why exactly he did things the way he did. Solidified his thinking on some moves, and had him think about options on others. Twice, Carl pointed out steps where Vincent could save time by using a different tool. "Hey," Vincent called, making Carl's head jerk in his direction. "You were good today. I'm going to use your suggestion about the stud finder." Carl grinned, nodding. With an answering nod, Vincent left.

Hearing a huge exhale, he smiled as he descended the stairs.

Climbing into his truck, he pulled out his phone. He wanted to call Hilary. Tell her about the day. Tell her about Carl. But he hesitated. He was her neighbor, nothing more. He scrolled through his contacts, looking for Tomas. All he had was an email address. None of the emails he'd sent had been returned. He tossed the phone on the dash, put the truck into drive, and headed to his mother's house.

Word spread. With the help of social media, there was no lack of work. Ali told him that Eddie pestered Iris, but he could not give a valid reason for getting rid of Vincent. He was very good and very popular, allowing him to pick and choose his clients. He preferred small, custom jobs that would make the lives of senior citizens easier. He installed pull-out drawers in the lower cabinets of Yvonne Cho's house so she would not have to get down on arthritic knees to search through a cupboard. He added handrails along the hallway of Anisha Singh's house so she could move from room to room without her walker. And he built more than one bedside step stool for little old ladies whose beds had gotten taller as they got shorter. Having a "Vincent" in your home became a much sought-after item. Though grateful for the work he found through the senior center, he refused to be auctioned off at their spring fundraiser, much to his mother's dismay.

He got out of the truck and went around to get his tools out of the back. Iris had booked this client and sent him the information. Jeanne Barclay wanted him to install a new showerhead. It should be easy enough, even by himself. Carl was helping Ali do an inventory. Eddie was rarely at the store, so couldn't complain. Gathering his supplies, Vincent headed up the walkway to the tidy ranch house and rang the bell. While he waited, his gaze roamed over the statuary littering the yard. Apparently, Ms. Barclay had a thing for naked nymphs. The door opened, and Jessica Rabbit stood there. He gulped; this was not what he expected. He was used to gray-haired old ladies in kitten sweaters, not vamped-out women in kitten heels.

He pulled a business card from his shirt pocket and handed it to the woman. "Ms. Barclay? I'm Vincent. I'm here to fix your showerhead."

Jeanne Barclay shook back her shellacked hair and thrust her D-cups at him. "Oh, honey, I think you should check out *all* of my plumbing." She turned and strutted down the hallway. He heaved a sigh and followed her. It was going to be a long morning.

A burst of laughter greeted Hilary as she opened the door. She forced herself to have lunch in the staff breakroom at least three times a week. She would much rather heat up her lunch and eat at her desk while reading a novel, but knew getting along with her coworkers was important. They were nice enough and had invited her to meet up with them outside of work, but she held back. She wasn't up to sharing personal stuff. She was happy to learn about their lives, families, and histories but did not want to discuss her past. It was still too raw, the scars, both figurative and literal, were too fresh. To make up for it, she brought in cookies or a fruit tray on Fridays and joined them for lunch.

She was settling in nicely at Keeney College. Work was challenging because she'd always worked in office management despite having a degree in marketing. Shortly after marrying David, she took over the running of his dental office. Getting the job at the college so soon after the divorce was a godsend. She thanked social media for that. Scrolling through Facebook one day, she saw an old friend was changing jobs. Hilary reached out and, within a couple of weeks, was packing her bags for Keeney.

Sherry from Human Resources waved at her and glanced back at the phone in Dana's hand. "Show that last one again."

"What are you looking at?" Hilary asked as she opened the fridge and pulled out her lunch bag.

"Are you following #HotAndHandy?" Sherry spared her another glance.

Hilary shook her head and peered over Dana's shoulder. It took her a moment to realize what she was looking at. When she did, she nearly dropped her lunch. An incredibly busty woman had taken a selfie of herself with Vincent.

"I know, right!" Dana smirked. "That's my sister-in-law and the guy who works out of Keeney Building Supply. She had him in today to do some plumbing work."

"He can clean my pipes anytime." Sherry snickered.

The next photo was of Vincent's butt as he bent over his toolbox. Sherry and Dana giggled again.

"Umm…" Hilary stammered. "I have to take a conference call." She scurried back to her office and closed the door. Pulling out her phone, she logged on to Instagram and typed in #HotAndHandy. There were *many* photos of Vincent. Most of them were of him standing next to a beaming geriatric, with comments attesting to his great work. But five shots of him were dated today. All but the selfie appeared to be taken without his knowledge. Hilary's face flamed as she scrolled through them repeatedly. There was one of him standing in a bathtub, working on a shower head, gripping a pipe wrench with both hands. His muscles were bunched with effort, and his T-shirt had risen to expose his lean belly and the V leading into his jeans.

"Holy cow," she murmured, leaning back in her chair and fanning herself while staring at the screen. The mix of pain meds and wine made the memories of their evening together foggy. She remembered the strength of his arms and the hard planes of his chest. All that muscle-bound goodness lived steps away from her. She glanced at the selfie, then down at herself, and sighed in frustration. With half the women in Keeney drooling over him, Hilary hadn't a hope in hell with the hot handyman. Was she avoiding him to protect herself, or was he avoiding her? She clicked off the link. Staring at pictures of him didn't make the frustration any easier.

CHAPTER 7

The slamming of a car door startled her, and she bobbled the box of clothing destined for Goodwill. "Oops, sorry about that."

The voice came from a man who appeared to be in his early thirties and didn't look sorry at all. Clean-shaven and well-groomed, he leaned against a late-model BMW, hands thrust into the pockets of pressed khaki slacks. It looked like an often-practiced pose.

Getting a firmer grip on the box, she nodded, conscious of the man's appraisal; he made no attempt to assist her. She put the box into the back of her car and turned to face him, not bothering to straighten her clothing or wipe the dirt off her hands.

"Can I help you?" she asked, meeting his gaze with raised eyebrows.

He pushed off the car and strolled toward her, scanning her from head to toe, lingering on her chest. She crossed her arms and tightened her lips, unconsciously stepping back to come up against the side of the car. She wasn't exactly alone, both Iris and Vincent were home, but she felt...vulnerable.

"It's Hilary, right? I've heard a lot about you," he said with a mocking smile. "My mother is quite smitten." He stopped an arm's-length away, chest thrust out, scanning Hilary's features as if cataloging them.

Bringing her feet together, she straightened her shoulders, pleased that she was slightly taller than the man, even without the benefit of heels. "Oh! You're Iris's son." She was well aware the statement sounded like a question. "It's Eddie, right?"

His smile faltered. "Yes, it is." He waited for her to respond like she should be thrilled to make his acquaintance. When she remained silent, he stiffened, nodded curtly, and headed toward his mother's door.

Hilary let out a breath and slumped against the car. She rubbed her sweaty palms on her thighs and, for good measure, ran them through her hair, making the curls spring up even more. The day wasn't hot, but she could feel sweat trickling down her back. God, she hated men sometimes. The freshly cut grass and neatly piled wood next to the garage gave evidence that for every Eddie in this world, there was a Vincent. Someone who wasn't a jerk. As if aware she had been thinking about him, Vincent materialized from his house, the sweat-stained T-shirt and unruly hair testifying to the work he had been doing. He caught her glance and came toward her, maintaining eye contact while removing his work gloves.

"I see you met Eddie," he called as he got closer. "What do you think?"

Pausing, she was about to say something dismissive but changed her mind. "Honestly? He seems like a prick." In fact, he reminded her a lot of her ex-husband, glossy and polished and as shallow as a saucer. It had taken years for her to realize how little depth there was to David. She'd been flattered by his attention and was caught up in building the business. Once the practice was established, he spent money on any shiny thing that caught his eye, tossing it aside when it lost its sparkle. She hadn't expected him to do the same to her.

Vincent snorted in surprised laughter. "He is that." He leaned against the car beside her, idly slapping his thigh with his gloves. Sweat and fresh sawdust blended with his usual scent of pine and leather. His jeans and T-shirt were stained, and he didn't seem to care. It was rather refreshing, and she inhaled deeply.

He raised an eyebrow at her. "Did you just…smell me?"

"That I did. I needed to wipe out the memory of Eddie's aftershave." Wrinkling her nose, she grinned up at him, pleased to see his smile.

He chuckled, turning completely toward her. "How's the thumb?"

She held it up for his inspection. "Much better. There's barely a scar. And thank you for looking after me that night. I was a bit out of it."

"Not a problem. That's what neighbors are for."

"You seem more relaxed. Is work going well?" She didn't mention that #HotAndHandy was her favorite hashtag on Instagram.

"It is," he replied, seeming surprised. "I like what I'm doing, and the clients have been great."

"Is your assistant working out?"

"It was a bit rough at first because he doesn't have a lot of experience, but Carl makes me think about what I'm doing and why I'm doing it. So, yeah, it's good."

Hilary widened her eyes in mock surprise. "Look at you being all teacherly."

He laughed and rolled his eyes at her. "Yeah, yeah yeah."

"I put aside some books for you to borrow."

"You did?" His eyes lit up, and he looked like a kid in a candy store. "What are they?"

"Come and see," she said, waggling her eyebrows.

He looked down at his clothes and made a face. "I'll track

dirt all over the place. Can you leave them outside your door, and I'll pick them up later?"

It was an impulsive thing to say, and he was in the middle of something, but she deflated nonetheless. "Sure."

"Thanks. I'm really looking forward to seeing what you picked out."

And with that, her world looked a little brighter.

A movement caused them both to turn. Eddie was carrying a bag of garbage to the bins. He nodded and smiled at her but did not acknowledge Vincent. After depositing the garbage into the bin, he dusted his hands off and sauntered over to the driveway, stopping a good six feet away from Hilary and Vincent.

"How's the garden shed, Ortiz? It must be bigger than your jail cell, especially without your roommate. Or do you miss kissing him goodnight?" He turned his smirk on Hilary. "Did you know your neighbor was a convicted felon? You might want to get your locks changed, and not by him."

Feeling Vincent stiffen beside her, Hilary surreptitiously nudged him before facing Eddie with big eyes. "Would you install it for me?"

Eddie puffed up like a peacock.

Vincent snorted. "Not if you want the lock installed this century. He doesn't know the difference between a screw-driver and a socket wrench."

Face red with fury, Eddie scowled up at the taller man. "Watch it Ortiz, I sign your paychecks."

Pushing himself off the car, Vincent slowly shook his head. "No, you don't. Your mother does. I'm still trying to figure out what you do at KBS besides twirl around in a fancy chair behind a big desk. The custodial staff knows more about building materials than you do. As far as I can tell, you're just a glorified pencil pusher."

Hilary expected Eddie's head to explode as he stepped closer to Vincent.

"Piss off, Ortiz. There's more to running KBS than hauling wood around like a Neanderthal. KBS is going to be mine. And so help me, God, I will get rid of you before then." He glared at Hilary, then stomped off.

Face screwed up in apology, Hilary looked up at Vincent. Steam was practically coming out of his ears. "I'm sorry, I shouldn't have teased him like that."

Hands on his hips, Vincent gusted out a huge exhale. "Not your fault. That's been building for years." When Eddie was back in the house, Vincent stepped closer to Hilary, eyebrows drawn together. "Iris doesn't see what a jerk he is. He uses her and treats her like a doormat. He's a total douche, but you can't dismiss him. And don't trust him."

Momentarily tongue-tied, Hilary gazed at his serious expression and clasped her hands before her. She really had stepped in something with her flippant remark and regretted it even more. If Eddie was able to manipulate his mother, living here could become difficult. "Thanks, I'll keep that in mind."

Thinking that the light had gone out of her day, she made for the stairs, only to be stopped by Vincent's hand on her arm.

"Hilary," he said, his low voice rumbling along her nerves. "Be careful, I don't want you to get hurt."

For a moment, their eyes locked, then she nodded and headed up the stairs. She was pretty sure it wasn't Eddie who could hurt her. Regardless, she made sure to lock the door behind her.

CHAPTER 8

The driveway was full; Marcia's Subaru Outback was parked behind Hilary's Prius. Vincent wasn't surprised. His mom hadn't been home when he dropped off the cooler at her place. He parked the truck and turned off the engine, debating his next move. As much as he enjoyed talking to his mom at the end of the day, he really didn't want to talk to Iris. Things were still kind of awkward, and Iris tended to flutter around him like a bird that didn't know where to land. He'd found two new KBS shirts on his doorstep the other morning, which he supposed were a peace offering, but her siding with Eddie over the need for supervision still pissed him off, despite how much he enjoyed working with Carl. He'd never thought he'd like taking on an apprentice, but it was kinda fun to—using Hilary's words—be teacherly.

He looked longingly at the tiny house. If he stuck close to the side of the garage, maybe he could ninja his way around the yard and make it to his place undetected. He shook his head and climbed out of the truck, muttering to himself, "Suck it up, princess."

Through the window of Iris's door, Vincent could see the

two women sitting at the table, scrolling through their cell-phones, a glass of iced tea in front of each of them.

He knocked once, then entered. "Hey." Marcia dropped her phone, and Iris clutched the table edge. Vincent cocked his head to the side. They looked more guilty than startled. "What's up?" He propped a hip against the kitchen counter and sipped from his ever-present water bottle.

Iris leaped up from the table and fluttered past him into the kitchen. "How was your day? You must be parched. Shall I get you some water?" She stopped when Vincent raised his water bottle at her with a small smile. "Oh," she said, turning toward Marcia with big eyes. Marcia grimaced in response.

Catching the furtive exchange, he asked again, "What's up?"

Iris found a spot on the counter needing her attention, grabbed a dishcloth, and started to scrub furiously. Marcia rolled her eyes and motioned Vincent to come and join her. When he was seated, she asked, "Have you been on the Keeney community Facebook page today?"

Vincent shook his head. "I haven't been on it at all."

Iris looked up. "You don't do Facebook?"

"It's a time suck. Besides, you and Ma tell me everything."

"You know I've made a website for your business and that people post photos and reviews?" Marcia asked, picking up her phone.

Vincent nodded, wondering what she was getting at.

"Reviews on social media lead to more work. You did work for Jeanne Barclay?"

Uneasiness skittered through him. "Yeah. What about it?"

"Were there any problems?"

Jaw tensed, he looked down at the table. "Nothing I couldn't take care of." And nothing he wanted to tell them.

"What happened?" Folding her hands in front of her, she gave him a hard stare.

He didn't say anything for a moment but knew she

wouldn't let up. When she wanted information, she was like a pit bull. Once she sank her teeth in you, she didn't let go.

Gaze fixed on a spot on the wall, he said, "I installed a shower head for her a few weeks ago. Everything was fine. I got this feeling, though. She didn't come out and say it, but she sort of let me know she would be interested in me personally."

Marcia nodded but didn't say a word.

"I got out of there as soon as I could. I don't need her kind of trouble." The lace panties he found in his toolbox seemed more like a threat than an invitation, and he'd put on rubber gloves before disposing of them. "Two days ago, she called me and said the shower head was leaking, so I stopped by yesterday morning to look at it." He scrubbed his hands through his hair.

He really didn't want to tell them about standing in the bathtub, arms raised overhead as he looked at the shower head, and feeling Jeanne's talon-tipped hands stroking his ass, then sliding around his front to grab his crotch. He'd turned, grabbed her arms, and all but threw her against the bathroom wall. Heart pounding, it took him a moment to realize it was a horny housewife and not a predatory prisoner in front of him. Jeanne's eyes were wide, and her tongue darted out to lick her lips. Vincent stepped out of the bathtub, lips curled in disgust. "The shower head is fine. Don't call me again," he'd declared before stalking out of the house.

"What was wrong with the shower?" Marcia's question brought Vincent back to the present.

"There's nothing wrong with the shower. I can't say the same thing about Jeanne Barclay. Why? Did she complain to you?" Vincent twisted around to address Iris, who shook her head vehemently.

His mother answered. "She went onto Facebook and trash-talked you instead. She claims you do shoddy work, are totally lacking in customer service, and she didn't feel safe around you."

Vincent's hands curled into fists as he swore softly.

Marcia had more good news to share. "Iris had two customers call today to cancel projects."

"Three." Iris clutched her necklace tightly.

"You told me two." Marcia frowned.

"I managed to convince one of them not to cancel."

Vincent focused on not losing his temper.

"Then the trolls came out," Marcia stated.

Vincent's brow furrowed. "Trolls?"

"Social media trolls," Marcia sneered. "People who lurk in the background and like to stir the pot by getting nasty. Trying to piss people off."

His knuckles whitened. "Are they saying lies about me?"

Marcia's lips thinned. "No, they're questioning the program you took in jail and whether it was legitimate. They intimate you're not licensed or insured."

"And they're wondering if you were part of a gang," Iris chimed in.

Vincent couldn't take anymore. He shoved his chair back from the table, wanting to hit something but not knowing where the target was. Of all the ways things to go sideways, he hadn't expected this. He headed to the door.

"You can't take off. We need to figure this out."

"Ma," he said. "I'm a little frustrated right now and I don't want to say something I might regret. So, please, just give me a few minutes."

*H*ilary coasted down the driveway on her bicycle. At the end of the street was a narrow path connecting to the Burke/Gilman trail, a wide, paved pathway that followed the Sammamish slough from Redmond to Lake

Washington and then into the neighborhoods of Seattle before ending near Ballard. The ride from the house to the college took fifteen minutes, and it thrilled her to get some exercise while commuting to work instead of adding to traffic congestion. She'd bought a cruising bike with no gears. It had a basket on the front, and she could sit upright and wear work clothes instead of cycling gear because she had no desire to show up to work in bike shorts. Helmet hair was a real thing, but her curls bounced back, and fresh air and exercise at the start and end of her day were better than therapy.

She'd just parked her bike beneath the stairs when Vincent exited Iris's apartment, moving at a fast clip. "Hey," she called, her heart beating a staccato rhythm. He flipped a hand but didn't slow down, didn't even look in her direction. Disappointed, she started up the stairs. She was only going to tell him that she'd enjoyed the book he recommended. He disappeared inside his house momentarily, then came back out and crossed to the garage. A minute later, she heard the lawn mower start up. Hilary was on the third step before she stopped.

Today was Thursday. He mowed the lawn on Saturday mornings. Always.

He attacked the grass with swift, jerky movements, unlike the smooth control usually a part of his routine. He was clearly agitated. Should she go to him? And what? He'd probably think she was a nosy old busybody. She continued up the stairs, digging her keys out of her tote bag.

After removing her work clothes, she hung her light gray pantsuit and pale peach blouse in the closet, then pulled on a pair of gray leggings and a baggy gray sweatshirt with Keeney College printed across the chest. Padding back up the hallway barefoot, she heard a tapping at the door. Iris stood there with another woman. The other woman was slightly younger looking and wore a bold, red quarter zip sweater over fitted, dark jeans and red ballet flats. A stark contrast to Iris's pale blue cardigan over a pale blue blouse, mom jeans, and orthopedic shoes. The dark hair, dark eyes, bronze complexion, and firm set of the jaw gave the other woman away as Vincent's mother.

Hilary glanced between the women on her doorstep and Vincent furiously attacking the lawn. This could not be a coincidence. She opened the door and smiled politely.

"Hi, dear." Iris bobbed her head and twisted her hands. "This is Marcia Ortiz, she's Vincent's mom. I hope we're not bothering you. Marcia wants to ask you a question. It shouldn't take long, but if you're busy—"

"Oh, for God's sake." Marcia thrust herself in front of Iris. "We'll be here all night if you keep that up." She switched her gaze from Iris to Hilary. "Can I talk to you about social media marketing?"

Hilary blinked in surprise. "Um…sure." She opened the door, and Marcia brushed past her, heading toward the table. Iris followed at a slower pace, patting Hilary's arm in passing.

"Would you like a glass of water, wine, or some tea?" She wasn't prepared for guests; she only had a half bottle of wine in the fridge that would not go far split three ways, so she was relieved when they declined. She got herself a glass of water before sitting at the end of the table with Iris on her left and Marcia on her right. Iris surveyed the room while Marcia scowled at her phone.

"What's this about?" Hilary asked, taking in the tightness of Marcia's posture.

Brow furrowed and lips thinned, Marcia looked directly at Hilary. "You know what my son does for a living, right?"

Hilary nodded, brow furrowed as well. "He's a general contractor, and does home repairs and renovations. He did this apartment and does really good work."

Marcia relaxed a bit while Iris beamed. "Do you follow his work on Instagram and Facebook?"

Her face heated up, but she wasn't about to mention her addiction to #HotAndHandy. "I've seen a few photos. It's obvious the local seniors love him." As well as the cougars.

"Someone posted a bad review on the Keeney community Facebook page that's practically gone viral." Marcia thrust her phone at Hilary, who took it and looked at the post. It was a photo of a tiny blue-haired lady beaming up at Vincent, who, in turn, looked very uncomfortable, with a stain on his shirt and a scowl on his face. The caption beneath it read, "Ex-con fleecing our elderly?"

"I'm assuming there's no truth to this." Hilary glanced up at Marcia with a frown before reading the rest of the post. "Do you know who it's from? Perhaps the person…" She stopped speaking when she found the profile. Jeanne Barclay loved taking selfies. She had mastered the head tilt-chin lift combo that hid double chins and accented cheekbones. She also appeared to have an endless wardrobe of cleavage-revealing tops.

"Vincent did some work for her, and he won't say it, but I think she hit on him, and he turned her down." Marcia's tone reflected her anger and frustration. "She doesn't hear no very often."

"Now you're repeating rumors." Iris tapped her on the arm in a gentle reprimand.

Marcia rolled her eyes at Iris. "Jeanne Barclay is a spiteful bitch, who goes through men like Kleenex."

Drawing both lips between her teeth, Hilary scrolled through the comments. "There are some supportive comments about Vincent's work."

"Yeah, but they're hidden by the mean ones. Someone else has jumped on the bandwagon and is gleefully crucifying Vincent."

"I don't know who wouldn't want Vincent to succeed," Iris said, shaking her head.

Marcia rolled her eyes again but wouldn't look at her friend. Hilary saw this and wondered what lay beneath the surface.

"What do you need from me?" Hilary asked, putting the phone on the table.

"Is there a way we can spin this? Make it go away?" Marcia leaned forward and took her phone back.

"This was on the Keeney community page?"

Marcia nodded.

Propping her elbows on the table, Hilary steepled her hands. "Most community groups have rules about trolling. You can approach the administrator about taking it down."

"That's Kush Patel from the senior center," Iris clarified. "I'll give him a call."

"You don't acknowledge the post itself, because that just gives it a longer life. Did Vincent do work for the lady in the photo?" At Marcia's nod, Hilary continued, "Was she happy with the work?"

Iris nodded like a bobble-head. "Oh, yes. Vincent replaced her rickety outdoor staircase. Phyllis couldn't say enough about how pleased she was."

"That's great," Hilary replied. "You need to include testimonials like that. Call her back and ask if you can quote her. Then post photos of the work itself, not of Vincent. Every couple of days, do posts of gleaming counter tops or whatever the job was. Consistently use a hashtag linking Keeney Building Supply and satisfied customers. Make sure the website address shows up. And keep your website up to date with before and after photos of jobs." She turned to her landlady. "Iris, for anyone who has canceled a job, offer them a huge discount in exchange for great reviews."

Iris stood from the table, smiling as if she were thrilled to have a specific task to complete. "I'll do that right now." She hurried off. Marcia was slower to stand.

Hilary rose at the same time and pushed her chair in, happy to have been able to help. Not counting the conversation in the driveway, she'd hardly spoken to Vincent since spiralizing her thumb, both relishing the memory of being with him and cringing at being tipsy and out of control.

"Thank you. I was so mad I could spit." Marcia sighed. "I'm pretty sure it was Iris's son Eddie who stirred the pot. He wants to see Vincent fail."

How was she supposed to respond to that? She'd seen firsthand how they felt about each other, but why would Eddie want to damage the family business? Marcia stopped beside her at the door, and, for a moment, they watched Vincent cut the grass. His movements less frantic, his shoulders sagging as he maneuvered around the yard. When his back was toward the house, Marcia said a quick thank you and goodbye before heading down the stairs to let herself into Iris's apartment.

Holding a glass of wine, Hilary stood by the kitchen sink, watching Vincent through the window, wishing she could walk out there with an offer of support and friendship. She caught her reflection. Thin, flat-chested, and gray-haired. Friendship was about all she had to offer.

*A*ss dragging from a sleepless night, Vincent hauled himself up the stairs to the KBS breakroom. Normally he entered through the front doors, happy to be seen in his company T-shirt. The checkout clerks would greet him and introduce him to customers. He'd picked up a few clients that way. Today, he parked at the back of the building and slunk past the guys at the loading dock, barely acknowledging anyone. The door to Iris's office was closed, and he sighed in relief, not wanting to face her this morning. He would grab his gear out of his locker, check out his job sheet with Ali—if in fact he had any jobs—and get to work. He had no interest in talking about the shit on social media. He had no interest in talking to anyone.

Carl was at the table scrolling through his phone. They'd been working together for six weeks and had fallen into an easy routine. The kid was quick, careful, and eager to learn. Not perfect, he accepted Vincent's critical eye and listened closely to instruction when faced with a situation his schooling hadn't covered.

"Ha! I beat you. This is the first time I've gotten to work before you." Carl sat up straight and beamed at Vincent.

Vincent eyed him sourly. "I'm not on the clock until 8:30."

Cocking his head to the side, Carl agreed, "Yes, but wasn't it you who said if you weren't fifteen minutes early, you were late?"

Vincent's narrow-eyed look was lost on Carl, who had returned to gazing at his phone. Vincent opened the door to his locker and froze. "Did you go into my locker?"

Carl didn't look up. "Yeah, I borrowed a carpenter's pencil."

"Don't go into my stuff. Hear me?" Vincent slammed the door.

Smile disappearing, Carl looked at Vincent. "Um, sure. It's just, I left mine in the truck yesterday and I knew you kept extras."

"I don't care if there were twenty of them, you don't touch my stuff without asking first."

Eyes big, Carl stared and nodded his understanding.

Vincent stalked toward the coffeemaker, then swore when he picked up the empty pot. "How hard is it to make a fresh pot. You're not the only person who works here. You—"

"I finished the coffee," Ali's hard voice came from the

doorway. He scowled at Vincent before shifting his gaze toward Carl. "Head on down and start loading the truck."

Carl bolted from the room, shooting Ali a look of relief in passing.

"Sit down." Ali placed his clipboard on the table and a fresh can of ground coffee on the counter. He took his time refilling the water reservoir and replacing the soggy, used filter with a clean one. The smell from the open can of coffee warmed the air but did nothing to dispel the frosty silence. Slowly scooping in the coffee, Ali asked, "What was that about?"

Vincent crossed his arms and scowled at the table. "Nothing."

"I don't care who cut you off in traffic, don't take your shit out on the intern." Ali put away the can and the filters, then wiped off the counter. Only the sputtering sound of the coffeemaker filled the silence. With skill borne of practice, Ali shifted the pot from beneath the spout, filled Vincent's mug, then shifted the pot back onto the burner. He placed the mug in front of Vincent, who glanced up in surprise and muttered his thanks.

Easing into a chair opposite, Ali pulled his clipboard toward him. "Do you think you can finish up that vanity install this morning? 'Cause, if so, Jerome Haskins wants you to take a look at his back deck. He thinks the wood is rotting. Definitely wants new stairs, but look at the deck itself." When Vincent didn't say anything, Ali looked up and settled back in his chair.

"You've got new work for me?" Vincent asked softly.

"Yeah."

"Didn't the shit hit the fan, and I lost some jobs?"

"Social media crap. There should be a special place in hell for internet trolls." Ali tapped his mechanical pencil on the table.

"You know about trolls?"

"Of course I do. Where the hell have you been lately?" Ali caught the hard look on Vincent's face. "Right. Sorry about that. Anyway, Jeanne Barclay's post disappeared, and there's been a lot of photos put up from satisfied clients." He fished his phone out of his shirt pocket, scrolled for a few seconds, then grunted in satisfaction and handed the phone to Vincent. Three posts in a row mentioned him by name. He recognized the interiors of two homes he'd worked on, but the last post gave him pause. He stared at the photo and then read the accompanying comment. *"Vincent Ortiz is a craftsman. His painstaking work is exquisite. He goes out of his way for his clients, focusing on their needs and safety. I would be happy to have him work in my home any time."* The photo was of the same bathroom pictured on the website. But the website photo was taken by Marcia when the work had just been completed, and Hilary hadn't moved in. In this photo, bright fluffy towels perched on a small stool next to the tub, and a glass bowl filled with colorful soaps sat on the vanity. A flash of guilt shot through him as he handed the phone back to Ali. He'd been short with his mom and Iris yesterday and knew they were behind the new flattering reviews. They must have put Hilary up to making that post, too. A warm feeling went through him, and he made a mental note to thank all three and an additional note to apologize to Carl.

Ali tapped at the clipboard. "We're not going to let the trolls win. Are you ready to get to work?"

Vincent nodded once and rested his arms on the table. "Let's see what you've got."

*I*ris acted like she'd never received flowers before in her life. She'd hugged Vincent, accepted his apology and the grocery store flowers, and clapped at his offer to take her, his mom, and Hilary out to dinner the following night.

Hilary was parking her car when he emerged from Iris's place and waited for her to get out of the car. "Hi," she said, giving him a small smile.

"Hi. How are you?"

"I'm good," she replied, her gaze moving past him to the stairs. "What's that?"

He snatched up the small houseplant and held it out to her. "This is for you. A thank you gift for cleaning up that mess on Facebook. I really appreciate your help."

"Oh! You're welcome." She accepted the plant with a smile that lit up her face. "It was no trouble at all. I'm glad it worked out."

Feeling mighty pleased with himself, Vincent beamed before noticing the tote bags Hilary carried. "Oh. Sorry. Let me take that for you."

"Thanks," she said, transferring the plant to his hands. "I need to get my keys."

He followed her up the stairs and waited for her to unlock the door. She dropped her bags inside and turned back to take the plant, admiring its bright green leaves.

"Thank you. The builder installed a garden window over the kitchen sink. I think this little guy will be quite happy there."

Vincent smirked. "That builder sounds like he knows what he's doing."

"Yeah, but let's not tell him so it doesn't go to his head."

Propping a shoulder against the open doorway, he watched her put the plant in the window, then remove her blazer and drape it over the back of a chair. She wore a high-necked, blue-gray sleeveless T-shirt tucked into loose, light gray slacks, a thin silver necklace, and small silver studs in her ears. She looked polished and professional, yet the outfit seemed to be chosen to blend into the background. Color stained her cheeks when she caught him looking, and she turned away, hunching her shoulders.

Hurt at her reaction, he blurted, "Want to go to dinner with me?"

"What?"

He cleared his throat and tried again. "I want to take you to dinner tomorrow night."

"Me?" She stared at him as if it were a foreign concept. Her shoulders relaxed, and her face brightened as the words sunk in. "That…that would be nice."

"Cool. We can—"

Iris's excited voice interrupted him. "Well? Did she say yes? Is she coming with us?" She clambered up the stairs not waiting for an answer. "Come with us, Hilary. Vincent's taking you, me, and Marcia to that new Korean barbecue place where you cook the food at the table. It will be fun."

"That does sound fun," she said brightly, but Vincent didn't think she meant it.

CHAPTER 9

All four went to the restaurant in Marcia's car. Hilary had suggested she drive herself, but Iris shot her down, so she sat beside her landlady in the back seat while Vincent drove, and his mother rode shotgun, giving him directions. Every now and then, Hilary's eyes would meet Vincent's in the rearview mirror, and she'd quickly look away. It wasn't a date, and there was no sense crying over it.

It turned out to be a fun evening with Marcia telling tales about Vincent's childhood. He blushed and fidgeted, rolling his eyes at Hilary. They polished off all the food and lingered long after the table was cleared. It was the most enjoyable time Hilary had had in a long while. A date would have been nice, but an evening with friends was probably better in the long run.

June was a day away, and the Pacific Northwest was drying out from a long, wet winter and spring. It was eight weeks since she had moved in, and she finally felt settled. The apartment no longer smelled like new paint; it smelled like home. She considered buying a houseplant to keep the one Vincent gave her company. She made an effort to chat with Iris, probably not as much as her landlady would like, but Hilary was not interested in baring her soul over coffee. Her interactions with Vincent were few and far between. A nod, a wave, a small smile. She could admit to herself she was definitely avoiding him. She was not prepared to make an overture only to be rejected. And if something were to happen…no, there was nothing to be gained from a relationship with the hot handyman. It would only end in disaster or, at the very least, awkwardness. So she avoided him as much as possible, knowing she was capable of making her own repairs, thanks to stubbornness and YouTube.

One warm Friday afternoon, she came home with a celebratory bottle of wine. She'd spent two weeks supervising the install of a new software program at the college. It had been up and running for three days without error as of two o'clock, so she headed home early. Changing into shorts and a tank top, she poured a glass of wine and headed out to the back deck to read her book. A vehicle approached as she settled in the shade. If she didn't make any noise, Iris wouldn't notice her.

But it wasn't Iris. Vincent moved slowly across the lawn toward the garden shed. She wasn't sure how much work had been done converting it into a livable home, so when he emerged, barefoot, shirtless, and clutching a towel and a shaving kit, she had her answer.

Head down, he passed out of her line of sight and used a key to enter Iris's home. A few minutes later, the shower started up. Excellent. Now she was imagining him naked, soaping up his lean, hard body. She gulped her wine like it was water, and she was dying of thirst.

The water shut off, and the door opened and closed a few minutes later. Setting her book aside, she craned her neck for a better view. When he entered her line of sight, the towel was wrapped around his hips. Warmth pooling low in her belly, she shifted in her seat, focusing on the water glistening on his shoulders. Her wineglass wobbled and then crashed to the deck. Vincent halted. She froze. He turned toward the house and, squinting against the sun, searched the deck until he found her in the shadows. Tipping his chin, he raised a hand in a silent salute and entered his house. She groaned and covered her face with her book.

Through the window on his front door, Vincent watched Hilary clean up the broken glass, broom and dustpan in hand. He hesitated, pulled the door open, closed it decisively behind him, and strode across the yard and up the stairs to her apartment.

She turned to face him as he reached the top, her expression unreadable. He was in clean jeans and a T-shirt, wearing flip-flops. Her gaze fixed on his still-damp hair.

He tilted his head toward the tiny house. "The caulking on my shower hasn't dried, so I had to use Iris's."

A blush bloomed on her neck and rose up her cheeks. She looked down at the deck.

Holding up the two beers in his hand, he asked, "May I join you?"

"Sure," she said with a one-shouldered shrug. In gray shorts that showed off firm, shapely legs that appeared to go on forever, and a loose white tank top highlighting smoothly muscled arms, she looked young and vulnerable.

Forcing his gaze to remain on her impassive face, Vincent flashed a hesitant smile. "I'm hoping you'll let me use your computer. I don't have one, and my phone is on the fritz."

She appeared to consider his request for a moment, then returned the smile, though hers was small and guarded. "Have a seat. I'll be back in a second." She skirted around him and carried the broom and dustpan into the house.

While waiting, Vincent scanned the yard, pleased with the work he'd done for Iris. Neat flower beds bordered the garage, healthy green lawn carpeted most of the yard, and the vegetable garden was coming along nicely. He recognized the furniture on the back deck; he'd helped Darryl build the sturdy, round, wooden table and six chairs as a wood-working project in high school. Running a hand over the smooth surface, he admired the grain of the wood shining through the clear enamel and picked up Hilary's book. It was an Elvis Cole novel by Robert Crais. He settled into a chair to wait for her return.

The seconds turned into minutes, and he realized he'd made a mistake. They weren't friends who met up for beers on a Friday afternoon after a long work week. They were neighbors. That's it. He was about to head back home with his tail between his legs when Hilary emerged from the house carrying her laptop and wearing a different outfit. The shorts and tank top were replaced by a long, loose caftan. Definitely appropriate for the warm weather, it also effec-tively hid her slim form from view. She looked nice, the pale peach color suited her, but a caftan seemed more appropriate for his mother than Hilary. He stepped forward and accepted the proffered computer from her. She went back inside and then emerged with two glasses and a bottle of wine.

He looked at the wineglasses and the two beers already on the table and smiled. "Looks like we're two-fisted drinkers."

"It's not like either one of us is driving, so why not." She set the glasses down and held up the wine. "Which would you prefer?"

"The wine is fine." Sitting back down, he watched as she filled the two glasses. She had graceful hands, with long, slender fingers, the nails short and unpolished. Accepting the glass, he noticed a small tattoo of a dove on the inside of her right wrist. He raised his glass and caught her eye. "Thanks. To Friday."

"To Friday," she repeated and glanced away quickly.

Perched on the edge of her chair, she looked like a bird ready to take flight at the first hint of trouble. When they'd gone to dinner with his mom and Iris, she'd been relaxed, quiet, but then no ever one got a word in when his mother started telling stories. Hilary had laughed, though, and seemed to genuinely enjoy herself. Obviously, being alone with him made her uncomfortable.

He pulled the laptop toward him, resolved to get his business done and get out of there. "This shouldn't take long, I need to order a new cellphone, and I don't like to use the computers at the store."

"Why not?"

"I know Iris wouldn't mind, but I walk a fine line with Eddie." He concentrated on the screen.

She played with the folds of her dress. "I've umm…heard you're doing well."

"Yeah, it's going good." He looked up to meet her gaze. "And thanks again for the testimonial. It means a lot."

"I'm glad I was able to help. Especially after you helped me." She held up her thumb for inspection, her lips rolled back between her teeth.

Vincent grinned. "I guess we're even now."

Shifting in her seat, she glanced down at her wristwatch, then up at him, biting the corner of her lower lip. "I was about to have something to eat. Would you…like to join me?"

A protest was on his lips, but his stomach growled in response.

She rose from the table and pushed her chair in. "I'll take that as a yes."

"That'd be great," he said, watching her enter the house. The caftan might be loose, but the soft fabric hugged her behind nicely. She needed more than loose clothing to hide her attractiveness.

When Hilary returned, he was finishing his purchase. He set the laptop aside and helped her with the tray of food, looking over the snacks. There was cheese, salami, crackers, olives, and peanuts. As well as chips and salsa. "Thank you." He popped an olive into his mouth before loading up a plate. He stopped. Had he taken too much? He glanced at her plate. She had about the same amount as him. Was this her dinner?

She must have sensed his thoughts. "This is my idea of the perfect meal; finger foods, no cooking." She scooped some salsa with a chip and took a healthy bite.

He loaded up a chip of his own. "No vegetables?"

She swallowed, then grinned. "That's what the salsa is for."

They munched away in silence, enjoying the food and the warm day. When the food was gone, he refilled her glass with the last of the wine, and opened a beer for himself. If she kicked him out, he'd take it with him.

Lounging in her chair, she pointed toward the laptop. "What happened to your phone?"

He rolled his eyes. "My assistant, Carl, dropped a hammer on it. I can take calls, but the screen is trashed, no texting or internet access." He pulled out the damaged phone and showed her the splintered screen.

"How did he do that?"

"He was hammer flipping."

"I don't know what that is," she replied, shaking her head.

Vincent shook his as well. "There's a guy on one of those home reno shows who flips his hammer, twirls around, and then catches it."

"You mean like a majorette in a marching band?"

"Exactly. Well, Carl isn't exactly light on his feet, and he flipped the hammer, stumbled over his feet, fumbled the hammer, and it landed on my phone while he landed on his ass. Like this."

Hilary snort-laughed when he pantomimed the less-than-graceful ballet. Sitting in a heap on the floor, he grinned back at her, feeling like he'd earned a reward.

"Will KBS pay for it?" she asked when she finally stopped laughing. "You do use if for work, after all."

"Yeah, I just need to fill out the damage claim without throwing Carl under the bus in the process."

"Oh, definitely— *Ouch!*" She winced, looking at her hand. Blood was seeping from a cut on the heel of her palm. She got up and went into the house. Following closely, he found her standing over the sink, squinting at her hand. "I mustn't have gotten all the glass." She looked annoyed rather than upset.

"Do you have tweezers?" Vincent headed down the hallway and caught her reply as he entered the bathroom.

"Left-hand drawer of the vanity."

Returning with the tweezers, a tube of antiseptic ointment, and a box of bandages, he took her small hand in his much larger one. "Here, let me look." He gently probed with the tweezers and found the offending piece of glass, removing it as she hissed. He smiled triumphantly at her. "No trip to urgent care this time."

"Thanks," Her soft green eyes met his own as he applied the ointment and put a bandage on the wound. Standing close together, he stroked his finger over the bandage and breathed her in. As if of its own accord, his finger moved toward the pulse beating furiously beneath her tattoo. She shifted her weight, giving him a direct view down the front of her caftan.

Freezing, he looked up into her eyes.

She snatched her hand away and stepped back, face going hard and impassive.

Not knowing what else to do, he said, "I'll bring in the dishes."

He brought the tray in and went back for the laptop. She was facing the sink when he re-entered the house. He placed the laptop on the table and turned to her uncertainly.

"I had a double mastectomy a few years ago," she said, her

back toward him.

Waiting for her to continue, he stepped forward and silently loaded the dishwasher.

"I reacted badly to the implants, so reconstructive surgery was not an option for me." Her words were matter of fact, her tone of voice without self-pity. He nudged her gently aside to wash the wineglasses in the sink and rinse out the beer bottles. "My husband reacted badly to a wife without breasts."

Vincent jolted but remained silent, reflecting on the boxes storing her medical records and divorce papers. Weren't you supposed to love someone in sickness and in health?

Beside him, Hilary sighed softly and gripped the edge of the counter.

"Is that why you changed your clothes? Because you didn't want me to notice?"

Her arms rose to cross her chest, and she hunched slightly. "Yeah."

As shitty as it was that her husband had treated her that way, a weird relief filled him. It wasn't fear of him that made her change. She hid herself away like a frightened fawn seeking shelter in the forest. Was it possible to coax her out? Convince her that she was safe with him? It was worth a chance, because her thinking she was less than perfect was unacceptable.

Taking her shoulders in gentle hands, he guided her to face him, and tipped her chin up with a finger. "I think you're beautiful," he stated. There was no arguing that fact. He liked her soft gray curls, her erect posture, thrust out chin, and her way of speaking when she wasn't guarding herself.

She swallowed and looked down. Her full lips called to him. He hesitated, then cupped the back of her neck, bringing her closer to press a soft kiss against her forehead. At her shuddering breath, he glided his nose along hers, stood back, turned, and quietly left the house.

CHAPTER 10

Sleeveless and patterned with bold, bright flowers on a black background, the blouse was made of a wrinkly fabric that looked chic rather than sloppy, and paired well with her gray slacks.

There was a shop on Main Street she'd passed a number of times, whose windows were filled with colorful clothing that called to her. She stopped in on an impulse and picked up the blouse. Now, she wasn't so sure. It was too much.

Hilary headed back to her closet to find something else, turning her head to see her alarm clock. "Crap!" Too much time was wasted dawdling in front of the mirror; she'd be late for a meeting if she didn't leave now. Scooping up a light cardigan in passing, she grabbed her lunch and purse and headed out the door.

Iris and Vincent stood at the bottom of the stairs, and she tossed them a wave on her way to the car.

"I love that shirt," Iris said, smiling brightly.

The compliment didn't make her feel any better, but she mumbled a thank you.

"Hey." Vincent stopped her before she closed the car door. "You dropped this."

"Thank you," she said, accepting the sweater.

"Not a problem. You really do look nice." He smiled and stepped back, allowing her to close the door.

His words warmed her all the way to work and through her morning meeting. His words *and* the memory of his kiss. Yes, it had been on the forehead, but he'd looked at her as if he wanted to do more. And she'd wanted it, too. Forty was too young to give up on life. Other people started over, why couldn't she?

At lunch one day, a coworker regaled Hilary and others with her adventures—and misadventures in online dating. It would get her out of the house if nothing else.

The prospective clients wanted to replace the flooring on their back deck. They'd emailed photos to Vincent, giving him an idea about the project's scope. He mulled over the idea of Carl taking the lead on the project as he ascended the stairs at the back of the store. The kid was turning into a real asset, and could at least do the measurements.

Iris was on the phone in her office, voice raised with concern. "Three days ago? Why am I just hearing this now?"

In the breakroom, he pulled his personalized coffee mug off the hook, filled it up, and then scrolled through the supply list on his new phone, listening shamelessly to Iris's side of the conversation. If she was upset, he wanted to know why.

"I'll let you know when my flight gets in."

Iris was in full mama bear mode and was determined to get to her cub.

"Of course, I should be there, I'm his mother. Fiona, I don't doubt he is getting good care, but I want to see him." Rising in volume, her voice bordered on a needy whine.

Drifting to the doorway, he saw Iris clutching the phone with both hands at the desk.

"I suppose you're right, there isn't much I could do there. But have Eddie call me as soon as he wakes up. Fine. Bye." Iris cradled the desk phone and pulled a tissue out of a pocket to wipe her eyes.

He backed away and texted his mother, knowing he was a coward for not speaking with Iris directly, but Marcia was better equipped to deal with the situation. She would be sympathetic and not call Eddie a useless tool.

Three pickups and an SUV were backed up to the loading dock behind KBS. Vincent filled his truck with supplies at one bay while customers waited for employees to load their purchases at the other bays. It was a carefully orchestrated ballet between moving forklifts and burly men as orders were filled.

"There you are!" Marcia called, coming through the door clearly marked Employees Only. Oblivious to the activity around her, she made a beeline for Vincent, causing more than one KBS employee to step hastily aside. Boxes were bobbled, and lumber was dropped, but no one challenged the feisty woman charging across the loading dock; however, exasperated looks were thrown at Vincent. He raised both hands in the air, calling out, "I'm buying a round for all of you tonight."

He removed his gloves and tossed them into the bed of the pickup, grabbing a water bottle and drinking deeply. Beside him, Carl stood with a tablet. Vincent clapped him on the shoulder. "Thanks. When I get done with this delivery, we'll talk about the Martin project. In the meantime, Ali wants you working in the store this morning."

"Okay," he said before turning to Marcia. "Hi, Mrs. Ortiz. You're a great cook. Thanks so much."

"Umm…you're welcome?" Marcia furrowed her brow at Vincent.

"I share my lunch with him." He draped his arm over his mother's shoulders. "He especially likes your calzones."

"Oh. Well, I guess I'll have to make more," she murmured, watching the younger man stop and chat with another employee.

Vincent smiled, knowing food was his mother's love language.

"What's wrong with Eddie?" he asked, raising the water bottle to his lips.

Marcia's knuckles whitened as she gripped the straps of the large purse slung over her shoulder. "He and his wife Fiona are down in Vegas. Eddie went to a racetrack where you can drive high-end sports cars. He didn't make a corner and crashed. He's got a crushed pelvis and a cracked collar bone."

Fumbling the bottle, Vincent wiped the resulting spill off his shirt. "Holy shit! How fast was he going?"

Marcia shook her head. "Don't know. The worst part is that the accident happened three days ago, and Iris just found out today. Fiona let it slip that Eddie didn't want her there."

Vincent winced. "How's Iris taking it?"

Rolling her eyes, Marcia's lips flattened. "You know she thinks the sun shines out of his ass. She's making excuses, as always." Her shoulders sagged as she moved closer to lean against the side of Vincent's truck. "I think Fiona called only to get some insurance information. Iris didn't get to speak to Eddie. Apparently, he was asleep."

It was Vincent's turn to roll his eyes.

He smiled briefly at Marcia, sure she was thinking the same thing he was; Eddie was avoiding his mother. Wrapping his own mother in a quick hug, Vincent reached for his work gloves. "You gonna feed Iris tonight?"

Marcia nodded. "Yeah. I'll keep her company, let her talk."

"Love you, Ma."

She waved over her shoulder as she retraced her steps.

Climbing into the truck, he stuck the keys in the ignition. It wasn't new but in good shape like all the KBS vehicles. About to pull out, he spotted Ali in the rearview mirror. He was waving as he jogged across the loading dock. Vincent turned off the engine and climbed out. He hopped up onto the raised platform, saving the older man from having to come down the stairs to meet him. Ali pulled a handkerchief out of a pocket and wiped the sweat off his balding head.

"Did I forget something?" Vincent glanced over the equipment and supplies in the back of the truck, mentally comparing them to the invoice form he had signed.

"No, no, you're good. These came for you." Ali thrust a small cardboard box at Vincent.

Stan, the forklift driver, saw the exchange and yelled from the moving vehicle, "Are you two getting engaged?"

"Bite me!" Ali yelled back. Stan laughed uproariously, and cut the forklift engine.

Vincent looked up from the box in his hand to see that he and Ali now had an audience. The other employees had ceased working, overcome with curiosity. Ali grabbed the box back irritably, opened it up, and displayed the contents for all to see. "Business cards! Are you happy now?"

"That's boring." Stan started up the forklift and trundled off, the other employees following in his wake.

Vincent laughed at the irritated look on Ali's face. "I would have said yes if I was into older guys."

"Asshole," Ali replied with a grin.

Taking the box back, Vincent pulled out one of the cards. It wasn't fancy. The KBS logo appeared in the left-hand corner, and in the middle of the card, in bold print, was his name, Vincent Ortiz, with his phone number and KBS email address underneath it. He beamed. "Thanks, man, this is seriously cool."

Ali waved away the thanks. "Leave a couple of these with each of your customers for them to pass out. A cheap form of advertising."

Vincent nodded as Ali continued, "Eddie thought hiring you was a stupid idea. But he's wrong. Business has picked up; we get lots of calls for your work." Ali crossed his arms and looked up at Vincent. "Having Carl sign off on you is wrong as well. That ceases as of today."

His shoulders straightened, relieved from a weight he didn't know he was carrying. "What about Eddie?"

Ali crossed his arms, tucking his hands in his armpits. "I'm glad he's laid up. That will give Iris time to get on a firmer footing here. She's much better at handling the employees than Eddie."

"Can I keep Carl as an assistant? He's pretty useful, and work goes faster with the two of us."

"Yeah, if he's working out for you. You're a good contractor and a good mentor. It's a damn shame you proved Eddie wrong." Ali winked, slapped him on the shoulder, and headed to the stairs.

The box of business cards may have been a cheap advertising tool to Ali, but they meant the world to Vincent. He took a picture of one and texted it to his mom, knowing she'd be pleased. On impulse, he sent one to Hilary as well and then kicked himself. There was no reason for her to care. She'd probably think he'd sent it by mistake.

Instead, she replied with a heart and clapping hands emoji.

Eddie was out of commission for six weeks, work was going well, and Hilary answered his text right away. It was a good day.

· · ·

*I*dling at a stop light, Vincent took in the development happening in Keeney. On his left was an office park broken up by green playing fields and winding paths. All but the walking paths were empty on a weekday morning, but on evenings and weekends, they teemed with kids and adults playing soccer, baseball, ultimate frisbee, and even cricket. Yep, Keeney was growing. On his left was Keeney Building Supply's competition, a large chain hardware store. The parking lot was full of cars, and he wondered if that worried Iris. Was KBS able to compete with the megastore? At the entrance to the parking lot stood a group of Latino men. Day workers looking to pick up some income. Odd that he never saw the same line of men outside of KBS.

A jolt of recognition went through him, and he turned his truck into the parking lot. Finding a parking space, he put the truck in park and was pulling the key from the ignition when his glance caught the box of business cards. With a shrug, he grabbed a handful and shoved them into his shirt pocket. He strode across the asphalt toward the group of men who turned with hopeful smiles at his approach. He nodded in return and said, "Hola," while his eyes remained focused on the man in the back.

"What the hell, when did you get into town?" He stopped a few feet before the man, hand extended, a warm smile on his face.

The man stiffened and stepped back.

Vincent's smile froze. "What the hell, Tomas?"

Tomas Alvarado met his confused look with a glare. Not as tall as Vincent but equally as imposing, with straight dark brows covering brown eyes, the hard line of his mouth mirrored the hard line of his jaw. Muscled arms crossed his chest as he planted his feet wide.

The men circled them as Vincent crossed his own arms.

He'd been in this position before, but at that time, Tomas was standing beside him as they faced a group of prisoners intent on breaking into the facility's storage shed. New tools had been purchased for the training program, tools another prisoner thought he could steal, smuggle out of the prison, and sell. Words were exchanged, punches were thrown, but ultimately, Vincent and Tomas prevailed. They had been a solid force in prison, and Vincent had expected them to be a solid force when Tomas joined him after his release.

"Where've you been?"

Tomas shrugged. "Staying with my cousin in Woodinville."

"You didn't call." He knew he sounded like a heartbroken teenager, but he was hurt. He'd emailed Tomas with details about working at KBS. He told him Ali would take him on and gave him the number for his cellphone.

Scowling, Tomas said, "What was the point? You lied."

Vincent held his palms up. "About what?"

Tomas dropped his arms and stepped toward Vincent. "I went to KBS. I met Ali. I was filling out the paperwork when an asshat in pleated pants and a polo came over. I told him I was a friend you recommended, and he sniffed. The asshat *sniffed* at me! Then he told me KBS wasn't hiring, took my paperwork, and walked off."

"Where was Ali? He knew Iris approved your hire." Vincent's fists curled at his side. He knew how proud Tomas was.

Tomas waved a hand in dismissal. "He'd taken off to help a customer. I didn't wait around. What was the point? The asshat was probably calling the cops."

Vincent rubbed one hand over his face while the other settled on his hip. *Goddamn Eddie had to stick his nose in.* Then his lip curled. Eddie was out of commission, and out of state.

"We can fix this. Climb in the truck, and let's go back to KBS."

Tomas shook his head. "Why? So I can be humiliated again? I don't think so."

"There's been a mistake. The owner knows about you and is expecting you. You'll be doing the same work I am. Small reno jobs and repairs so we can earn money and develop a solid reputation. Meanwhile, we can work on our business plan."

Tomas pushed past him, hands curled into fists.

Vincent reached out as he turned away. "Please."

Tomas glanced at Vincent's hand on his arm. The forgotten men surrounding them looked back and forth between them like spectators at a soccer match.

"Fine," Tomas muttered as he turned and headed toward the truck.

The trip to KBS was not long, just painfully quiet. Tomas answered Vincent's questions with monosyllables. He'd been out for six weeks and couldn't find work, so he'd joined the group of day laborers who hung around the hardware store.

Pulling into the parking lot behind KBS, Vincent frowned. "There aren't any workers here."

Tomas looked at the busy lot and then at Vincent. "What do you mean?"

Vincent waved at the entrance to the lot. "Day workers. There aren't any here." He turned to Tomas. "Why's that?"

Tomas snorted. "They used to be here. I hear it used to be *the* place to find work. Up until about a year ago. Then some guy, I'm assuming the asshat, threatened them. Said if they continued to show up, he'd call ICE and report them as illegal immigrants."

Vincent reared back. "Seriously?"

A muscle ticked in Tomas's jaw. "Even if you have the papers to prove your status, no one wants to get caught up in an ICE raid. You don't work, you don't get paid."

Fucking Eddie.

. . .

incent entered Eddie's office with a perfunctory knock, closely followed by Tomas. Iris and Ali were on either side of the desk, a mass of papers between them. Both looked up at the interruption, curiosity on their faces.

"Iris McCleod and Ali Haddad, this is Tomas Alvarado. He's the friend I told you was coming in for a job."

Iris nodded while Ali stood up to face them. "I remember you came in a few weeks ago. But you didn't fill out the paperwork."

Through gritted teeth, Vincent said, "That's because Eddie told him KBS wasn't hiring."

Ali placed both hands on his hips and shook his head. All three men looked at Iris, who sat behind the big desk, eyes wide and mouth open. "There must be a mistake. Eddie wouldn't—"

Vincent worked hard to keep the anger out of his voice, saying, "Yes, Iris, he did. As soon as Tomas mentioned my name and that I'd recommended him, Eddie took the paperwork and told him to take off."

Iris stood and faced the window over the store's floor. "I'm sure it was a misunderstanding. He must have…" She looked at Ali, but he didn't say anything, didn't back her up. Vincent placed a large hand gently on her shoulder. Being the bearer of bad news sucked, but Iris needed to take her rose-colored glasses off when it came to her son. He was hurting too many people.

"I'm sorry, Iris. I know you love him, but Eddie and I—"

She blinked rapidly, sniffed, and pulled away. "It doesn't matter." She stepped toward Tomas and extended her hand. "Welcome to KBS. Vincent has been extolling your praises. Can you start tomorrow?"

Tomas took her hand and nodded, returning her smile. Iris patted his arm and moved back to the desk. She settled into her chair, saying, "You two go with Ali to straighten out the paperwork. I've got to get back to this…this…" without looking at them.

Ali cleared his throat. "Right, we'll leave you to the new regulations." He followed the others out the door and turned. "Do you want the door open?"

Iris didn't glance up, two bright dots of red on her cheeks. Her answer was barely audible. "Please close it."

CHAPTER 11

The ding of an incoming text message was a nice distraction for Hilary. Reading another report had her just this side of a headache. Her heartbeat quickened as she saw the text was from Vincent. The content, however, caused her to sigh.

Vincent: *Are you familiar with the new state requirements for family leave?*

Hilary: *Yes. Why?*

Vincent: *Iris is having trouble with it. Any chance you can help her?*

She heaved another sigh, contemplating her response. Yes, of course, she could help Iris. Whether she *wanted* to help was a different matter. It would mean more contact with Vincent. He was so sweet, thoughtful, kind, and gentle. The kind of man who could easily steal her heart. She really needed to stay away from him. Before she could reply, another text came through.

Vincent: *I'm better with building forms than government forms.*

The text was accompanied by a GIF of a desk covered with paper.

She snorted; the GIF looked oddly similar to her own desk. She groaned and relented.

Hilary: *Sure. Tell her I will come by KBS after work.*

He responded with a thumbs-up emoji as well as a kissy face emoji. Hilary was trying to decipher the significance of the kissy face when another text came in.

Vincent: *I meant happy face.*

Hilary: *I know.*

Tossing her phone on the desk, she rubbed her temples. He was just being friendly. Trying to draw her out. And she appreciated it. She *did* need to do more besides work and hole up in her house with a book. Her profile for a dating site was complete, but she was too chicken to pull the trigger. What if only creeps responded? What if no one responded at all? She wouldn't know until she tried. But not today. In the back of her mind, she heard the squawking sounds of a chicken.

It was too difficult to work together at the imposing desk, so Hilary and Iris sat on the equally imposing leather couch with a laptop on the coffee table in front of them. Hilary suspected Eddie had shopped at a store that specifically sold pretentious furniture. He probably had his own parking space.

Blowing out a gust of air, Iris shoved her glasses up on her head and leaned back against the cushions. "What a pain this is," she said, rubbing the inner corner of her eyes. She held up a hand before Hilary could launch into a lecture on the importance of paid leave for new parents. "Oh no. I am in full support of this. Paid leave is good for everyone. It's the logistics of the implementation that frustrates me. Eddie told me to leave it for him to take care of, but when he comes back, I don't want him to have a huge pile of work. He needs to concentrate on healing."

Hilary shifted in her seat to face Iris. "If you are going to take over the accounting, working on this will help you in the long run. Eddie must be thrilled to relinquish some responsibilities." She'd only met Eddie the one time. He may be a class-A jackass, but he was still Iris's son and had been badly injured. "How much longer will he be in the hospital?"

"They initially said six weeks, but he's developed an infection they are having a hard time treating. Not sure how much longer it will be." Iris sniffed and rubbed at a stray tear.

She wasn't a hugger, but Hilary knew the benefits of human touch. She put her arm around the older woman and gently squeezed her. "Don't fret. They'll get a handle on it."

Iris fished a tissue out of a pocket and wiped her nose. "I just don't know why Fiona doesn't want me to visit. I would feel so much better if I could see him."

Remaining silent and feeling woefully inadequate, Hilary was ill-equipped to cheer people up. Dealing with family drama made her think of her own mother-in-law, a lovely woman she missed greatly. Her eyes filling with tears, she glanced around the room, seeking a distraction. "Can you see the whole store from the windows?"

Iris got up stiffly from the couch. "Except for the area directly beneath us, so Darryl installed a couple of mirrors." She chuckled while sharing the memory. "The day he hung them, he was up on one ladder over to the right, and Ali was on another ladder on the left. We had Marcia and Vincent down on the floor, and I was up here calling out instructions on positioning the mirrors to the best angle."

Hilary joined Iris at the window and looked out to find the two mirrors. "That sounds efficient."

"Yes, it was, except Marcia and Vincent were dancing around and making faces. I was laughing so hard I couldn't speak. Darryl was so annoyed he banished me to the cash register and had one of the other employees take my place."

Looking down, Hilary watched Iris's face relax with the memory. "What about Marcia and Vincent?"

"Ali told them that if they behaved, he'd buy them ice cream cones."

Hilary smiled. "I would think Marcia couldn't be bribed with ice cream."

With a wink and a nudge, Iris said, "She kind of liked Ali, and Ali was good to Vincent."

They watched the activity beneath them. Two women were comparing one power tool against another, a pregnant woman pondered flooring samples, and an employee was stocking shelves. Ali was strolling through the aisles, stopping now and then to adjust a product. As if sensing their presence, he glanced up and saluted. Iris smiled and waved.

"He's such a good man, Darryl thought the world of him."

Ali's attention switched to something directly below her. Through one of the conveniently placed mirrors, she saw Vincent come through a doorway and approach the older man. Beside her, Iris sighed with pleasure. "I am so glad this has worked out."

Hilary looked down at her quizzically.

"What do you know about Vincent's past?" Iris asked.

"I know he was convicted for possession of stolen goods and learned construction while he was at a minimum-security prison. People seem to think it was a wrongful conviction."

Head bobbing in agreement, Iris watched the two men beneath them. "Marcia hired a lawyer who was able to reduce his sentence but couldn't get the conviction overturned."

"Vincent is fortunate to have you and Marcia behind him." Hilary placed a hand on Iris's shoulder and squeezed.

"They have been very good to my family. There isn't much I wouldn't do for them."

Below, Vincent and Ali were focused on a tablet. Whatever Vincent was saying seemed to please Ali. "Vincent seems close to Ali as well," Hilary murmured.

"There was a time I hoped Ali and Marcia might get together." Iris was silent for a few minutes but then responded. "She left Vincent's dad when he was seven. It was a long time coming. Ray was not a good parent, he had a wandering eye and would rather chase after women than chase after his son. It took Marcia a while before she was finally convinced she would be better off without him. She worked here at the store for a while, and I know Ali was interested, but…" Iris shook her head. "Darryl told me not to meddle."

Continuing to watch the conversation below them, Hilary asked, "Did Ali ever ask her out?"

"I don't think so. He would do things for her, though: fix things around her house and take Vincent to ball games. I don't know why it didn't go further. She's my best friend, but I didn't want to pry," Iris trailed off.

Another man joined the pair below, looking stiff until Vincent said something that caused all three to laugh. Ali pointed to the window, and the men looked up and waved. Vincent's smile widened when his eyes connected with Hilary's, and he mouthed a *thank you*. Her heart did a stutter step, but she ignored it and simply nodded and waved back.

Iris shifted beside Hilary. "That's Tomas. He and Vincent met in prison."

"Oh. Did he do the same contracting program?"

Iris nodded.

Hilary crossed her arms and cocked her head, watching the three men below. "They're fortunate to have learned a trade while they were inside."

"Um-hum."

Glancing between the men and Iris, Hilary commented, "The hard part is finding a job when you have a criminal

record. Now…a joint program between an educational insti-
tute and a local business would be a great idea."

"Carl, Vincent's assistant, is from the college." Iris
gestured at the store below. "We've been taking interns from
them for years."

"Really? Hmm."

It was Iris's turn to cross her arms and cock her head.
"What are you thinking? I can practically see the gears
turning."

Ideas were indeed swirling around inside her brain that
popped and sizzled enticingly. Hilary tapped a finger against
her chin. "Not quite sure yet. Let me get back to you."

"That should do it," Vincent said, slapping the side of the Hobart dishwasher. "If it causes you any more grief, call me." He fished a card out of his shirt pocket and handed it to the kitchen manager of Denali's main restaurant before hoisting his toolbox. He was glad he'd eaten a big lunch; otherwise, he'd be tempted to sample the mouthwatering breads currently being baked for the evening diners. Weaving through the gardens of the hotel complex, he passed a bicycle rack on his way to the truck. Two steps on, he halted mid-stride and looked back. The lone bicycle looked familiar. Canary yellow with a white wicker basket covered in fake daisies, it had to be Hilary's. All by itself, it was listing to the side and seemed slightly forlorn. He wondered what she was doing but continued on. She was a grown woman, and it wasn't his business to check on her.

But wasn't that what he was doing with the text messages? He'd shoot her a silly meme that made him smile, and they'd talk about books they were reading. Anything to draw her out, to ease the pain she'd suffered through her divorce. It was good that she was here at Denali's rather than at home. He should be thankful.

He should mind his own business. He thrust the toolbox into the truck's cab and stood staring at the interior, hands on his hips. Then he moved quickly. Off came the KBS shirt, on went the flannel button-down hanging from the back of the passenger seat. He slammed the door of the truck and headed back to the hotel, running his hands through his hair and hoping the restaurant didn't have a dress code.

The hotel complex was initially the first elementary school in Keeney. Now, it boasted three restaurants, a pool, a movie theater, and multiple bars and lounges. He found Hilary in the third place he looked. All by herself, she was listing to the side and seemed slightly forlorn. He wasn't sure how he felt about that. She shouldn't be alone in a bar, but then again, he was happy he hadn't found her with a man.

"I'll have what she's having," he called out at the woman behind the bar, slipping onto the stool beside Hilary and raising a hand to hold the bartender's attention.

Hilary looked up at his voice, not appearing too surprised by his presence, and closed the book in front of her. He lifted his chin in acknowledgment and waited for his drink. When it arrived, he tapped it against her glass, took a long pull of the liquid, and promptly spit it back into the glass. "It's tea!"

"Yeah?" Hilary frowned at him.

"Unsweetened iced tea with no booze in it," he said in disgust.

She shrugged. "I got here a while ago, and they don't serve alcohol until after four p.m."

"Well, it's after four now." Vincent waved the bartender over again and ordered two beers.

There was no awkward silence with Hilary, just a quiet companionship. Vincent sat back and relaxed. The back of the bar was a mirrored wall with shelves of liquor bottles. He could see the empty room and Hilary in the open spaces between the bottles. His gaze kept returning to her. Her hair had grown a bit longer since he first met her four months ago, the curls relaxed, the silver-gray contrasting sharply with her dark eyebrows. His gaze moved from her face to her long, slim fingers idly playing with a coaster. He spotted the tattoo.

"Why a dove?"

Hilary glanced at the inside of her wrist as if seeing the tattoo for the first time. She traced it with a finger from her left hand. "It reminds me to seek peace and love myself."

Surprised by the honesty of her remark, it took a moment to think of a reply. "Does it work?"

She shrugged. "Probably not enough. It's way too easy to focus on what I don't have and brood over the past. Do you know what I mean?"

"Um, yeah," he answered. Images of his time in jail, followed by the fruitless job search, came to mind. Again, he thanked the universe for having good people in his corner. He didn't think the woman beside him could make the same claim.

The beers arrived as Hilary turned to him. "I've shown you mine, now you show me yours." The bartender placed the bottles down abruptly and scuttled off.

Vincent caught Hilary's smirk in the mirror. "I wonder what she was thinking?"

"Huh," she said with a wide-eyed look of innocence.

They tapped their beers together and drank.

"Weren't you required to get a prison tattoo?"

He shook his head. "I had a deal with my mom."

Her brow furrowed. "You'll have to explain that."

Turning his stool, he rested an arm on the bar and held his beer with the other hand. "I wanted a tattoo when I was seventeen. Ma said sure, but she would be getting the exact same thing in the exact same location, so I had better choose wisely."

"What did you have in mind?"

He tilted his head back and smiled at the memory.

"Starting with the local ones, I was planning on having the names of all the ski hills I'd been to tattooed down the side of my ribs." He looked at Hilary to see her eyes following the path of his hand as it absently moved down the side of his chest. She glanced away when their gaze met, coloring slightly.

She cleared her throat. "Was Marcia not on board?"

Vincent snorted. "Oh no. She was ready to make the appointment for us to get the first one done. The deal was that she would watch me get my tattoo, and I would watch her." He shook his head. "I didn't want to see her topless while some guy was touching the side of her boob."

Hilary choked on a laugh. When she recovered, she said, "But now you're a grown-ass man. What's stopping you?"

His gaze moved over the bar's surface, then came back to meet hers. "I haven't seen anything I want permanently inked on my body." He reached out and touched her wrist. "I like this. The workmanship is lovely." He traced the outline of the tiny bird and gently pressed on her pulse point before removing his hand. He watched in fascination as her heart rate increased in tempo.

She dropped her hand in her lap, and turned away to fiddle with an earring. "The woman was good. I may get her to tattoo my chest."

"Another dove?"

Watching him through the mirror, she shook her head and waved at her chest. "If I can't have breasts, I figured I'd get the scars tattooed over."

Meeting her gaze in the mirror, he saw her hand pressed tightly against what would have been her cleavage. He nodded slowly, his gaze remaining on hers. "I've heard of that. Have you picked out a design?"

Her shoulders relaxed. She placed both elbows on the bar and rested her chin on top of her hands. "Some. It's expensive. Insurance covers reconstruction, not tattoos, so it won't happen for a while."

"I know nothing about reconstruction. Is that implants?"

"Either implants or using a woman's own tissue. My implants didn't take. My husband wanted me to try the other, but I didn't want to face another surgery and decided to live flat. He didn't like that decision. He wanted the old me back, when I was—" she cupped her hands in front of her to mimic large breasts, "—and that person isn't coming back." Downing the contents of her beer, she placed the empty bottle on the bar.

It didn't say much about her husband that he rejected her because she no longer conformed to his idea of a woman. She was perfect, exactly the way she was. Vincent signaled the bartender for another round.

She slid off the barstool. "Thank you, but not for me. I'm on my bike."

Reaching out, he stayed her with a hand on her arm. "I'll take you home. We'll throw your bike in the back of the truck."

Ducking her head, she considered his hand for a moment, then sat back down. "Alright."

He squeezed her arm gently before letting go. "What are you doing here? Late lunch?"

She blew out a gust of air that ruffled her bangs. "Sort of. It was a date, but the guy didn't show."

"Jerk," Vincent muttered but hid his satisfaction behind a drink from the bottle. He was glad she wasn't seeing anyone. Indicating the novel in front of her, he said, "At least you had something to do while you waited."

"Yep." She flicked at the bookmark wedged between the pages. "But I was kind of hoping I wouldn't get this far in the book. That I wouldn't need it for more than a conversation starter."

"Have you dated much since your divorce?"

"Nope. This was going to be my first dip in the pool."

He winced inside. Watching through the mirror, he could see what it was costing her to appear like she didn't care. He wanted to comfort her but didn't know how. He settled for a shoulder nudge. She looked up to meet his eyes. He tilted his chin. "I know some guys. Just say the word, and I'll take care of him."

Throwing her head back, she slapped the bar and snort-laughed. It was the best thing to happen to him all day. "Right! What are you gonna do? Have the guy spackled?"

He waggled his eyebrows. "It could be arranged."

She shook her head, but the smile remained on her face. It was a pretty smile on a pretty lady. She sat up straight, her shoulders moved back and down as she turned her stool to face him. Seeing the humor in her eyes, he decided to make it his mission to make her smile every day. "I didn't know Keeney's local wise guy was living in my backyard."

Swiveling to face her, he said, "I made connections when I was in the joint."

Thunk!

They looked up to see the bartender drop off their beers and swiftly disappear.

Vincent nudged Hilary's knee with his. "What does she think of us?"

"The worst, probably."

They were facing each other, her legs primly tucked together, his spread wide and bracketing hers. She wore a short white skirt and a gray and white striped shirt. It had a wide boat neck and sleeves ending at her elbows. She looked fresh and summery and didn't seem to care that he was in his work jeans and an old flannel shirt. He suddenly felt self-conscious about not cleaning up before coming to find her. He hoped he didn't smell bad. He tapped his beer against hers, nudged her knee, and gave her a wink. Winking? When did he start winking? Mentally, he shook his head.

Hilary giggled. Okay, maybe he would wink more often. She was sitting up straight. She wasn't crossing her arms or doing anything to cover up her chest. Good.

"Iris says you've taken on another assistant."

"Yeah, but not really an assistant. A guy who was inside with me. Did the same program."

She played with the edge of her coaster. "How's that gonna work out?"

He stretched out one long leg and rubbed his thigh. "Tomas and I wanna start our own contracting business. We need seed money to get started, though. For now, there's enough work at KBS for both of us to go out on jobs separately. Tomas will take Carl with him, and Ali will find another kid to work with me."

"Will that be a new hire?"

"Nope." He shook his head. "KBS has connections with the college. Kids who are going through the building trade programs can get work experience at KBS."

Cocking her head to the side, Hilary sent him a calculating look.

He watched her through narrow eyes. "What are you thinking?"

Grinning, she slid off the barstool. "I have an idea for you and Tomas." Looking pretty pleased with herself, she headed off to the restroom.

*A*fter washing her hands, Hilary fluffed up her hair and slicked on a fresh coat of clear lip gloss. She smiled at her reflection. Drinks with Vincent was more enjoyable than lunch with a stranger. As wounded as she'd been when the guy hadn't shown up, she felt much better now. Vincent didn't seem repelled by her lack of breasts, and the age difference didn't seem like such a big deal. She sauntered back to the bar only to stop short. He stood with his back to her, stuffing his wallet into his back pocket while the pretty bartender smiled up at him. It looked like the date was over.

What made her think she could hold the attention of a man like Vincent? He was hot, sexy, and young. She was... not. With faltering steps, Hilary moved closer. Watching his handsome face through the mirror, she forced a smile when she caught his eye.

Smiling tentatively, he turned around. "It's kinda early, but would you, um, like to get some supper?"

The bartender gave a friendly wave and walked away. Looking up, Hilary realized Vincent was focused solely on her. "The bartender said the food here is good. We could sit outside and maybe talk about your idea?" Was this...what? Her head slightly fuzzy from the two beers, her belly swooped as she considered the implications.

"Shit, I suck at this." Vincent shoved a hand through his hair and sighed. "I haven't asked a woman out in over four years. Can you give me some help here?"

A smile bloomed on her face, and she cocked a hip and crossed her arms. "It's been more than twelve years since I've been *asked* on a date. My reaction time is a little off. Now that I know what's going on, try again."

"Okay," he replied slowly. He stepped closer, lowering his voice and capturing her eyes with the intensity of his own. "Hilary, are you free this evening? I'd like to take you out for dinner."

"Sure, I'd like that." She uncrossed her arms and put her hands behind her back, bouncing on her toes and smiling like she was back in high school, the nerdy bookworm being asked out by the captain of the basketball team. It felt that good.

"Yeah? Cool." Vincent rubbed a hand over his face and

released a breath. Picking up her book in one hand, he placed the other on her arm and walked her to the door.

"So…this is a date, then." She half expected Iris and Marcia to join them and was thrilled to feel his hand move from her arm to her upper back, secretly hoping it would move lower.

"Yes, it is." He smiled down at her. He stepped away as they walked from the bar out to the patio. Reaching a table, he pulled out a chair for her and then sat caddy-corner to her. When the waiter brought them water, Vincent raised his glass to Hilary. "To our first date."

She sipped from her glass and met his eyes over the rim.

Not just a date, a *first* date. Nice.

*V*incent offloaded the bicycle and rolled it over to the side of the garage where Hilary usually parked it. As impromptu as it was, the date had gone fairly well, in fact, quite well. She was easy to talk to and easy on the eyes. When she smiled, her whole face lit up. And when she laughed… He vowed to make her laugh at least once a day because it made him feel so good. They didn't get around to discussing her idea until the drive home. Apparently, when she got excited, she moved her hands a lot. Now, she was standing in front of him, bouncing on her toes, and waving her hands in front of her.

"We should have no problem getting a grant to fund the program."

While she seemed to think it was a no-brainer, he was having a hard time wrapping his head around the idea. Why would someone want to fund a program taught by two ex-convicts?

"From who?"

She tucked a wayward strand of hair behind her ear.

She'd done it more than once during the evening. He propped his hands on his hips to prevent himself from doing it for her.

"Okay," Hilary ticked items off on her fingers. "The trades are screaming for apprentices. There's lots of training available, but construction is hard work, and few want to go into it. If we focus on at-risk youth, those who have already had a brush with the law, we're golden. We get sponsors like KBS who can help with job location, we get non-profits on board who work with youth, the school districts to help with tutoring, then add you and Tomas as instructors for the sexy component."

"Sexy component?" His lips quirked up.

"Well, yeah, there's nothing sexier than a reformed bad boy." She placed her hands on her hips and gave him a grin as she swept wide eyes up and down his long body.

He threw his head back and laughed. God, this woman. He wanted to throw her over his shoulder like a caveman and take her to his bed. He also wanted to spend hours listening to her and watching her face light up with the enthusiasm of her ideas.

Iris poked her head out her door and looked at them. "You two okay?"

"Just fine," he answered because he couldn't find the words to describe how good he felt.

"I'm convincing him to think bigger than being a handyman," Hilary called.

"Oh," said Iris. "Will KBS be losing its best employee?"

"Probably not. She has more convincing to do." He guided Hilary to the stairs with a hand on the small of her back. They waved as Iris ducked back into her place.

A few hours later, twilight set in, and they were comfortably ensconced in chairs on Hilary's deck. They'd kicked around ideas for the program and thoroughly enjoyed each other's company. An incoming text lit up his phone, making him glance down and grimace. "Ugh. I have to pick up Tomas at seven tomorrow morning." He rose to his feet. "I should get going."

Hilary rose as well and busied herself with the empty cups and teapot. "Yes. You…umm… head on home. I'll…just—"

He took the items out of her hands. "I've got this." He carried them into the house and placed them on the counter. Turning, he found her behind him, twisting her fingers and looking everywhere but at him. She was like no woman he'd known. Competent and accomplished but so incredibly vulnerable. She pulled at him as if he were a puppet, and she held the strings. He wanted to explore this attraction but knew moving slowly was the key to being with Hilary. He stepped closer, shoved his hands in his pockets, and leaned against the doorway, forcing her to look up at him. "Thanks for a great first date."

"You're welcome." The words came out in a whisper.

He shifted his weight, drawing closer still. "Although, we *have* eaten together many times now, including the trip to urgent care and when you let me use your computer."

"Oh," she said softly, her big eyes widening further.

He reached up to tug on a curl. "But I'm hoping instead of you needing stitches or a band-aid, this time you'll let me kiss you."

"Oh," she said again, with a slow blink.

Vincent leaned down, touched his lips behind her ear, and whispered, "May I?"

Hilary turned her head toward him. He guided her closer with a fingertip to her chin and touched her lips softly with his. Once. Twice. And then cradled her face in the palm of his hand, and deepened the kiss. Her lips parted, his tongue found hers, and her hands came up to rest on his chest. When a small sigh escaped her, Vincent pulled back. He wanted to pull her close enough for her to understand exactly what she did to him. Instead, he rubbed his hands up and down her arms. He turned their bodies so she was inside the house, and he was outside. "I'd like to do this again. Would you?"

At her silent nod, he smiled and headed for the stairs. At the door to his house, he turned. She stood framed in her doorway. "Good night, Vincent," came softly through the quiet darkness.

"Good night, Hilary."

It was Friday, and Vincent hadn't seen Hilary all week, even though they shared the same address. They'd texted, though, and agreed to happy hour on her deck, with him bringing the drinks and her providing the food. Taking the stairs two at a time, he smiled at his own eagerness. Last week was great. Her enthusiasm for setting up the training program was contagious. Tonight, they would work on a proposal to present to Iris and Ali, to get KBS on board. And hopefully, they'd do some more kissing. He stopped himself from thinking beyond that. After all Hilary had been through, he did not want to rush her. His cock argued otherwise; thus Vincent started and ended each day with a cold shower.

He shifted the six-pack of beer and bottle of wine in his arms to rap on the door. No one answered. Glancing over to the driveway, he confirmed Hilary's car and bicycle were both there. Through the windows of the French doors, he saw her purse and car keys sitting on the counter so he tried the doorknob. Unlocked, he pushed the door open and called, "Hey, you okay?"

"Not really. Can you come back here?"

Dropping the booze on the table, he hustled to the bedroom, expecting more blood. The room was empty. "Hilary?"

Her voice came from the en suite bathroom. "In here."

He peeked in to find her rooted to the floor, arms crossed over her chest, facing away from the door. Seeking her reflection in the mirror, he caught the disgusted look on her face. "What's wrong?"

"There was a huge-ass spider. It startled me, and I dropped my glass, which shattered on the floor. I can't move because I'm afraid I'll cut myself."

"I'm thinking you should give up day drinking," he said, taking in the broken glass and Hilary's bare feet.

"It was a glass of water."

"Maybe buy plastic stuff. You and glass don't seem to get along." He grinned at her growl of annoyance.

From his examination of the floor, his eyes moved upward and widened. She wore bright pink panties and a matching camisole. Nothing else. He swallowed. With clothes, she was hot. Without, she was dynamite. Long firm legs, tight rounded ass, flat belly, and toned arms. She may not have tits, but Hilary was sexy as hell.

"Are you going to stare, or are you going to help me?" Bright red dots sat high on her cheekbones.

He cleared his throat. "Yeah, umm…give me a second." He pulled off his T-shirt and placed it on the floor at the base of Hilary's bed. Then he leaned into the bathroom and grabbed a hand towel from the rack. "I'm going to wipe down the backs of your legs in case there are any pieces of glass on them." Glass crunched beneath him, and he was thankful to be wearing shoes. He crouched, and carefully ran the towel down the backs of her thighs and calves. She tightened at his touch, and he heard a sharp intake of breath. He spoke gently as he would to a wild animal, "Your legs look fine. I'm going to pick you up and put you on the end of the bed. We'll do the fronts of your legs, and then your feet." He glanced up to catch her nod, then tossed the towel over his shoulder as he rose to stand next to her. A pulse beat rapidly in the hollow of her throat. He grinned at her reflection. "I promise not to drop you." With one arm behind her knees and one arm around her shoulders, he scooped her up and carried her to the bed. He placed her down so her feet were above his T-shirt on the floor, and knelt in front of her. Her slim foot was silky smooth, and he concentrated on looking at the skin of her legs and feet, trying not to inhale the provocative scent emanating from the juncture of her thighs. "I didn't know you were afraid of spiders."

She huffed and crossed her arms again. "I'm not afraid. It startled me. Did I not mention it was a huge-ass spider? It had to be the size of a dinner plate."

"Really?" He sat back on his heels, trying not to smile. "And what happened to it?"

"I don't know." She waved an arm in dismissal. "It probably scuttled back down the drain, laughing at me. I'm surprised you didn't hear me scream."

He picked up his T-shirt and wrapped the towel in it, chuckling as he stood. "I didn't see any glass, but I'm going to shake these out over the garbage can and put them on the washing machine. Then I'll grab the vacuum cleaner. Don't move until I get back. There might be bits of glass in the carpet by the door." Looking up, he caught her gaze on his chest and abs...and lower. He slowly straightened, not bothering to conceal the proof of his arousal.

The red spots were back in her cheeks. "Fine. I'll be here."

❄

*H*ilary flopped back on the bed when Vincent left the room, then, when her heartrate returned to normal, she turned and crawled to the headboard. A noise from the doorway drew her attention. Vincent stood there, staring at her ass. He entered the room and placed a glass of wine on the bedside table. "I'll umm…go get the vacuum," he muttered and backed out of the room, continuing to look at her.

Did he just lick his lips?

Groaning in embarrassment, Hilary seated herself and gulped the wine. She grabbed the afghan from the bottom of the bed and draped it across her legs. This was not how she wanted the evening to go. She'd planned on wearing a nice dress, putting some makeup on, doing her hair, and looking presentable. Not greeting Vincent in her underwear, and then posing like she wanted Vincent to do her. Absently, she rubbed her scars, wincing slightly.

"Do they hurt?" Vincent leaned against the doorway, holding a beer in one hand and the vacuum cleaner in the other. Unfortunately, he'd taken the time to put on a fresh T-shirt.

"Not really. They feel a little tight. I'm supposed to massage them with Vitamin E oil."

Tipping his chin at her, he placed his beer next to her glass of wine and plugged in the vacuum cleaner. A weird warmth went through her as she watched him meticulously clean the bedroom carpet—picking up the clothes she'd left on the floor in the process—then move on to do the bathroom floor. He didn't frown, didn't sigh heavily and make a big deal about it, just took care of her like he was happy to help. After finishing, he stepped into the bathroom and reappeared, holding a small bottle. "Is this it?" At her nod, he placed the bottle on the nightstand then stood back, looking down at the floor. "I'll um, put the vacuum away," he said, turning away.

"You can stay," Hilary replied quickly. "It's not like there's anything to see."

He gave her another chin tilt, but his lips were thinned.

He moved around the bed, toed off his shoes, and settled beside her with his back against the pillows. She pulled the camisole up over her head and gasped when she felt warm skin against her belly. Whipping the fabric off so she could see again, she was face to face with a frozen Vincent, his arm extended, reaching for his beer. Her stomach tightened. He removed his arm.

Both of them were red-faced.

Other than the plastic surgeon, the nurses, and her douche of a husband, no one had seen her scars. *Can he take it?* No longer angry and red, the scars were thin, running from one armpit to the other, right where her nipples had been located. Vincent stared at them for a moment, then turned away. Obviously not. Hoping to hide her disappointment, she closed her eyes. Only to open them when she felt his arm move across her belly. He reached for the oil and settled back; his torso twisted toward her. "May I do it for you?"

She took in the softness in his eyes and the softness in his smile and nodded wordlessly.

Sitting up, he poured some oil into his hand. Again, he moved across her body, placing the bottle on her bedside table. *Why didn't he put it next to his beer, on the table on his side of the bed?* He rubbed the oil into his hands and slowly reached out to touch the scar over her heart. She jerked. He pulled back. "Did I hurt you?"

"No!" She closed her eyes, lowered her head, then spoke in a rush, "No one has touched me there in almost a year. And that was for a follow-up appointment."

"Okay," He lifted her chin with one finger. "We'll do this slowly."

His hand moved toward her chest. While the scars had no feeling, the tissue around them did. The combination of his rough calluses and the slickness of the oil was magical. A tingle went through her that she'd thought she'd never feel again. A tingle leading from her missing nipples down to her core. She relaxed against the pillows and watched him through heavy-lidded eyes. He stroked from the center of her chest outward to her armpit. Then he sat up and moved a leg to the other side of her body, somehow managing to remove the afghan. Straddling her, his denim-clad legs pressed against her bare legs. "Is this okay?"

Words escaped her, so she nodded.

Both of his hands stroked her chest as he looked up and met her heated gaze. He smiled slowly and spread his fingers wide, encompassing more of her skin, stroking her belly as well. His hands moved up and out, thumbs dragging across the scars to her armpits, down her ribs, and back up again. The feeling was delicious, and she wanted him to experience it, too.

Her tongue darted out, and she licked her lips. "I um, saw you had a scar, just above your ribs. Do you want me to massage it?" *Where the hell did that come from?*

He pulled his shirt over his head in answer. Her eyes traveled over the expanse of his chest, up over his shoulders, and down his arms. The ridges of his stomach muscles and the dark hair arrowing down to his jeans captivated her. With a small amount of oil in her hands, it was her turn to explore his warm, velvety skin as he leaned into her touch. His eyes closed as he groaned out a sigh, then opened, and he held her gaze, smiling encouragingly. She grew bold and found his nipples. Small, tight, and dark against his bronze skin. He groaned again when she tweaked them. His head descended, and she watched his lips come toward hers. There was nothing tentative about the kiss. His lips were firm. When his tongue darted out, hers was there to welcome him. She shuddered at the contact and opened more. Not just her lips but her thighs. He repositioned himself. With her hands on his shoulders, she drew him down and felt his erection press against her center, the fabric of her panties drenching with the contact.

The denim of his jeans abraded the soft flesh of her inner thighs as he settled against her. He traced kisses across her jaw and down her neck to nuzzle her throat, lowering himself completely over her. Her head fell back, and she reveled in the feel of the hard body touching her, their skin sliding against each other in the slickness of the oil. Of their own volition, her hips rose, and she rubbed herself against his erection through his jeans. It had been too damn long. The heat and the friction sent flames shooting from her aching core throughout her body. She stiffened and clutched his shoulders, arching her back to press harder against him, then released a long groan of pleasure.

She opened her eyes to find him smiling at her. He reached down between them and unzipped his jeans, freeing his erection to rub it against the wet fabric of her panties. Levering himself up until he was on his knees between her legs, he grasped his cock and watched her. Tentatively, she reached out. This, too, had been a long time. Her hand moved over his, and she learned his rhythm. His hand fell away as she stroked him from root to tip, watching the passion play across his face. Hot and hard, his cock felt like iron encased in silk. He strained against her, hands gripping her thighs, and she increased the tempo of her strokes until a stream of cum burst forth to paint her belly. The smell of sex and satisfaction filled the air, and he bent down to kiss her softly. Once. Twice. Then, once more.

With a quirk of the lips, he got off the bed and went to the bathroom. When he returned, his cock was tucked away, the button of his fly undone, and he held a warm, wet cloth in his hand. With gentle strokes, he cleaned off her belly, then placed soft kisses over her scars. He returned the cloth to the bathroom and came back to the bed to lie on his side and scoot close. Head propped up on one hand and the other splayed across her belly, he kissed her shoulder. She tilted her head toward him, meeting his satisfied smile with her own.

Having half-expected him to leave, she chewed the corner of her bottom lip, not knowing what to do next. "Thank you," she said. "It's been a long time and…"

He stroked her ribs lightly, and dipped a finger into her navel. "And what?"

She pressed lightly against her breastbone and then waved her hand in the air. "This isn't what a man wants."

"No?"

"No!" She now held her hands in front of her as if cupping a pair of breasts. "They want boobs that jiggle and nipples to suck on."

His hand trailed up between her scars, stroked her collarbone, and cupped her chin. "Tits are nice, but they're not what I want." He leaned in and kissed her softly, flicking a tongue at the seam of her lips.

"What do you want?" she asked in a husky voice.

He lay back, pulling her with him until her head rested on his chest. His hand moved through the curls of her hair and down across her back. She didn't want him to stop. "I want a woman who laughs, has a good ass, and lets me get to third base on the second date."

She giggled. "Was that third base?"

"Wasn't it?"

"I don't know. It's been a while since I played bedroom baseball."

He laughed and squeezed her ass. "Is it too soon to try for home plate?"

His stomach growled before she could answer. Pulling herself away from his hold, she dropped a kiss on his chest, then climbed off the bed to head to the bathroom. "We can talk about it after I feed you." She grinned at her reflection in the mirror, knowing he was watching her ass.

They sat at the table on the back deck, the remains of their meal in front of them. Vincent put his beer on the table and cleared his throat. "It's been a long time since I've had sex. I don't have any condoms. Do you have any?"

Leaning her elbows on the table, Hilary shook her head, smiling slightly. "No. The last time was with David, and that was more than two years ago."

"If you're on birth control…I'm clean…or I can go to the store and buy some."

She placed one hand on her chest, unconsciously rubbing her scar. "I can't have children. Something happened during chemo and…" She shrugged and looked away.

"Ahh." He had no clue what to say, so he grabbed her chair and pulled it closer to his, then intertwined his hands with hers, pulling them in to kiss her on the knuckles. "You wanted kids?"

She shrugged again. "I don't know. When we got married, David was a dentist building a new practice. I ran the business part of the practice, and we were super busy. We never really talked about having a child, just assumed that it would happen in time. But then I got sick…" She looked away and shook her head. "It was after the mastectomies and after the reconstructive surgery failed that we found out. And…it was too much for him. We separated shortly after."

Separate. What a polite word for such a heartbreaking action. Aloud he said, "Did you consider adopting?"

"I suggested it, but David wasn't interested in buying a baby." She grimaced. "His words, not mine. So…"

"What a douche."

Hilary barked out a surprised laugh. "David the douche. That's a good description for him."

Vincent squeezed her hands, glad to make her feel a bit

better. But he could feel the tension in her and didn't want the night to end with her thinking about her ex-husband. "Not only is he a douche, he's a moron."

Letting go of her hands, he shifted around to scoop her up and position her in his lap. He looped her arms around his neck, and stroked a finger across an eyebrow before sifting his hand through her hair. "I like everything about you. I like your smile, your laugh, your ideas, your cooking, even your bicycle." He spoke softly, looking deep into her eyes, his other hand stroking up and down her back. When he felt the tension easing from her, he slid his hand over her bottom, stroking along her hip, up her belly, with the lightest touch. He rested his hand on her chest for a moment before moving it up and over her shoulder to stroke his thumb up her throat and across her bottom lip. Wanting to erase the wariness in her expression, he said, "There is nothing I would change about you."

She pulled her hands apart, and she traced his shoulders with her fingertips, bringing her own thumbs down to flick his nipples. His eyes blazed as she nipped at his thumb. "The dishes can wait until later."

He kissed her lightly. "Is that an invitation?"

At her nod, he stood and carried her into the house and to the bedroom.

CHAPTER 14

The idea of a training program was little more than an outline of a dream, but Hilary knew she could bring it to life if she framed it correctly. She and David had started a community program in Olympia where patients paid what they could for dental cleanings, simple extractions, and fillings. The first event proved so successful that other dentists joined in. Now, it was a community event that occurred four times a year and included other healthcare providers and social service agencies. It pleased Hilary to no end that she'd been on the ground floor of something that had benefited so many, and she'd love to be able to do it again.

The office of the college's program coordinator was on the ground floor in a part of the building Hilary had yet to visit. She'd scheduled an appointment for two o'clock and stood in the hallway waiting for the woman to finish her phone conversation. When the call ended, she counted to twenty, then knocked on the open door. "Hi, Ms. Cho? I'm Hilary Banks."

The woman waved a hand while not looking away from

her computer screen. "Yes, come on in, and call me Valerie. Take a seat, and I'll be right with you."

Hilary sat and mentally reviewed her talking points while waiting.

Valerie heaved a sigh and smiled before pushing back from her desk. "Done," she said, pivoting her wheelchair to roll to a small refrigerator. "I feel like I've been on the phone all day. Would you like some water? I'm parched."

"I'm good, but thanks."

Valerie returned to her desk with a bottle of water, smiling again. "You said in your email that you have an idea for a training program for the trades?"

"Yes," Hilary replied then shared the outline of her idea. "What do you think?"

Valerie hadn't interrupted but took notes the whole time. Now, she put her pen down and sat back. "I think it has merit, and you're correct. You will need community partners to get it off the ground."

Hilary opened her mouth but closed it when Valerie raised a staying hand. "The sticking point will be the community partners aspect. Finding ones who will collaborate without wanting to dominate."

"It sounds like you're speaking from experience," Hilary said.

"Indeed. Lots of people want to get involved with higher education and are willing to donate generously, but they put such tight restrictions on those donations that they're totally useless." She shook her head. "To the point that only redheaded, left-handed people who can tap dance and speak five languages may participate in the program."

Hilary laughed at the exaggeration. "So you're saying I should approach agencies that have proven their ability to play well with others."

"Bingo! I'll send you the names of non-profits that I think

would be interested. What businesses are you planning to approach?"

"So far, it's just Keeney Building Supply. They already take on our students, and I've spoken to one of their contractors."

Valerie bobbed her head, then narrowed her eyes. "Wait. Isn't that the #HotAndHandy guy?"

Heat rose up Hilary's neck. "Yes, that's Vincent."

"Well, well." Valerie waggled her eyebrows. "I'd sign up for classes with him."

It was on the tip of her tongue to say, "He's taken. In fact, he's mine," and wipe that smirk off Valerie's face. Instead, she smiled tightly.

Sitting in the breakroom, Vincent and Tomas each pulled out their notebooks to record the details of the day's job. They had hung kitchen cabinets in three new condos for a developer and were excited at the prospect of doing more work for the company.

"Water or coffee?" Vincent asked, going to his locker to put away his gloves.

"None. My back teeth are floating. I gotta go to the john." Tomas headed out the door while Vincent moved to the coffeemaker.

"Oh, good. You're here." Iris stood in the doorway.

"Hey, what's up?" Vincent raised his coffee mug in greeting.

She looked frazzled. A pair of glasses rested on the top of her head, and another pair sat on the end of her nose. "Payroll is messed up. For some reason, both you and Tomas are entered twice. But with different social security numbers. Can you write yours down? I want to confirm which is correct."

He was writing on a pad of paper when Tomas returned. "Hey, write down your social security number. Iris needs it."

Tomas froze in place. "Why?"

Vincent looked up at the wary response. "You've got one, right?"

"Of course I do. I was born here." Tomas scowled at Vincent and Iris, who backed up against the counter, clutching a printout against her chest.

"No one said you weren't. This isn't an immigration issue. Right Iris?"

Eyes wide, she nodded.

Jaw tightening, Tomas grabbed the pen and pad of paper on the table, and wrote down his number. Vincent pulled out a chair for Iris then sat beside her before shooting a glare at Tomas. "Show me both of the entries."

Iris pointed out where she had highlighted Vincent's name and number twice in pink. He glanced between the printout and the numbers on the paper. He pointed to one of the numbers. "This is the one that's correct." She put a checkmark beside it. "Now, let's look at the ones for Tomas." He compared the yellow highlighted names and numbers with Tomas's handwriting. He tapped the printout. "This one here." Iris dutifully checked one off. She was about to stand when Vincent said, "Huh."

"What is it?" Both Iris and Tomas spoke at the same time, then smiled at each other.

"The incorrect social security numbers are almost identical. Only the final digit is different." Vincent looked up at the others, eyes narrowed.

"What does that mean?" Tomas asked. The two men looked at Iris, who was shaking her head.

"I've never seen that before." She stacked the papers together and made to rise from the chair but gasped and grabbed the table.

"What? Is it your back?" Vincent stood quickly. He didn't like the lack of color in her face.

"Just a twinge. I'm fine." She hurried to the door, throwing a quick thank you over her shoulder.

The men looked at each other and shrugged before returning to their notebooks, intent on their next project.

CHAPTER 15

"When are you going to show me your tiny house?" Hilary nudged his foot with her own as they sat on her back deck eating nachos. Since the previous week, they had made it to home plate every night. He'd returned to his house the first two nights, and they'd slept separately. The third night, she asked him to stay, and he did.

To his surprise, he was a cuddler, cradling her against his chest or spooning against her back as they fell asleep. In the mornings, he'd awake surprised and delighted to find her still there. And more delighted to discover she was an enthusiastic fan of morning sex.

When she was a boneless heap of satisfaction, he'd kiss her neck, set her alarm, and leave to shower at his place. It was a great way to start the day, and more than one person at KBS commented on his perpetual smile.

"Whenever you want." He slid his fingers through her hair. That was another thing, he was a toucher. If they were in the same room, he wanted some form of contact with her.

"Cool!" She set down her wineglass and leaped up. "I'm ready for the tour."

He stood more slowly, rolling his eyes and heaving a sigh.

"Oh, come on." She moved toward the stairs. He grabbed her hand and pulled her back against him, burrowing his nose in her neck.

The sound of a car door closing caught their attention, making them jump apart.

"Hey, Iris," Hilary called, peering over the railing.

Iris looked up, gave a quick wave, and darted into the house.

"That's weird. She's barely spoken to me this week." Hilary held his hand as they walked across the grass. "Is everything okay at work?"

He shrugged. "I think so. I've been so damn busy I've barely seen her."

The conversation stopped as they approached his door. The upper half was frosted glass, framed with bright red paint. The bottom of the door was black. He pushed it open and stepped back to allow Hilary to enter. Propped against the doorway, he crossed his arms over his chest and watched her. She gasped and clasped her hands together, then kicked off her flip-flops and stepped onto the polished concrete floor. He had pushed out one end of the garden shed and raised the peaked roof. It was now about eight feet wide by twenty feet long. To his left was a compact bathroom: toilet, shower, and a sink with storage underneath it. To his right was a comfortable built-in couch, upholstered in denim, with bright red throw pillows. Across from it was a bookcase and flat-screen TV. Farther down was a decent-sized kitchen, separated from the main room by a counter with two stools tucked beneath it. To the right of the counter, beside the entrance to the kitchen, a staircase led to the loft bedroom.

Hilary was busy opening the doors to the cupboards beneath the stairs and oohing and aahing. He released the breath he didn't know he was holding and settled on the couch. Besides Iris and his mom, she was the first to see it, and he hadn't realized how much her opinion mattered. When she grinned at him and headed up the stairs, he followed her. She kneeled on the bed, examining the books on the shelves surrounding his bed, and turned on and off the lights mounted in the wood.

She fell back against the pillows, stroking the chenille comforter and gazing at the skylights in the peaked roof. "You designed this, didn't you?"

He nodded, proud of the work that he'd done, and thankful for Iris's trust and support.

She shifted her gaze to focus on his face. "It's really lovely. Can you teach others to do this kind of thing?"

"Probably, but I haven't really thought about it."

"Isn't that what you're doing with Carl?"

It hadn't started out that way, but Carl was curious and full of questions about products, methods, and techniques. Vincent was now in the habit of starting each project with an explanation of the whys and the hows. And God bless him, Carl paid attention, took notes, and rarely made the same mistake twice. "Yeah, I guess I am."

"Do you like doing it?"

"I do. As much as I like working on a project, seeing him do well makes me feel good."

"I think you are very good at what you do." Her eyes crinkled with her smile.

He gazed at the woman on his bed, thinking life was pretty much perfect except for one minor detail. He prowled toward her, ripping his T-shirt off and tossing it to the floor. His hands went to his fly. He wrestled his jeans, underwear, and socks to the floor, then stood naked in front of her. "Why are you still dressed?"

"Just enjoying the show," she said with a saucy grin.

He stood tall, palming his cock as he watched her eyes watching him. When they fell to half-mast and her tongue darted out to touch her lips, quick as a snake, he reached out and grabbed her ankles, drawing her to him. Before she could blink, her shorts and panties were down, and his nose was rooting in her heat. He couldn't get enough of her. When she sighed, he settled between her legs, and started lapping up the wetness seeping from her seam. When she groaned, fisting her hands in his hair to hold him to her, he smiled, happy to know there was something else he was good at.

Much later, he stroked a lazy hand over Hilary's hip and thigh, thinking about Iris's odd behavior. "What do you know about social security numbers?" Frazzled didn't begin to describe Iris; she jumped like a scared rabbit whenever he approached her. Worried that either he or Tomas was doing something wrong, he'd asked Ali. The older man had waved off his concerns, assuring him that their clients were happy and there was lots of work lined up for them.

Hilary was sprawled across him, limp as a noodle. She may have said, "Not a damn thing," or she may have said, "What do you want to know?" Her face was buried in his neck, and her words were muffled, so he continued. He relayed the moment with Iris and Tomas and the duplicate, almost matching numbers. "How do you think that happened?"

Pulling back, she propped herself up on an elbow. "Well, it's perfectly understandable for someone to make a data entry error and enter someone's information twice. But for two people to have multiple numbers so similar? That's a little hinky?"

"Hinky?"

She moved a hand through the air in a so-so gesture. "Questionable. Not an accident."

He pondered her response, absently running a hand up and down her spine.

"How many people have access to the payroll program?" she asked quietly.

It was a few moments before he responded, "Not many."

CHAPTER 16

Without a doubt, Iris was avoiding him, so Vincent called in the big guns. He talked to his mom.

The ice chest was sitting on the kitchen table, an insulated cooler next to it. Something new. He opened it to find bottles of milk, orange juice, and water. He lifted the lid of the ice chest. It was filled to the top with sandwiches and baggies of cut-up fruit and vegetables.

Marcia bustled in, heading to the coffeemaker. Her office was in a bedroom Ali redid for her many years ago. She might work from home, but Marcia was completely dressed with full makeup. No pajamas for her.

"No pop?"

"That boy needs to eat healthy foods. He doesn't need the sugar. It won't hurt you, either."

Vincent's eyes narrowed as he poked at the bag of veggies. Underneath, he found a container of ranch dressing and a baggie of cookies. He *could* eat the veggies, but he definitely *would* eat the cookies.

He joined his mother at the coffeemaker and planted a

kiss on the top of her head. She leaned into him and smiled. "Do you have a few minutes?"

"Is this about Hilary?"

"What?" He jerked back.

"The woman you're seeing?" She handed him a full mug of steaming, black coffee. "Are you practicing safe sex?"

"Ma!"

Marcia grinned evilly and leaned against the counter. He shook his head at her. "Yes, we're being safe." The truth was, they weren't using anything. It was the first time in his life he'd ever done so, and he felt honored that Hilary had let him do so. But his mother didn't need to know that.

"You deserve someone special, and she seems like a nice woman. But are you sure she's not on the rebound and only using you? That's what divorcées do you know."

Great. Like he needed that thought rolling around in his brain. He glared over his coffee at her. "What the hell, Ma?"

"Sorry, sweetheart. Just messing with you. Hilary doesn't seem like the kind of person who would do that. More like the relationship type."

Now he had that thought in his brain, which felt a hell of a lot better. A relationship with Hilary? He pictured himself taking her to the movies or out to dinner. Spend the day hiking or maybe skiing. He made a mental note to ask her if she skied or snowboarded. Snuggled up with Hilary in front of a fire after a day on the slopes sounded perfect.

Marcia patted his arm and made to leave the room.

He shook off the image and said, "It's not Hilary I want to talk about. It's Iris."

Now he had Marcia's full attention. She moved to the table and sat down, cradling her coffee mug between her hands. "She hasn't called me for a while. I didn't see her at church yesterday, either. But then I got busy…"

"I'm not sure what it is, but something is going on at KBS, and Iris is avoiding me." At Marcia's anxious expression, he held up a hand. "Tomas and I are busy, and lots of work is coming in. Ali told me we're doing great. Eddie is still out of commission. Maybe it's him. When I get done this afternoon, would you come by the store? Maybe grab Ali, and we'll talk to Iris together?"

She nodded, deep in thought.

Giving her another kiss, he slung the cooler over his shoulder and hefted the ice chest. "I really appreciate you doing this, but I can feed myself."

Her face brightened. "But then I wouldn't get to see my boy every day. It's not a hardship at all."

"Thanks, Ma," he said and headed out the door.

It was close to five when he heard his mother enter the breakroom. "What is it about EMPLOYEES ONLY you don't understand?" he asked.

She waved a dismissive hand. "Is Iris in her office?"

"Yeah. With the door closed."

Marcia's eyes narrowed. Unlike Eddie, Iris never closed the office door. She always wanted to know what was going on. "Right. Let's go."

"Should we wait for Ali?" Vincent asked, leaning back in his chair. He really wasn't looking forward to this.

Marcia shook her head. "He'll be here shortly. Might as well go rip the bandage off."

Vincent trailed her the few steps between the two rooms. She grabbed the knob and opened the door without hesitation. He smiled slightly. His mother *never* hesitated.

Iris looked up and burst into tears. Marcia rushed to her and wrapped her arms around the sobbing woman. Propped against the doorway, he knew he'd done the right thing. He turned at the sound of footsteps.

"Oh boy. That's bad," Ali muttered.

"No shit," Vincent replied.

Ali shouldered past him to sit in one of the two chairs facing the desk. Vincent sighed and moved to the other.

Eventually, Iris's tears stopped, and she sat back in her chair, wiping her eyes. Marcia remained beside her. They might be best friends, but the two women were unalike. Bird-like, Iris was nervously energetic and slightly apologetic. The word for Marcia was robust. Short, rounded, and full of color, she was a force to be reckoned with. Her upright posture was a sharp contrast to Iris's slumped form.

"Eddie's embezzling." Marcia stared directly at Ali and Vincent. They both jerked but didn't say anything.

Throwing a crumpled tissue into the wastebasket, Iris heaved a sigh before speaking. "As far as I can tell, he's been doing it for the past year. He adds a fake employee and sets up a direct deposit to a bank account. After a few months, that employee 'quits.'" Iris air quoted. "And another takes their place."

Hands tightening on the arms of the chair, Vincent shared a look with Ali and knew the same thought was going through his head; *fucking Eddie.* The guy had everything handed to him on a silver platter, yet he was screwing over his own mother.

Ali cleared his throat. "How…um…did you catch it?"

Iris glanced up and shifted in her chair. "The new state family and medical leave program. I had to account for each of the employees, and I noticed duplicate social security numbers. When I did some more digging, I saw those numbers were linked to the same bank account."

"In Eddie's name?" Vincent fought to keep the anger out of his voice.

Covering her face with her hands, Iris nodded. "Why would he do this?" she asked through her sobs. "We gave him everything we had. What did we do wrong? It must be Fiona's doing. She must have taken advantage of him when Darryl died. I'm sure she put him up to it."

Vincent leaned forward in his chair, but Ali's hand on his arm stopped him before he could speak. He looked up to see Marcia scowling at him. He sat back and crossed his arms, feeling impotent and wishing he could throttle Eddie.

"You and Darryl didn't do anything wrong." Marcia sighed and rubbed Iris's shoulder. "You loved that boy and raised him the best way you knew how. As for the whys? Only Eddie can answer those."

"How many fake employees are there?" Ali asked.

Iris dropped her hands into her lap and sniffed. "Two. A fake Vincent and a fake Tomas."

"Before them, how many were there?"

"Never more than two at a time."

Ali rubbed a hand over his bald head. "Full-time or part-time?"

"Part-time," Iris answered, wiping her eyes. "Why?"

He blew out a breath. "Two part-time employees working at minimum wage isn't a huge amount of money. A few grand a month, I imagine." He said the last statement as if it were a question.

Iris nodded.

"Why would Eddie need the extra cash?" Ali squinted, looking up at the ceiling. "He makes a damn good salary."

Vincent leaned forward, switching his focus between Iris and Ali. "I thought Eddie was an owner. Why is he drawing a salary?"

A blush moved across Iris's blotchy face. Her attention was on the pages in front of her when she spoke. "KBS was originally set up with Darryl and me as joint partners. When it became obvious that Darryl wasn't going to get better and Eddie came home, Darryl had our lawyer change our corporate structure. He was afraid Eddie would run roughshod over me. We changed it so Ali is the operations manager, I'm the CEO, and Eddie is the marketing manager. The three of us together were to make decisions." She looked up at

Marcia, tears welling in her eyes again. "After Darryl passed, I was lost and didn't want to come in. Eddie would bring papers by for me to sign. And I...I just signed them without reading them."

Shooting an evil look at the two men, Marcia wrapped her arms around Iris without a word.

"It never occurred to me to verify that Iris knew what she was signing," Ali said, gripping the arms of the chair with white-knuckled hands. "Eddie said you were feeling poorly, so I let things go."

Iris gave Ali a watery smile. "No one is blaming you. I...I trusted my son."

"Did *he* change the corporate structure?" Marcia asked.

"No, but he gained signing access to the bank accounts," Iris answered.

Vincent stared helplessly at his mother's best friend, grinding his teeth with the effort of keeping his mouth shut. Iris certainly wasn't perfect, but she did not deserve a bastard for a son.

"Is Eddie still in Vegas?" Ali asked.

Iris shook her head. "No, he's been back in Kirkland for the past week. But he developed a reaction to the antibiotics and has a serious case of diarrhea. That's why he hasn't been coming into KBS."

Eddie with a case of the trots. Good karma. Vincent chewed on his inner cheek to prevent himself from laughing. "What are you going to do?" He looked pointedly at the phone.

Iris's mouth opened and closed, but no sound came out. The other three waited for her to speak, not coming to her rescue. "I don't want to bother him when he's not feeling well," she murmured.

Marcia rolled her eyes.

Ali's lips thinned.

"Oh, for Christ's sake," Vincent said. "Pick up the phone

and ask him. It's your business, and you have a right to know."

"You should also hear his side," Marcia pointed out.

Silence. Iris looked at each of them in turn, then slowly reached for the desk phone. She dialed and put the phone on speaker when Eddie answered.

"Hi, honey, how are you feeling?"

"Awful." The voice on the other end sounded groggy. "I'm pretty sure I've crapped out five pounds. I can't move more than ten feet away from the toilet. My ass is chapped—"

Red-faced, Iris cut him off. "That's too bad hun, but umm…there's something I need to ask you. It's umm…about payroll."

"I told you to leave payroll alone, I can take care of it from here. Don't worry."

"Well, hun, it's just that…there's two extra employees on the payroll, and their paychecks are going into a bank account in your and Fiona's names." Iris heaved a sigh after she got it out.

"Fuck," Eddie said softly.

Vincent stirred in his chair and made eye contact with Marcia and Ali. He shifted his gaze, and it caught on a leather-bound book sitting on the corner of the desk. Why did that look familiar?

There was a strained laugh on the other end of the phone then Eddie said, "Oh! I know what that is. Fiona and I were test-driving a new automatic deposit system and used our account for the test run. She forgot to transfer the funds back. I'll get her to do it tonight."

Marcia nudged Iris and frowned at the phone. Iris cleared her throat before speaking again. "But, honey, it's been happening for over a year. Didn't you notice the extra money in the account?"

"That account belongs to Fiona. I've never looked at it."

"But—"

"Mom, I gotta go, I feel another crap coming on. I'll call you later."

The line went dead.

"He threw Fiona under the bus?"

"Yep."

"His wife. He threw his wife under the bus?"

"Yep."

"Who does that?"

"Eddie McLeod."

Vincent was downing the pot roast she had cooked like he hadn't eaten in days while her plate was untouched. She was too busy trying to process all he had told her.

"But—" She gazed at him earnestly, hands clenched on either side of her plate.

"Babe, I know." Vincent placed his knife and fork down and reached over to take one of her hands. "Eddie thinks only of himself. He doesn't have a soul." He kissed her knuckles, released her hand, and went back to his meal.

It had been a long time since she had cooked a meal for a man. Her lips tipped up, she watched him butter a slice of bread and mop up the rich gravy. "I take it you like pot roast."

"No shit. I've never had a better pot roast." He narrowed his eyes at her. "And don't you dare tell my mother."

She laughed, and finally started on her own meal. She'd been worried about cooking dinner, setting the table, sitting across the table from him. Chips and salsa on the deck on a Friday night were one thing, pot roast on a Monday was something else. Something people in a relationship did. *Not* friends with benefits.

He'd showered before coming over, and smelled of soap and clean laundry instead of sawdust. Stepping up behind her, he'd kissed her lightly and squeezed her waist as she stood at the counter making the salad. She'd turned back to the salad but glanced over her shoulder when she heard a sound. Vincent had re-set the table, so instead of sitting across from each other, the place settings were now at right angles to each other. He'd caught her look and shrugged slightly. "I like being near you." Her knees had all but given out at his explanation.

Now, he got up from the table to refill their water glasses and serve himself another helping. He looked relaxed, totally at home in her apartment. Looking around, she realized he *had* made himself at home. His library book was on the coffee table, one of his flannel shirts hung on a peg by the door, and his travel coffee mug sat on the counter near the sink. Seating himself at the table, he settled the full plate in front of him, and began eating with quick economic movements as if expecting someone to take the plate away from him.

"After supper, I thought we would go over the outline for the course. See if there is anything we've missed before we give it to the curriculum department." Putting the training program together excited her. Too many post-secondary schools concentrated on university level academic courses, ignoring the trades. A program that combined class work with on-the-job training backed by a local builder would serve the college well. Working with Vincent on it was the icing on the cake.

He swallowed a mouthful before speaking, "I thought it wasn't due until next week."

She toyed with her fork. "True."

"So we don't *need* to work on it tonight."

Without working on the proposed construction course, there wasn't a reason for him to be there. Not looking up from her plate, she shook her head. She tried not to show her disappointment, expecting him to leave at any moment. She startled when his finger dipped into the gravy on her plate.

Looking up, she saw him bring his finger to his mouth and slowly lick the gravy off it. Her mouth formed an O.

He leaned into her, eyes at half-mast. "How about we do the dishes, and then find something to entertain us?"

Hilary nodded.

"You finish eating, I'll be right back." He rose and kissed her on the forehead.

Hilary was loading the dishwasher when he returned with a Scrabble game. She laughed, not sure if she was relieved or disappointed.

Vincent moved beside her, started running hot water to wash the pots, grabbed the dishcloth, and wiped down the table. "I used to play regularly with this guy. I'm damn good."

"Was that when you were in…" Hilary was never quite sure how to refer to his time in jail.

"Inside?" Vincent quirked an eyebrow at her. "Yeah. Bill would organize tournaments. I never won, but I came close a few times."

Hilary picked up a tea towel and started drying the pot lid Vincent handed her. "Huh. I pictured you lifting weights or playing ping pong."

"Did that too, but Scrabble is good for the brain. Have you played?"

"Not for a while. I might be a bit rusty."

Vincent gave her a wicked grin. "I'll try not to take advantage of you."

The tiles were not presenting in Hilary's favor. The best she could come up with was PLAY. Vincent was fast. He'd built on that before she retrieved her new tiles. He added FORE in front of the P. She didn't look at him, instead arranging the tiles on her rack before slowly spelling out FLIRT.

Vincent used the A in PLAY for LAP.

She hung the word KISS off the bottom of the T, shifting in her chair and pressing her thighs close together.

He watched her silently as he placed COC above the K.

She turned an S into SLIDE.

He added USSY to a P.

The letters were barely on the board when he stood and advanced. He pushed her chair back and bent down, thrusting his tongue into her mouth. She reached for his fly. In moments she was inside his pants, one hand on his ass, the other stroking his cock. He growled. She leaned forward and stroked the pre-cum with her tongue. "I like this game," she said, licking her lips.

Scooping her up and heading to the bedroom, he said, "Oh, but it gets better."

She bounced when he tossed her on the bed, staring at her with predatory eyes. His jeans hanging open, his hard cock bulged over the top of his underwear. Expecting him to move on her quickly, she shifted her legs restlessly with anticipation. After years of drought, she was happy to be getting sex on a regular basis, and Vincent didn't disappoint. He was passionate and generous while playful and gentle. Unlike David, he didn't shy away from her scars, learning where she was most sensitive and what pleased her.

What pleased her was watching him undress. He did so now, revealing acres of taut muscle under smooth skin. Skin she was allowed to explore.

Rising on her knees, she shed her sweatshirt and tossed it aside to reveal a turquoise camisole edged with gray lace.

A slow smile curved Vincent's lips as he ran a finger under the satin shoulder strap. "I like this one. Does it have matching panties?"

She nodded.

"Will you show me?"

Keeping her eyes on him, she slowly slid her pants down her legs, and bent over to kick them off.

"Wait. Turn around," Vincent ordered.

She shuffled around to display the pretty bow that covered the back of the panties, looking over her shoulder when he sucked in a breath.

"Yes," he hissed, palming her butt cheeks with both hands. "A present just for me."

A shiver went through her as he drew the panties down, trailing his fingers between her cleft.

He clambered onto the bed behind her and walked her up to plant her hands on the headboard. "Don't move," he said. Ever so slowly, his hands traced up her legs, over her hips, and around her waist. Pulling her back against him, she felt his cock press between her thighs to drag through her wet folds. Gripping a hip with one hand, he used the other to glide his cock back and forth, edging her until she saw stars. "Such a good girl," he murmured in her ear.

"Such a jerk," she gritted out in response.

"Yeah?" he replied. "Do you want something?"

She sighed out a yes.

"I can't hear you. You have to tell me what you want." He teased the head of his cock against her clit mercilessly.

She groaned. "Inside. I need you inside."

Vincent fell back, leaving her gasping. Then he widened her legs to pull her down on top of him, driving into her sheath in a hard thrust.

"Yes," they cried out together.

The angle was new, and she squirmed to accommodate all of him. He slid one hand inside her camisole to stroke against the underside of her scar while the other snaked down to play with her clit.

The orgasm hit her like a freight train, and she sagged in his arms. He eased her off him to lay her on the bed. Glassy-eyed, she smiled, opening her arms and legs to take him in. He entered her in one long, smooth stroke. His eyes remained on hers as he slowly moved in and out until he stiffened and found his release.

Replete, she took his weight and held him close, kissing the side of his neck and believing she truly was the luckiest woman in the world.

CHAPTER 17

Idly playing with her hair, Vincent was on his back as she lay across his chest. This was good. He'd had partners but never girlfriends. He smiled to himself and gently squeezed Hilary's ass. Yep, this was good. He looked around the room he had grown quite fond of. Unlike the rest of the apartment, the colors of the bedroom were muted and restful. Her camisole and panties stood out against the pale yellow club chair on which they'd been tossed. She was a contrast as well. A bright, passionate woman who dressed in drab clothes under which she wore sexy underwear.

His phone rang. Shifting Hilary, he grabbed his jeans from the floor and dug his phone out of his back pocket.

"Hey, Ma. Umm…sure. Here, just a second." He handed the phone to Hilary. A muscle ticked in his jaw in his effort not to laugh at the look on her face.

She sat up, one hand clutching the phone to her ear, the other clutching the sheet to her chest. "Hello?" Her expression moved from confusion to concern. "Sure. I'll see you in half an hour. Bye."

Hilary dropped the phone and leaped out of bed, grabbing her clothes as she raced to the bathroom. "Get up and get dressed! Your mother is going to be here in half an hour," she called over the sound of running water.

At a slower pace, he followed her, taking the wet washcloth from her hand as she moved to clean up. "That's my job," he said, wrapping one arm around her waist, and using the cloth to wash gently between her legs. He met her frantic eyes in the mirror. "What's up?"

She waved her hands in front of her. "She wants my help with something. She didn't want to get into it over the phone." Her voice rose with each word.

"Okay. So why the panic?" He dropped the washcloth in the sink and wrapped his arm around her shoulders, kissing her neck.

She practically danced in place. "Because she'll see us. She'll know we've been having sex."

His lips twitched. This time, he kissed her on the temple. "She already knows." When Hilary's eyes widened, he continued. "Iris must have told her we were together, then she asked me. I said yes."

Hilary covered her face with her hands and groaned. "Oh God. This is awful."

He stiffened. "Why?"

"She's gonna think I'm taking advantage of you. That I'm a cougar!"

Relaxing, he turned her in his arms. He pulled her hands from her face, and kissed her gently. "Babe, I'm thirty. You can't take advantage of me." Her eyes remained closed, and she gently banged her head against his chest. "And she's not going to think you're a cougar. She's seen both your bicycle and your wardrobe."

Hilary reared back and narrowed her eyes. "What's wrong with my wardrobe?"

"You don't wear provocative clothes. You dress like a professional woman." He felt her relax, then whispered in her ear, "A professional woman who wears seriously sexy underwear."

She grinned and pushed away from him. "Well, let me get dressed in my professional-woman-relaxing-at-home clothes to greet your mother."

He stepped back. "Just don't forget the Sexy AF underwear."

"She's here," Vincent called. He'd volunteered to put the Scrabble game away while she freaked out over what to wear.

Hilary hurried from the bedroom, adjusting the loose pale pink tunic she wore over capri-length leggings. She'd debated putting on shoes, but it was summer, it was her place, and she had pretty pink nail polish on her toes, so she went barefoot. She stopped at the dining room table, gripping her hands together behind her back, unsure what the protocol was. Marcia was Vincent's mother. He was her...*what?* Mentally, she gave her head a shake and pasted on a smile as he opened the door and hugged his mother.

"Hi Marcia, can I get you something to drink?"

The older woman turned toward her. Vincent had the same coppery skin tone and looked exactly like her, but much taller, leaner, and definitely more masculine.

"Sure. White wine if you have it."

"I'll get it," Vincent offered, moving to the refrigerator. He pulled out a bottle of chardonnay as well as a bottle of beer. Pouring the wine into two glasses already on the counter, he handed them to the women, then snagged the beer for himself and motioned to the living room.

Hilary let Marcia precede her, noticing the small smile playing on her lips. Marcia took the armchair, and Hilary perched on the couch with Vincent beside her. He relaxed against the pillows, cocking his legs and brushing one knee against Hilary's thigh. She shifted slightly, putting a little distance between them and glaring at him over her shoulder. He ducked his head, but not before she caught the twitch of his lip.

She forced herself to sip her wine and not gulp it. "What is it I can help you with?" she asked.

"Did Vincent tell you about Eddie?" At Hilary's nod, she continued, "I want you to prove he took the money."

Hilary choked on her wine and coughed a few times before giving Vincent and Marcia a watery smile. He rose to get her a glass of water, which she gulped gratefully. "Seriously? I can't do that!"

Marcia leaned forward, her gaze fixed on Hilary. "I know you know your way around a payroll system." At Hilary's startled expression, she said, "Relax, I didn't stalk you. Iris told me you worked as an office manager. It shouldn't be too hard to figure out whose bank account the money is really going into."

Hilary shook her head. "It's not that easy. Payroll systems are only concerned about whether an account exists, not who set up the account."

"Can't Iris ask Fiona about the account?" Vincent asked.

Marcia grimaced. "She's not ready to do that yet. She and Fiona are...not close and never have been. They rarely get together which I think is Eddie's doing. He doesn't seem to want them to bond."

Tapping a finger against her glass, Hilary leaned back against the couch. Immediately, Vincent's arm went around her shoulder. "I know nothing about Fiona McLeod. What's she like?" She looked between Marcia and Vincent.

He shrugged. "I've never met her. I was inside when they got married."

"It's Han. Fiona never changed her name. I met her at the wedding...briefly." Marcia placed her wineglass down on the table to pull out her phone and scroll through photos. She found one and handed the phone to Hilary. Vincent leaned in to look as well. The screen showed an image of the bridal couple, Eddie and Fiona. An older couple stood on one side of them, and Iris on the other. Marcia pointed at the couple. "Those are her parents."

Hilary zoomed in on Fiona, a tiny, dark-haired woman dressed in a traditional red Vietnamese wedding dress. Eddie beamed next to her in a black tuxedo. Iris beamed as well, while the other couple wore strained smiles.

"Wait. I know her. Fiona Han is the director of Keeney Works. She and I have been playing phone tag for the past week." At the blank looks on Vincent and Marcia's faces, Hilary explained, "Keeney Works is a local non-profit that provides job training and assists with finding jobs for under-served populations. I'm trying to connect with her to explain our program and get her on board. She would be a valuable ally." Hilary took a breath. "I'd hate to think she was stealing from Iris."

"That would be a huge scandal, the director of Keeney Works embezzling from her mother-in-law." Vincent's eyebrows rose.

Marcia snorted. "You're not kidding. Keeney Works is the result of a lot of effort. Churches, non-profits, the city council, and the senior center spent a couple of years getting it off the ground. A lot of heads would roll if this were true. It's a model for other communities."

"Which is why a collaboration between them and our program would be a selling point for the college."

"I'm remembering Fiona now," Vincent nodded. "She was a senior when I was a freshman. Student council president, leader of the debate team, and seriously hot." He smirked at the glares from the women. "What? I was a hormonal teenager."

"Fiona's parents are first-generation Americans and very

successful," Marcia ignored Vincent, taking back her phone. "They started with one nail salon, opened four more in the area, and then opened a school for training nail technicians and cosmetology students. Both of the Han kids worked in the salons during school, attended university on scholarships, and worked in the family business. Fiona was the accountant before taking on the director's role at Keeney Works."

"So, she could have set up the false bank accounts," Vincent speculated, then shook his head. "But that doesn't sound like the Fiona I knew. She was seriously a straight arrow."

"She could. But she has so much to lose. Why would she do it?" Hilary frowned.

Vincent rose from the couch. "Why marry *Eddie* is a better question," he called over his shoulder on his way into the kitchen. He was back in a moment with the bottle of wine and a fresh beer for himself.

Marcia put a hand over her glass and shook her head. "When he wants to be, Eddie can be quite the charmer. She was obviously blinded to his asshole-ness." She caught Hilary's eye and smiled innocently.

Hilary looked up at Vincent. "You went to school with both of them. What was Eddie like?"

Vincent carefully filled her wineglass, then looked at his mother, who nodded. "Cocky and condescending. He was always the first to have the newest thing—cellphones, sneakers, video games, and would rub your nose in it. Nothing I wanted, but I could see how it bugged other guys."

"Was he popular with the girls?"

"I guess. He obviously overwhelmed Fiona at some point. They've been married for three years. Do you think he's done with her already?" Vincent sat on the couch and handed Hilary her refilled glass. He rewarded her thank you with a kiss on the nose.

Hilary darted a look at Marcia to see her reaction. The older woman wore a pleased grin. Hilary did not know how to feel about that but decided to drink her wine and worry about Marcia's reaction later.

"It's possible. I doubt Eddie married for love. It threw me that he didn't marry a white girl." Marcia pondered the question. "And I wouldn't be surprised if he's ready to move on. There was an article recently in the *Keeney Courier* about Fiona's parents. They've set up a trust stating their fortune will go strictly to charity, and that none of the children will inherit."

Hilary eyed Marcia speculatively. "I wonder if Fiona knows what Eddie is up to? Or even suspects."

"No idea. But I have a friend who plays Scrabble with her mother. Let me see if I can find out what the scoop is."

Hilary choked on her wine again. Vincent hid a smirk as he handed the glass of water to her.

"Are you okay?" Marcia asked, looking up from her phone.

"I'm fine. I just…didn't know Scrabble was so popular in this town."

Marcia resumed looking at her phone. "Yeah, competition can get heated at the senior center."

Vincent snorted. Hilary gave him the side-eye and elbowed him in the ribs.

"Aha!" Marcia looked up and beamed at them. "I just bought tickets to Keeney Works' fundraising gala. You'll have a chance to meet Fiona Han next Saturday."

"Oh! Wow," Hilary said and gulped her wine. "That's good. Good idea."

incent's eyes narrowed. Why had Hilary shut down? She was clutching her wineglass so hard he was afraid the stem would break. He stroked the back of her neck. She jerked up and gave him a quick smile that didn't reach her eyes. Fortunately, his mom didn't notice. She chattered on about the fundraiser and convincing Ali to wear a suit jacket.

Standing up from the couch, he announced, "Ma, I'll walk you out to the car."

Marcia stuffed her phone into her purse and rose as well. "Thanks, honey. Hilary, I'll call you tomorrow. I bought six tickets so we can figure out who all will be at our table."

Still clutching her wineglass, Hilary stood and moved woodenly toward the door. "Sounds good."

After kissing his mother goodbye and watching her pull out of the driveway, he walked back up the stairs to find the kitchen and living room empty. He followed the light coming from the bedroom to find Hilary standing in her walk-in closet, arms wrapped tightly around herself. He leaned against the doorway and checked out the closet as well.

It was a damn fine job. On the cedar-lined wall to the left were shelves for sweaters and shoes, with a bank of drawers beneath them. On the right were three rods for hanging clothes; one for dresses and longer items, two mounted, one above each other for shirts, jackets, blouses, and the like. Directly across from the pocket door was a full-length mirrored cabinet for jewelry.

Hilary didn't have many clothes. Unsurprisingly, they were arranged neatly and by color. Not that there was much of it. She seemed to wear mostly muted tones.

He followed her gaze, which was fixed on the rack of dresses. There were three of them. All conservative, all rather shapeless, all dark. Vincent didn't know much about women's clothes, but he could guess…

"Do you need to go shopping?"

She caught his eye in the mirror and grimaced. "I have nothing for a gala."

Vincent pulled his hands out of his pockets and stepped forward to wrap his arms around her, and rest his chin on her shoulder. "Neither do I."

She rolled her eyes. "Yeah, but you're a man, and you look like you. Pants, a shirt, and your good to go. Me, on the other hand…"

"So, buy a dress. There's more than a week before the event."

"Um-hum," she agreed but didn't look happy.

"And maybe some killer shoes to show off those gorgeous legs of yours." He waggled his eyebrows. She smiled slightly at that.

"What is it?" He kissed her behind the ear, and squeezed her gently.

"Are we going to this together?"

"Yeah. I figured you and I would meet Ma and the others there. Or we could pick Ma up on the way."

Hilary shook her head. "No. I mean, are we together? Are we a couple? Because if we're not, if this is just us hanging out and having sex, I'm okay with that. But if we go to the gala together, people might wonder. It will be the first time we go out in public and…" She wasn't meeting his eyes, and it didn't feel like she was breathing.

He kissed her behind the ear again, then tilted her chin until she met his gaze in the mirror.

"We *are* together. We *are* a couple. We are walking into the gala holding hands. I want everyone there to know you are *mine*."

Her eyes widened as she took in the possessive tone in his voice. "Okay," she whispered, "but I still don't have anything to wear."

Turning her in his arms, he kissed her soundly. "You've

got time," he muttered before wrapping his arms around her and cradling her against his chest. He stared at their reflection. Her riot of silvery curls against his own raven-dark hair. It didn't bother him at all. He couldn't care less how old she was or that her body didn't conform to society's view of femininity. Now, if only *she* could be comfortable with that.

CHAPTER 18

$\mathcal{H}$ilary answered the ringing phone in a breathy voice, "I'm naked and in bed, where are you?"

Silence.

She checked the screen of her phone. Unknown number. Crap! She'd thought it was Vincent. She hung up. Thirty seconds later, it rang again. Unknown number again. This time, she let it ring three times before answering as professionally as possible, "This is Hilary."

"Hi, it's Marcia. I just tried calling and got some phone sex operator. I must have misdialed."

Hilary slid down on the bed pillows, her toes curling in embarrassment. "That's weird. They must have a number similar to mine."

"Yeah." Marcia laughed. "I hope you don't start getting pervy phone calls."

Hilary forced out a chuckle and reached for her glass of wine. She'd eaten by herself as Vincent was on a job, which was taking longer than anticipated. He texted her with instructions she'd followed through to the letter, including the two cans of whipped cream. Now, she was naked and talking to his mother. Gah!

"Anyhoo, I won't keep you. I chatted with Iris today. KBS will pick up the cost of the tickets, but Iris won't be going."

"Really, why's that?" Hilary focused on the conversation rather than her lack of clothing.

"She hemmed and she hawed, but when I pushed her, she told me that Eddie told her that Fiona didn't want her anywhere near her. Apparently, Eddie told Iris that Fiona told him that Iris and Darryl said something derogatory about Vietnamese nail salons being fronts for massage parlors. And I'm using air quotes around *massage*." Marcia paused to take a breath, and it sounded like a sip from her own glass of wine.

Staring at her toes, Hilary thought about the hard-working women who worked in nail salons and how easy it was to spread false information.

Marcia continued, "I think it's a crock. Darryl may have been rough around the edges, but he would never think that, and he sure as hell wouldn't say that. Regardless, Iris does not feel comfortable asking Fiona to endorse the program."

"I don't blame her," Hilary murmured. She couldn't imagine having an antagonistic relationship with her in-laws. In fact, she still exchanged emails with her ex-mother-in-law, a lovely woman who was not at all to blame for her insensitive douche of a son.

"So, you're going to be riding point."

"What!" Hilary sat up so fast that wine sloshed down her chest. She placed her glass on the nightstand, then palmed her face. This wasn't good.

"You represent the college, not KBS. Keeney Works will benefit from this relationship, and that is the point you have to drive home."

Speechless, she listened as Marcia went on. Though good at public speaking, Hilary hated it. It made her heart race. Crap. *This is what happens when you have a good idea.*

She was off the phone and staring sightlessly at the

ceiling when Vincent entered. He leaned against the door, taking a pull from the beer in his hand. "Yum."

Rolling her head to the side, she gave him the side-eye, closed her eyes, and sighed.

"What happened?"

"Your mother just steamrolled right over me. I have to buttonhole Fiona at the gala and sell her on the proposal. Arrgghh! And I still have nothing to wear!"

Vincent walked to the side of the bed and leaned over to kiss her on the nose. She scowled at him. He grinned at her. He toed off his boots, put his beer down, and made short work of removing his clothes. "Ma's right. You're the perfect person to talk to Fiona. You have no history with her, and you have the backing of the college."

He lay on the bed, snagging her around the waist and pulling her close. He frowned when his hand came away wet. "What's this?"

"Chardonnay," she responded absently.

"Okay…I'm not sure how that's gonna work with whipped cream, but I'm game to try."

Before she could reply, he leaned over and licked her from her navel to her collarbone. She forgot about Marcia, Fiona, and the dreaded gala, discovering that whipped cream and chardonnay *did* pair well together.

"What the hell are we doing here?" Ali whispered, following Vincent, Tomas, and Carl into Boutique on Main. They'd been next door assessing an empty store whose owner wanted it renovated for a combination bookstore, coffee shop, and wine bar. The four men in dusty work boots looked out of place as they huddled in the entryway of the incredibly feminine dress shop. Vincent ignored the question. "I'll just be a moment. Don't touch anything." The men huddled closer as Vincent wound his way through the displays of silky blouses, sexy dresses, and stiletto shoes to the counter at the back of the store. He certainly wasn't comfortable in the shop, but he wasn't about to show fear in front of the guys.

"May I help you?" A gauzy pink curtain parted, and a tiny older woman entered the shop from a back room. Dressed all in black, she had cropped gray hair, enormous gold earrings, and thick glasses framed in rhinestones. She tottered around the counter on three-inch, leopard-print heels. Possibly not her best choice of shoes.

He held out his hand. "I'm Vincent. We spoke on the phone this morning." When her forehead wrinkled, he added, "I'm here to buy a dress for my girlfriend."

The woman nodded. "Oh, right! I'm Betty Anne." She took his hand in both of hers. "What lovely calluses you have." She smiled up at him through her lashes. "I bet you're very good with your hands."

What the hell was he supposed to say to that? "Umm…yes?"

He felt a wall of testosterone behind him.

"You're buying a dress?" Ali asked.

"You've got a girlfriend?" Carl asked.

Tomas grunted.

Ignoring them, Vincent pulled out his phone. He found a photo of Hilary and showed it to Betty Anne, who was immediately swarmed by men looming over her shoulder. They studied the image in silence. Vincent had caught Hilary unaware. She was in profile, reaching up to water a hanging basket. Standing on tiptoes, in shorts and a tank top, her curly gray hair tucked behind her ears.

Betty Anne tapped the screen. "Does she pad?"

"No," Vincent said. "She wears loose shirts in public."

"How tall is she?"

Vincent held his hand up to his chin. "About this high, I guess."

"Hold still," Carl pulled out his tape measure. He gave one end to Vincent and dropped to the floor with the other. "Looks like 5'9"."

"Shoe size?" Betty Anne asked. "And how high of a heel?"

"She wears a size nine and as high as you've got," he said with a grin.

Betty Anne gave the phone back. Perfume wafted behind her as she tottered to a rack of dresses. "Come back in an hour," she ordered.

"Yes, ma'am," Vincent replied, turning to the front door. Tomas plucked the phone from his hand and studied Hilary's picture as they exited. The men moved toward Vincent's truck, where he liberated the cooler from the back seat. Ali unlocked the door to the empty store and held it open for the others to precede him.

"Put the cooler down. I need to talk to you." Ali glowered at Vincent. Carl cleared off the counter for Vincent, who placed the cooler on top. He headed back out the door to Ali, who propped one hip against the truck, crossing his arms and tucking his hands in his armpits.

"Look, son, I know what you're trying to do for Hilary, but how the hell are you going to pay for it?" He jerked his chin at the dress shop. "That ain't Walmart."

Hands on his hips, Vincent snapped at Ali, "Not that it's any of your business, but I've made an arrangement with Betty Anne." He narrowed his eyes at the smirk on the older man's face. "Not that kind of arrangement."

Ali's white teeth gleamed against his weathered skin. "You said it, not me."

"She asked me to make a rolling step stool with a handrail for her. She has a hard time hanging displays and reaching items in her storage area."

Ali squinted off into the distance. "Okay, but one of those

dresses and a pair of designer shoes is gonna cost more than that."

Heat crawled up Vincent's neck as he mumbled quickly, "I agreed to be a model in the fall fashion show."

"I'm sorry, did you just say you're going to be in a fashion show?" Ali's eyebrows arched high.

Vincent pinched the bridge of his nose. "Yes. The senior center holds a fashion show in September, and Betty Anne wants me to escort the ladies down the runway."

Ali doubled over in laughter. Vincent crossed his arms and stared at the ground, waiting for him to recover.

"Wait 'til the guys hear about this," Ali said, wiping his eyes.

"Not one word," Vincent ground out.

"Oh, son, that is going to cost you big time." Ali strolled into the empty store, a scowling Vincent following close behind.

"Finally," Carl said. "I'm starved." Opening the cooler, he handed hoagies around to the others. Tomas ignored his, still studying the phone.

"What's the dress for?" Carl asked after swallowing his first bite.

"That fundraising dinner next week," Ali answered sourly. He and the others had been informed that morning they would be attending. Iris came up with a lame excuse, so the party would be Marcia, Vincent, Hilary, Ali, Tomas, and Carl. When informed of the dress code, no jeans, no work boots, jacket and tie suggested, Ali scowled, Tomas frowned, and Carl grinned. Vincent wasn't concerned. He had a suit from his trial if it still fit. If not, he'd get another.

What did concern him was Hilary and making her feel good about herself. Keeney was a small town, and interest would be high when an ex-con showed up at a public event. The woman with him would be scrutinized, and Vincent knew Hilary was not up to public scrutiny—yet. He'd shared his concerns with Tomas, who came up with the idea of buying the dress. Vincent hadn't intended to take an entourage with him, but needs must.

"Can Tomas and I bring dates?" Carl asked. At the quizzical looks he received, he continued. "You and Ali are taking dates. Why can't we?"

Ali practically did a spit take and vehemently shook his head. "It's not a date. Marcia and I are attending the same business function. That's it. It's not a date."

Vincent eyed the other men. "You'll have to buy their tickets, but sure. You got someone in mind?"

Carl's head bobbed up and down. "There's a girl in one of my classes. She really rocks a tool belt. I'll text her now." He looked over at Tomas. For the most part, Carl didn't talk to Tomas. Mostly because Tomas barely spoke to anyone. "Do you umm…think you can find a date?"

Tomas's lip curled. "Yeah, I can find a date. I'll buy a ticket tomorrow." He handed the phone back to Vincent with a smirk. "You're right, she's out of your league. My cousin does hair and makeup. Do you want her number? Give Hilary a Cinderella day?"

"Yeah, sure." Scraping a hand across his jaw, Vincent said, "She'll either be thrilled or want to kill me."

Ali spoke around the sandwich in his mouth. "She'll love it. Women love grand gestures. Don't forget accessories—jewelry, purses, all that stuff."

Vincent winced. This was bigger than he thought.

After insisting he didn't need help choosing the dress, Vincent returned to the dress shop. He tucked his hands in his back pockets and walked to the back of the store, praying he hadn't made a mistake. Since they'd started sleeping together, Hilary dressed more casually, with closer-fitting tops. But when she dressed for work or was headed somewhere public, the conservative loose shirts in muted shades were very much in play, like she was doing her best to disappear.

A headless mannequin was posed beside the counter, wearing the dress. It was royal blue, sleeveless, with a high neckline. It bloused loosely to the waist, coming together snugly around the hips and ending slightly above the knees. Vincent circled the mannequin and took in the back of the dress, which wasn't much. It was tied at the neck, then hung open in loose folds to the waist. Vincent imagined Hilary's ass filling out the snug fabric. "I'll take it."

Sitting behind the counter on a high stool, smoking a cigarette and sipping a martini, Betty Anne looked like a fashion Yoda. "Of course you will. Now, shoes." She nodded at the counter in front of her. Three pairs of shoes were laid out for his inspection. Two pairs with four-inch heels, one flesh-toned and the other red with both the toes and the heels cut out, and the last pair had a low heel but were leopard printed with a pointy toe. Why did those look famil-iar? He remembered and raised his eyes to Betty Anne, who winked before sipping her martini.

He ran a hand through his hair. "I'd like to get her all three pairs, but I don't think I can afford to."

"Can you work them off doing future projects for me?"

Wondering if he'd just sold his soul to the devil, he met the shrewd gaze of the tiny woman. It looked like he'd be giving up his free time for a while, but Hilary was worth it. "Yes," he answered slowly.

"Excellent!" She climbed down off the stool. She reached for a bill of sale and filled it out with a rhinestone-studded pen. "I had a double mastectomy thirty years ago. It was expected I'd get implants, so I did. I had them removed about three years later. It was the best decision I ever made." She peered at Vincent over her glasses. "Tits aren't everything."

. . .

He'd placed the boxes right in front of her door and expected her to be home any moment. Not that Vincent was spying on her. Finally, she arrived, parked her bike, removed her helmet, and finger-combed her hair. She grabbed her tote bag and started up the stairs.

He eased out of his house and watched. She stopped at the top of the stairs, obviously seeing the boxes. Unlocking the door, she carried everything inside. He couldn't wait any longer and hoofed it across the lawn, taking the stairs as quietly as possible.

She chose to open the shoes first. Holding up the red sling-backs, she heard him at the door and grinned. The nude pumps got a nod of approval, the leopard-print heels a laugh. Shaking her head, she opened the large box and pulled aside the tissue paper. Her eyes went wide as she reached in and lifted out the dress, then she dissolved into tears.

He rushed forward to hold her. "It's just a dress. You can return it. You can get anything you want." She wrapped her arms around him and buried her face in his chest. "Shh. It's okay. It's okay. I knew it was too much. I'll take it back."

With a violent shake of her head, she stepped away from Vincent, sniffed, and wiped her eyes on her sleeve. "I love it. It's beautiful. It's just…" She waved her hands up and down in front of her loose gray sweater and loose gray skirt. "This is me. And that's…"

"Who you are inside," he said softly, stepping closer and cupping her cheek in his hand. "Everything about you is color. Your dishes, your bed sheets, your throw pillows, your artwork, even your underwear. I don't know how long you've been hiding in the dark, but don't you think it's time to step into the light?"

She gave him a watery smile, and leaned into his hand. She touched her chest. "Before this, I was a freaking peacock. Even after the mastectomy and the chemo, I wore bright colors. But when the implants failed, and David left me, I just…faded away."

"But you're coming back. I've seen it. When we're together, you drop this dull disguise, and a vibrant woman is revealed. I want the rest of the world to see her. I want the rest of the world to see *you*." The fingers of one hand curled into a fist at his side. He wanted to find her ex-husband and beat him to a pulp for wounding her.

Hilary moved her hands up to cup Vincent's face. "Okay, we can say goodbye to the gray. But I'm not coloring my hair! I'm allergic to hair dye, and I won't—"

He silenced her with a kiss. "I love your hair. I don't want you to change it." Unclenching his hand, he stroked her ass. "I can't wait to see this in that dress."

Her smile was a little bit bigger. "I can't wait to show it to you."

CHAPTER 19

The place was packed, half the population of Keeney in attendance. At least, it seemed that way. Hilary scanned Vincent and his friends. They cleaned up well. Carl and his date Julia both wore tuxes. Marcia displayed a surprising amount of cleavage in an ivory cocktail dress. Ali was in a suit, but when spotting Tomas in his black jeans, black shirt, and black cowboy boots, he promptly removed his tie. Tomas's date was the same cousin who did Hilary's hair and makeup. Anjelica's dress was full-skirted, red, with small white polka dots, and looked like something from the '50s.

Standing next to Vincent, a nervous thrill went through Hilary. She looked fabulous and felt amazing. Anjelica wielded a makeup brush like a magic wand. She'd given Hilary smoky eyes, high cheekbones, and a choice between bright red lipstick and a nude gloss. She chose the nude gloss to match the nude heels. After Vincent took her home, she planned to switch to the red heels and red lipstick, and lose the dress. He looked like a god. While off the rack, his dark suit, dark shirt, and dark tie appeared to be made for him. He hadn't let go of her hand since they parked the car.

"You guys, go find our table, we'll be with you in a few minutes," Vincent said.

With a lift of his chin, Tomas led the others away, leaving Vincent and Hilary standing near the door. She looked up at him expectantly. "What's up?"

Maneuvering her into a corner, he positioned himself so his back was toward the room full of guests. He reached into his pocket and pulled out a small silk bag. Wordlessly, he handed it to Hilary.

Eyes narrowed, she slowly opened the bag and removed a wide silver cuff bracelet. She bit her lip, blinking rapidly, then raised her head to place a soft kiss on his lips.

He released his breath in a whoosh. He took the bracelet and opened the clasp. Inside was an exact replica of the dove tattooed on Hilary's wrist. "Tomas made it."

"It's lovely. Thank you." She held her wrist out for Vincent to put the bracelet on, waving her other hand up and down in front of her. "Everything you've done…thank you."

Lifting her hand, he kissed her knuckles and whispered, "You're worth it." Stepping back, he turned toward the room, still holding Hilary's hand. "Let's do this thing."

Over tequila shots in the parking lot, Marcia shared her plan with the rest of the group. Carl, Tomas, and their dates would distribute postcards to each place setting. It was a bold move, but Marcia explained that she would rather apologize for distributing the postcards than ask to do so.

The front of the postcard showed the Keeney Building Supply logo and the Keeney Community College logo super-imposed over a blueprint of a house. On the back side were the details of the course Vincent and Tomas would teach to underserved students.

Ali and Marcia would chat up the board members, find out if they'd heard about the program, and extol its benefits to the community.

Hilary's assignment was to introduce herself to Fiona.

Easy peasy. She had her elevator speech down pat, she looked fabulous, and Vincent was ready to provide backup if needed. *Easy peasy.*

With the benefit of four-inch heels, Fiona Han stood slightly above five feet. In a navy sheath, black hair up in a chignon, pearls in her ears and around her neck, she looked every inch the executive director of a worthy non-profit organization as she spoke to someone across the room.

For a brief moment, Hilary panicked. Her shoes were too high, her dress was too short, her makeup was too heavy, her jewelry was… She touched the cuff on her wrist. Vincent's gift. His many gifts. He believed in her, and now it was time for her to believe in herself. She squared her shoulders, let out a breath, and sallied forth, only to be brought up short when a man stepped in front of her.

Without looking at him, she moved to go past him, but he moved the same way. The same thing happened when she tried the other direction.

"Hey, pretty lady, what's your hurry?" Eddie McLeod asked, grinning crookedly and holding a drink she suspected wasn't his first.

She replied, "There's someone I need to speak to," and tried to move past him only to be stopped when he held out his arm.

"Who do you want to talk to? I know everyone here. Well, everyone *worth* knowing. Tell me who it is, and I'll come with you." He looked her up and down and winked. "Then we can go get a drink."

Giving him her most disarming smile, she said, "Thanks. An introduction to your wife would be wonderful."

It seemed to take a moment for him to register what she said, and then he blinked and mumbled something before taking off in the other direction. She exhaled her relief, and looked around for Fiona, hoping she hadn't seen the interaction. Fortunately, Fiona was just finishing up a conversation.

Hilary approached with a smile and an outstretched hand. "Fiona Han?"

The diminutive woman looked up, a polite smile on her lips.

"I'm Hilary Banks, we've been playing phone tag for the last couple of weeks."

Fiona took her hand, and her smile brightened. "Yes. Preparing for the gala has consumed me. It's nice to put a face with a name. I promise to call you next week." She withdrew her hand and began to move away.

"I'll walk with you. I know you need to get to your guests, and won't take much of your time." Hilary marveled at her own boldness, continuing to speak. "Keeney Community College is planning a skills course for entering the building trades. We're focusing on at-risk students and are teaming up with Keeney Building Supply to provide students with an internship opportunity. Students would work under the supervision of the two contractors KBS has on hand. KBS would then—"

Fiona stopped, forcing Hilary to stop as well. "I've heard about the contractors at KBS—they're criminals."

Hilary eyed her warily. "They did serve time in a minimum-security facility. However, while doing so, they completed a contracting program, have earned their licenses, and have reputations for doing good work. Customer reviews—"

Fiona's lips thinned. "They are slick cons who intimidate old ladies," she scanned Hilary from head to toe, "and prey on divorcées."

"Excuse me?" Hilary's eyes went wide.

Fiona shook her head. "You seem like a nice woman. But don't let yourself be taken in by that scheming low life. He takes advantage of vulnerable women and has been stringing my mother-in-law along for years. Iris is too soft-hearted and should listen to Eddie because Victor Ortiz will rob her blind and take away her livelihood.

"Now I must go. Enjoy your evening." She turned abruptly, waving like a prom queen to a group of well-heeled businessmen.

"Vincent. His name is Vincent Ortiz," Hilary mumbled to Fiona's retreating back. With slumped shoulders and brimming eyes, she stumbled her way through the crowd to the restroom, thankful to find it empty. What would she tell Vincent? She'd been so positive Keeney Works would support them, support *him*.

Eyes swimming with tears, she faced herself in the mirror. The bold blue dress no longer set off her silver-gray hair, giving her confidence. It mocked her. Who was she to think she could wow the head of a major non-profit? She was a joke. She didn't belong here. With shaky hands, she pulled her phone out of her clutch and exited the restroom, intending to call an Uber. Head down, she walked into a solid wall of muscle.

"Oh, sorry," she said, looking into Tomas's dark scowling face. His eyebrows went up in silent inquiry as he loosely held her arms.

"Silly me, I wasn't paying attention. I'm just…going to get a glass of wine," Hilary muttered, unable to meet eyes that seemed to see every thought in her head. His face softened, and he squeezed her arms gently before releasing her.

At the end of the hallway was a T-junction. Left to the entrance and freedom, right to the bar and purgatory. Looking back, Hilary saw Tomas watching her, arms crossed, head cocked to the side. She gave him a finger wave and turned to the bar.

The low hum of conversation filled the dimly lit bar of the Keeney Country Club as gala attendees fortified themselves before the dinner. Hilary stood just inside the entrance, breathing a sigh of relief. No one she knew.

Finding a table farthest from the door, she huddled on the bench in the dark corner. She ordered white wine from an attentive server, and settled back with hands clasping her upper arms. She shivered from the air-conditioning, wishing she'd brought a wrap with her. But it was a gray pashmina, and she'd deliberately left it at home.

Vincent texted: *How'd it go?*

Hilary stared at the screen, heaving out a breath. *Can't talk. Busy right now.*

Vincent responded with a thumbs-up and a kissy-face emoji.

Closing her eyes, she leaned back against the wall, wondering what she would tell him and knowing she didn't have long before she'd have to do so. The air filled with the cloying scent of aftershave as someone sat next to her. She opened her eyes to find Eddie McLeod seated close beside her, much too close.

"Come here often?" he asked, leaning in and leering at her. What was once a pristine white cotton shirt was stained, his navy silk tie hanging loose around his neck.

The combination of bourbon and Brüt nearly made her gag. She pulled back, then Eddie pushed in. He placed one arm along the top of the leather seat back, letting his fingers brush against her bare shoulder while his gaze roved over her face, down the front of her dress, and zeroed in on her crossed legs. The fabric had ridden up, exposing a length of her thigh. Eddie licked his lips. He traced a finger down the column of her neck. "You look familiar, but I can't quite remember…" He placed his drink on the table and moved his hand toward her leg. She intercepted it with her own, dropping it back on the table. Could the night get any worse?

"Nice to see you again, Eddie," she muttered.

He moved his gaze slowly up her body then fixed on her face. "Remind me where we met."

If she needed confirmation that she was forgettable, this was it.

His hand was headed back to her leg. She plucked it away and put it back on the table. Wrong move. Grinning like this was a game, his other hand slid down the back of her neck, stopping when he encountered the bare skin of her back. Hooded eyes glittered, and he shifted closer. She grabbed his leg, just above the knee, and squeezed hard. He hissed and licked his lips again. Shit! Feeling his right hand sliding down her back, she leaned forward, gripped the thumb of his left hand, and yanked it back.

"You fucking cock tease! I'll—"

Eddie flew back and crashed into a table, toppling it to the floor and landing in a tangle of limbs. Vincent yanked him up by his neck and plowed his fist into Eddie's nose. The crunch of cartilage breaking made the bar patrons wince. Hilary leaped up, grabbing Vincent's arm before he could inflict any more punishment. "Stop!" she shouted. Vincent whirled around, shaking her off and sending her stumbling back.

"Back off," he snarled.

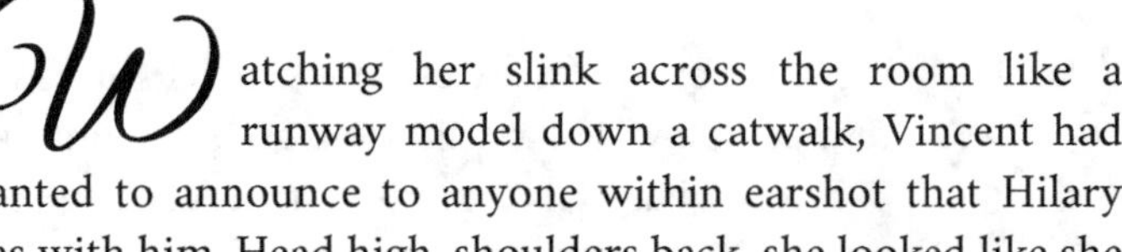

atching her slink across the room like a runway model down a catwalk, Vincent had wanted to announce to anyone within earshot that Hilary was with him. Head high, shoulders back, she looked like she owned the room and wouldn't let anyone take it from her.

Something cold and wet pressing against the back of his neck startled him from his thoughts.

"Here." Tomas thrust a beer at him.

"Asshole," Vincent replied, taking it.

"You're welcome," Tomas smirked.

They moved to stand with their backs against a pillar and watched the people around them.

"Did you finish handing out postcards?" Vincent asked.

Tomas made a disgusted sound. "One guy asked me to get him a drink, and the catering manager demanded to know why I wasn't in uniform, so I gave the cards to Carl." He gestured to his black shirt and jeans. "Apparently, I look like the help."

It was Vincent's turn to smirk. "I told you you should have worn a jacket."

"Whatever." He used his beer to point across the room. "Who's that with Hilary?"

"Shit. It's Eddie."

Tomas stopped him before he could take two steps. "Hang on. Don't go all Neanderthal."

Bristling with impatience, Vincent waited. If Eddie did anything to Hilary…

"He's gone," Tomas said. He turned Vincent toward a server carrying a tray of appetizers after Eddie walked away. "Let's get something to eat while Hilary does her job."

He took Vincent's arm when he hesitated and said reassuringly, "Relax. She'll be fine."

*Y*ears of pent-up frustration were released with that one blow. Hilary flinched, grabbing onto the back of a chair. His face filled with fury and pain, he leaned into her. "What the hell are you doing in here? I warned you about him, but I find you in the corner squeezing his thigh. You pass me over for Eddie McLeod? That's why you were busy?"

Rearing back as if struck, her mouth opened, but no words came out. She looked past him to the people gathering behind him and snapped it shut. Reaching for her clutch, she cast him one last tearful look before lowering her eyes, and pushing her way through the growing crowd.

Eddie groaned at Vincent's feet. "You broke my nose." A server reached down to help him up, and he struggled to stand, blood pouring down his face.

"You put your hands on my woman," Vincent ground out between clenched teeth.

Eddie snorted, blowing a bloody snot bubble out of his nose. "Your woman? That dried-up flat-chested bit—"

This time, it was a shot to the jaw. Eddie went down and stayed down. Vincent loomed over him but was grabbed from behind and held back.

"Stop! Get a hold of yourself," Ali ordered as Tomas pinned his arms to his sides.

Vincent's chest heaved as the haze in his head was replaced by a painful throb in his hand. Jesus, that hurt. "I'm fine," he said, looking up to see a crowd staring at him in horror.

"That's my husband, out of my way!" Fiona Han pushed her way through and kneeled beside Eddie. "What did you do now?" she muttered as he turned bleary eyes toward her.

"Nothing, " Eddie slurred. "He decked me for no reason. I asked a woman what time it was, and he hit me."

Fiona's eyes narrowed. "You just wanted to know the time?" She flicked her gaze up at Vincent.

"Yep," Eddie answered, splashing blood over his shirt with each bob of his head.

"Why? Did your watch stop?" Fiona grabbed his left hand and pushed up the sleeve.

Crying out in pain, Eddie cradled his hand against his chest. Fiona leaped to her feet and confronted Vincent. "You punched my husband then stomped on his hand when he was down. I will press charges!"

"Not so fast, Fiona."

Vincent looked past Fiona to find his mother approaching. He shifted his attention to the servers following closely behind her. Two women flanked a third, their arms protectively around her waist.

Fiona glared at Marcia. "My husband is injured, someone call 9-1-1. We need the medics and the police."

"They're on their way," Marcia announced. "The bar manager called when one of the servers said Eddie assaulted her."

A murmur went through the crowd. Fiona glared down at Eddie.

"I didn't! I was just standing there, and her ass fell into my hands. Then she wiggled it."

"Bullshit!" The server in the middle stepped forward, mascara running down her tear-stained face. "I bent to pick up a glass, and he ground himself into me and wouldn't let go. Then he laughed and went over to the woman in the corner."

The server on the left, a slightly older woman picked up the story, staring directly at Fiona. "Your asshole of a husband hit on that woman. He backed her into the corner and kept pawing at her. When he wouldn't stop, she bent his thumb back. I hope it's dislocated." The crowd shifted, and the woman kept going, this time looking each man in the eye. "I hope she presses charges. A woman should be able to go into a bar by herself. She should be able to have a drink without men thinking she's there to get picked up." She delivered her parting shot at Vincent. "She deserved better than that."

It didn't take long for the paramedics to show up, followed closely by the cops. Eddie loudly insisted he should be the one pressing charges. Fiona told him to shut up and stood back as the cops hauled him away in handcuffs.

In the same corner where Eddie hit on Hilary, Marcia didn't hold back, spewing her anger and disappointment. Vincent sank lower with every word.

"She was assaulted. Do you get that? Assaulted!"

"Ma, I got him off her."

Marcia flung her arm out. "Yeah, and then what did you do? You assumed the worst. You didn't let her speak. You didn't bother to find out what really happened. Now she's gone." She took a breath. "Do you remember the night you were arrested?"

The change of subject nearly gave him whiplash. "Of course I do. How could I forget it?"

Marcia moved closer to cup his chin so he couldn't look away. "You were so angry and frustrated, telling me over and over how they wouldn't listen to you."

Looking back at his mother, Vincent let the memory wash over him. Being pressed against the wall while his apartment was ransacked. The cops talking over him and not letting him speak, ignoring his protests and questions, already convinced that he was guilty.

Closing his eyes and nodding, he realized the magnitude of his error. Motivated by anger and jealousy, he'd lashed out before knowing what was happening. Not caring about Hilary, not caring about the truth, caring only for his wounded pride.

"I love you, sweetheart," Marcia said, releasing his chin to run her hand through his hair. "But you messed up, and as bad as you are hurting, Hilary is hurting even more. You need to fix this and fast."

Vincent sat at a round banquet table in an empty events room, staring at the floor. He'd given his statement to the police, and charges wouldn't be pressed, but he couldn't move, anchored in place by shame and frustration. He'd screwed things up with Hilary, and he'd screwed things up for Hilary, having all but destroyed her grand plans.

Cutlery clinked against china in the distance. The gala was in full swing, applause breaking out occasionally. A pair of tiny high-heeled shoes entered his line of sight. He looked up to see Fiona Han approaching, her dress pristine, not a hair out of place. He straightened but didn't stand.

"I only have a moment until..." she gestured behind her. "May I sit?"

Vincent jerked his head at a chair and turned to face her.

She fiddled with the jade bracelet on her slim wrist instead of looking at him. "Eddie...my husband...deceived me."

Vincent released a mirthless laugh. "You think? Eddie McLeod is a first-class liar and has been since grade school. Yet you married him." He shook his head sharply. "You could have had anyone."

A mask descended over Fiona's face. "You don't know anything about me," she said in a tight voice.

Lips twisted, he remained quiet. After a few tense minutes, Fiona broke the silence.

"Your team has been very effective in their campaign. The board members of Keeney Works want to invite you to make a presentation at their next meeting."

"Me?"

"You and your partner, a representative from KBS, and Hilary Banks." She sat back and cocked her head to the side. "I hope you can make that work."

Pretty sure she wasn't referring to the board meeting, he muttered, "I do, too," staring at the busted knuckles on his hand. He glanced up to see Tomas enter the room. Fiona looked over her shoulder as well. Vincent raised a hand, and Tomas stopped.

Looking down at her bracelet again, Fiona said, "I know very little about Iris. Eddie intimated his parents didn't like... um...immigrants. I'm guessing that was a lie as well. I haven't seen Iris since her husband passed away." She looked up, flags of color high on her cheekbones. "I intend to rectify that." She stood to leave.

"Did you look after the books for KBS when Darryl was sick?" Vincent watched her closely.

Brow furrowed, Fiona shook her head. "I offered, but Eddie declined."

"You never helped with payroll?" Vincent pushed.

Her frown deepened. "No. Eddie said his parents wouldn't like it, wouldn't want me close to their money," she said in a low voice. "Why?"

Standing, Vincent waved Tomas over, then looked down at Fiona. "Eddie's been embezzling for the past year. Iris asked him about it in front of me and two other witnesses. He said you did it."

Fiona rocked back on her heels, sucking in a breath. She met Vincent's gaze, then looked away. She spoke through pinched lips, "I see. I really must speak with Iris. Soon."

Tomas passed her and handed an icepack to Vincent, then stepped back, hands clasped loosely in front of him, and nodded at Fiona.

"Please bring a club soda and lime to my table." She spun on her heel and headed to the door.

"Fiona," Vincent called.

She stopped and glanced back.

"He doesn't work here. This is my partner, Tomas Alvarado."

Tomas cocked his head to the side and stared at her. Shoulders hunched, Fiona dropped her gaze and continued out the door.

Vincent threw Tomas a crooked smile. Tomas scowled, "Entitled women piss me off."

"Yeah, but that entitled woman wants us to make a presentation to Keeney Works."

"Us?" His eyebrows rose.

Vincent sighed. "We need Hilary." His shoulders fell, and he stared at the floor. "I screwed up."

"No shit. I saw her before she went into the bar. I don't know what happened, but she looked upset."

"Fucking Eddie." Vincent fisted his hands, then hissed at the pain in his knuckles. He joined Tomas.

Walking toward the banquet room, Tomas asked, "Why did you think Hilary was with him? She's into you, only you."

Vincent shrugged and shifted the ice pack. "Did you see her? So sure of herself. She spoke to all these people like she owned the place. She belongs here, drinking martinis and playing squash." He shook his head slowly.

"Hilary plays squash?"

Vincent shoved him with his shoulder. "You know what I mean."

"Yeah, I do, but isn't that what you wanted? For her to have her confidence back? And you haven't answered my question. What made you think she was with Eddie?"

"I walked into the bar to get a beer, thinking Hilary was with Fiona, which was good. It meant she was making progress. It surprised the hell out of me when I saw her sitting with Eddie, and I thought they must have been making plans when they were talking earlier. She had one hand holding Eddie's leg, the other holding his hand. And I…lost it."

"Holding his hand? She was breaking his damn thumb," Tomas muttered.

Vincent groaned in frustration. "I didn't know that! I saw Eddie's hands all over my woman, trying to screw me over again."

Tomas took Vincent by the arm and led him into an alcove. Holding him by both shoulders, he leaned close and spoke fiercely. "That's twice tonight I've heard you say *your woman*. Do you really feel that way?"

Vincent nodded.

"Does Hilary know you feel that way?"

Vincent grimaced. "I don't know. I've never said it to her."

"Do it. Tell her what you told me. And apologize."

Vincent shook off Tomas's hands. Shoulders slumping, he stared at him. "I'm such an idiot. Do you think she'll forgive me?"

Tomas pulled back and looked him in the eye. "You won't know until you try."

"I hear you. Now let go so I can go to her."

Tomas grinned and pushed Vincent away. "Get the hell out of here." He sauntered into the banquet hall, as Vincent tore off to the parking lot.

"*I*ris! Iris, it's Vincent. Open the door, please."

Finally, a light went on, and the door opened. Vincent sagged against the door frame.

"Iris, Hilary's not answering her door, and I don't have a key, can I use yours?"

Clutching her robe around her, she looked up at him, her gaze filled with apology. She shook her head. "I can't give it to you."

"What? She's upset, and I need to talk to her." He stood up straight.

"I know, Vincent. But I can't give you the key. I promised her I would not let anyone into her place without her consent." Iris looked sympathetic, but her tone was firm.

Voice rising, he said, "The lights are off, her car's in the driveway, but she's not answering her phone. I need to know she's safe."

Iris bobbed her head. "She made it home safely. I heard her go up the stairs."

Grabbing his hair with both hands, he squeezed his eyes shut and pleaded, "Iris, please, I need to see her. I screwed up so bad. I just…"

Iris sighed. "I know what happened." She stared at the damaged knuckles of Vincent's hand.

He blew out a sigh and stared at the woman who had loved him his whole life. Hilary wasn't the only woman hurt this evening.

Iris shook her head. "Your mom called. I've…I've had my head in the sand for a long time. Eddie is…" Tears filled her eyes, but she wiped them on her sleeve. "He called from the police station to tell me he's been charged with drunk and disorderly, and sexual assault." Her voice broke on the last word, and Vincent stepped forward to wrap her in his arms.

Holding her as she cried softly, he stared over her shoulder into her cluttered home, filled with photos of her, Darryl, and Eddie, and wondered where it went wrong. No family was perfect, but from the outside looking in, it sure seemed like Eddie had it good. KBS was a thriving business and would come to him eventually, so why screw over his mother? And screw around on Fiona, too. Because Vincent wasn't convinced this was the first time Eddie's hands went wandering.

Pulling back, Iris stepped into the kitchen, and reached for a paper towel to wipe her eyes and blow her nose. "I'm leaving him there overnight."

Vincent nodded, not that she needed his approval. He spotted Iris's cellphone and picked it up.

"Would you call Hilary for me? Please? I have to know that she's alright."

Iris took the phone from him, saying, "I won't give you the key. I will, however, call and check on her." She kept her eyes on him while it rang. "Hi…Hilary, honey, Vincent is here and wants to see you." Her shoulders drooped. "Alright, sweetheart. I'll tell him. Call if you need anything." Putting the phone down, she touched Vincent's battered hand. "She's not ready. Try again tomorrow."

Vincent nodded, tried a smile, and headed out into the night.

"Vincent," Iris called.

He looked back to find her framed in the doorway, a dark shape against the light from inside. "Don't give up on her. She'll come around."

Will she, though? He'd like to blame Eddie, but it was his own damn fault. Hilary didn't like drawing attention to herself, and his lashing out without waiting to hear her side of the story had put her squarely in the spotlight.

"I hope so," he mumbled, looking up at the darkness shrouding Hilary's home. For the first time in weeks, he walked to the tiny house to sleep alone.

CHAPTER 20

*M*ost of her night was spent on the bathroom floor. Nausea hit in the wee hours of the morning, and the bed was too far from the toilet, so she grabbed an afghan and pillow, and lay curled in the fetal position on the cool tile, staring at the baseboards Vincent installed. Her heart was a shriveled-up barren wasteland, and her stomach was a twisted knot of discomfort. In her despair, Hilary felt destroyed, defeated, defiled, and defective. After the nausea and diarrhea passed, the words dehydrated and desiccated came to mind.

Around mid-morning, she felt able to leave the bedroom. Huddled in the afghan, she grabbed her dead phone and dragged herself to the kitchen to paw through her briefcase, only to discover that she'd left her charging cord at work. Lovely. Never mind. Wallowing was the only thing on her agenda for the day.

Putting the kettle on to boil, she searched the cupboards for herbal tea, something without caffeine that she could keep down. Food was the last thing on her mind. She didn't know what made her ill but suspected the stuffed mushroom cap appetizers served at the gala. She hadn't eaten much else.

The gorgeous, sophisticated nude heels she'd strutted around in less than twenty-four hours ago sat by the door. They and the others should be boxed up, as well as the dress, and returned to Vincent. She touched the bracelet on her wrist. She couldn't take it off because the clasp was tricky, and she didn't want to damage it. At least, that's what she told herself.

Sunlight through the window mocked her as the water boiled. How could it be such a beautiful day when she felt so awful? Glancing to the side, she saw her Prius in the driveway, an empty space, and then Vincent's truck. That space between them seemed so significant today. Was it her imagination? Because it seemed to be getting wider.

A flicker of movement caught her eye. In tight jeans and a white T-shirt, Vincent exited his house and strode across the yard to the garage, not bothering to glance her way. A minute later, he reappeared with the lawn mower and went about his usual day, totally unaffected by the events of the night. She should have known. Why would he want her anyway?

She unplugged the kettle. Wrapping herself in the afghan, she shuffled to the living room, and faceplanted into the couch.

A knocking at the door penetrated her fog. Wincing against the sunlight, Hilary brushed hair out of her eyes and waited for the interloper to go away. The knocking persisted. With a sigh, she heaved herself up off the couch and walked to the door, still wrapped in the afghan.

The stupid French doors meant Fiona freaking Han could see her. Gah!

Hilary didn't trust herself to speak. She opened the door, eyebrow raised in question.

"Hi… Doesn't Iris McLeod live here?" A frown marred Fiona's perfect features. She'd gone casual on the sunny afternoon; crisp, sleeveless white blouse tucked into cropped, red trousers and red espadrilles. Pearls around her neck, and her hair in a French twist completed the look.

Hilary didn't have the energy to care about her own appearance. "Iris lives downstairs. I'm her tenant."

"Oh." Fiona colored. "I didn't know." She flashed a tiny smile at Hilary, and turned to the stairs.

"She's not home right now. She goes to the church on Saturday afternoons to teach cooking classes." Hilary glanced at the clock on the stove and back at Fiona. "She should be home in half an hour or so."

"Thanks. I'll go wait in the car."

While there was no sign of him, Vincent's truck was still in the driveway. He'd punched out Fiona's husband last evening, it was doubtful that an encounter would go well.

"Would you like to come inside and wait?" She wasn't sure who she was protecting, but the words were out of her mouth, and she couldn't take them back.

Fiona shifted from one foot to another. "If it's not too much of an imposition."

A soft fragrance drifted in her wake as she entered. Hilary hoped Fiona couldn't smell the aftereffects of a night of nausea on her. Fiona stopped next to the fireplace, her gaze moving around the room before settling on Hilary. "Were you ill?" she asked, cocking her head to the side.

Hilary shuddered. "Something didn't agree with me. Maybe the mushrooms." She shuffled into the kitchen and plugged the kettle in again. "Do you have a charging cord with you? I left mine at work, and my phone is dead."

Fiona scrunched her face up in apology. "No, I don't. Sorry."

Hilary heaved a sigh. "That's okay." She focused on the electric kettle, willing the water to boil faster in the awkward silence. Without the energy to make polite conversation and seeing a piece of dried-up something on the afghan, she said,

"I'm going to have a quick shower. Would you please make the tea?"

Fiona nodded, and Hilary disappeared down the hallway to the bedroom.

Thirty minutes later, she was back, dressed in loose linen trousers and a loose linen shirt, both white with thin gray stripes. Getting dressed pretty much sapped what little strength she had, so she hadn't bothered with makeup, and her damp hair curled around her face.

Fiona looked up from where she sat on the couch and placed her phone in her purse. She smiled wanly. "I owe you an apology. It was definitely the mushrooms that made you ill. So far, thirty people who attended the gala last night have contracted food poisoning."

With a sympathetic grimace, Hilary said, "That's not good." She moved into the kitchen, where Fiona had set out two bright blue ceramic mugs that matched the teapot on the counter. She poured herself some tea. It was an orange/ginger herbal tea. Perfect for a dicey stomach. Holding up the pot in silent inquiry, she poured another cup at Fiona's nod.

"I have no idea how to fix this. You invite people to give you money, and in return, you make them sick. This is a nightmare." Fiona raised both hands and massaged her temples.

A tiny hint of satisfaction bloomed inside Hilary at Fiona's obvious distress. It lasted only a moment before her usual desire to help others rose to the surface. "You put together care packages with tea, Imodium, etc. Include a handwritten apology and a coupon worth two hours of free labor from a Keeney Works student for the project of their choice. You deliver the packages yourself today." It was always easier to fix other people's problems.

Fiona's mouth hung open. "You're brilliant," she whispered.

Hilary handed a mug to Fiona and rested a hip against the counter. She shrugged. "When crap happens, you acknowledge it, apologize, and make amends. Blaming others for a bad situation never does any good." Running away, though, that had merit. She flicked a glance out the window then back at Fiona. She'd start looking for another place as soon as Fiona left. As far away from Keeney as possible. Maybe Drumheller, where she could hang out with dinosaur bones.

"I'm not sure if you've heard, but the board of Keeney Works wants you and your team to present to them at their next meeting. They're very interested in the program you've designed."

Hilary continued to sip her tea in silence, too worn out to care.

Fiona cleared her throat. "This is a lovely apartment you have. It doesn't look at all like it did when Iris lived here. I mean, it's not that Iris didn't have a lovely house. It's just that this looks so different. The kitchen cabinets look custom-made."

"They are custom-made. Vincent designed and built them to Iris's specifications."

"Oh. I didn't know." Fiona dropped her gaze to the countertop.

Hilary moved to stand on the other side of the peninsula from Fiona. "You don't know much about your mother-in-law, do you?"

Fiona shook her head. "I was led to believe I was not welcome in her home."

"Eddie?" Derision dripped from Hilary's question. "I'm sorry, I believe in giving people the benefit of the doubt and that every person has some redeeming quality, but I seriously doubt that pertains to Eddie McLeod."

Straightening her back, Fiona placed her cup on the counter with a clatter and opened her mouth like she was about to defend her husband. Nothing came out. Her shoulders slumped, her mouth closed, and she fiddled with her bracelet.

Taking this in, Hilary watched Fiona stroke the green jade. "I was married to a man I thought had my back and would stick with me through thick and thin. Then I got breast cancer. He was kind and supportive through the chemo, the hair loss, and the mastectomies. We didn't sleep together when I was going through the treatments and after the surgeries. We would go to bed together, he would hold me, and then after I fell asleep, he'd move to the other bedroom. When I was healed, he returned to spending the night with me. I wanted to have sex, but he'd just hold me, saying that if we waited a bit longer, it would be more comfortable for me. I agreed, thinking he was the most generous man in the world." She sighed.

"When we found out I couldn't have implants, he wanted me to wear bras with fake boobs. He got some for me. Did you know you can order them on Amazon? Bras with built-in boobs and fake nipples. I couldn't do it. We argued." Hilary sipped her tea, continuing to stare at Fiona's hands. "Apparently, a wife with fake boobs was preferable to a wife with no boobs. He stopped touching me. He moved out of the bedroom. And then I found out he'd moved on to another woman. Young, blonde, busty. All the things I wasn't anymore." Hilary looked up at Fiona, and bitterness filled her smile. "She was also fertile, another thing I lost to cancer. The last I heard, they were expecting baby number two."

Hilary pushed past Fiona and sat at the table, wrapping her hands around her mug. She gestured at another chair in silent invitation.

Fiona brought her mug with her but did not drink from it.

Hilary propped her head in her hand. "I have no idea why I told you that."

"Have you told your story to anyone else?"

Her gaze drawn out the French door to the tiny house, Hilary answered, "Yes, but I left out a few details."

Fiona placed her hands flat on the table, either side of the mug, and fixed her gaze on it as if memorizing the pattern of the flowers etched into the ceramic. "Eddie is the only man I've ever had sex with. Six months ago, I was diagnosed with an STD. When I confronted him, he accused me of having an affair. He went on and on, twisting things around until I almost confessed to it. While I spoke briefly with Vincent last night, I realized how much and how often my husband has lied to me."

At the sound of Vincent's name, Hilary's heart leaped, and then did a deep dive. She buried the feeling and concentrated on the conversation. "If things were falling apart, why go to Vegas with him?"

"I didn't. Eddie told me he was going to a trade show. I flew down there when the hospital called me." Glancing up at Hilary, she said sadly, "I think he had someone with him."

Silence descended for a few moments, then Hilary pointed her chin at Fiona's hands. "You're not wearing your rings."

Fiona lifted her hands as if noticing them for the first time. "My parents did not want me to divorce Eddie. They said it would be shameful. After last night…I now have their permission." She met Hilary's gaze, cocking her head to the side. "The evening wasn't a total loss."

A door closed in the distance. Both women turned to see Vincent exit his home, look up at the apartment, then walk to the driveway, head down, hands fisted loosely at his sides.

"You're not speaking to each other, I take it?" Fiona asked.

Hilary bit her lip and switched her gaze from Vincent to the blue sky mocking her misery. "I didn't come to the door when he knocked, and he may have called or texted, but my phone died, and I don't have my charging cord."

Fiona switched her gaze to Hilary. "Does he know you were ill?"

She shivered. The nausea may have passed, but she felt like she would never be warm again. Hilary shook her head, still looking out the door.

The garage door opened, announcing Iris's arrival.

Fiona rose from the table. "Thank you for the tea." When Hilary didn't move, she said, "I'll let myself out." She pushed her chair in, picked up her mug, and took it to the sink. She paused at the door and looked back at Hilary, still seated, still cradling her mug of tea, head bowed. "I saw you two walk into the gala last night, holding hands. He looked at you like you set the sun in the sky. Don't make him wait too long. Even the good ones screw up." She slipped through the door and closed it behind her.

The grass was cut. Weeds were pulled, and the flower beds were watered. Now, Vincent stood at the back of his truck, organizing the tools in his already organized toolbox. How else was he supposed to keep tabs on Hilary? Both her car and her bike were there, but she wasn't answering the phone. Peering through the windows was too stalkerish so he settled for lurking in the driveway.

A late model Audi was parked behind Hilary's Prius, which he hadn't seen arrive. He had no clue who it belonged to, but whoever it was, they'd been with Hilary for a good half hour. Iris returned from church, threading her Subaru between the other vehicles, and inching her way into the garage. At a snail's pace, she exited her car, and gathered her purse and cloth grocery bag. She emerged with her eyes screwed up against the brightness of the sun, and acknowledged him with a brief wave.

"Thank you, sweetheart," she murmured as he relieved

her of the bag and shortened his stride to walk beside her. "Has she…?" She patted him on the arm at the shake of his head, then dug into her purse for her keys. "Give her time," she murmured.

They looked up at the sound of light footsteps on the stairs. Iris gasped, then gathered herself and said, "Hello, Fiona."

Vincent took the keys from Iris, opened the door to her place, and put the grocery bag on the counter. He emptied it, putting the perishables into the fridge, killing time, giving the women privacy. When the crying started, he rushed outside. Locked in an embrace, the two women sobbed on each other's shoulders. Iris's handbag gaped open on the ground, Fiona's clutch leaning against it in sympathy. He heaved a sigh. The inaugural meeting of the "Eddie McLeod Destroyed My Life" club was now underway. He headed to his house, with *I'm sorry*, and *it's not your fault*, echoing in his ears. He settled on the couch, keyed up his cellphone to his audio library, picked up his crocheting, and tried to get lost in an audiobook.

When a knock came, he bolted to open the door, then sagged in disappointment.

"Hi," Fiona said.

"Hey," He wasn't in the mood for polite conversation and had no idea what to say to this woman. He glanced up at Hilary's apartment. There were no signs of life.

"This is probably none of my business, but I thought you should know," Fiona tilted her head back to look directly at him, "Hilary was sick with food poisoning during the night."

"Oh, shit." He went rigid, then shifted to move past Fiona, intent on getting to Hilary.

She reached out a staying hand, hurrying her words. "She's better now. But her cellphone died, and she doesn't have a charging cord, so if you texted or called her last night, there's a reason she didn't respond."

He stared down at her, then switched his gaze toward the house. Sunshine bounced off the windows, not allowing him to see inside. He swallowed and looked back at Fiona. "I should…"

"Yeah," she said, mouth turned down in sympathy. "She's still hurting."

"Wait here a moment," he said and disappeared. Returning, he reached behind and pulled the door shut as he stepped outside. "Are you and Iris okay?" he asked the tiny woman beside him as they walked to the driveway.

"We will be. I'm going with her to the police station to see Eddie."

"Are you going to bail him out?" he asked, thinking they should throw away the key.

Fiona pulled her keys out of her purse and stood beside her car. "I don't know yet. Neither one of us is sure that he deserves it."

Iris appeared, looking fatigued yet determined. He opened the passenger door and waited for her to get in and buckle her seatbelt before leaning in to kiss her on the forehead. When the car was gone, he climbed the stairs to Hilary's apartment two at a time, lifted his hand to knock, but hesitated. Would she answer? He'd been such an ass he wouldn't blame her if she never wanted to see him again. The thought curdled his stomach. She'd left Olympia after the last person hurt her. Was anything stopping her from doing so now?

He knocked loudly, pulled a small package out of his pocket, and left it by the door. Retracing his steps, he climbed into his truck and drove off.

CHAPTER 21

$\mathcal{S}$he'd hidden in the hallway waiting for him to go away, walking to the door only after hearing his truck leave. Opening it, she looked down and retrieved the package. It was a cellphone charger wrapped in notepaper. She smiled, pocketed the charger, and smoothed out the paper to read the words written on it. In Vincent's precise handwriting, it read:

I was proud to walk in with you. You looked so strong, and confident, and beautiful. You turned heads the whole evening, and my pride in you turned to possessiveness.

You are too good for me. I was afraid you realized that and decided to move on. Then to see Eddie beside you...

You did nothing wrong, which isn't telling you something you don't know.

I didn't give you a chance to speak.

I didn't ask if you were okay.

I didn't think about you.

I was wrong.

I am sorry.

Please forgive me.

. . .

With shaking hands, Hilary placed the note on the dining room table, then smoothed it down. A tear fell, quickly followed by another. She wiped her eyes with her sleeve and sniffed, her heart in her throat. Leaving the note on the table, she headed to the bedroom.

❆

Vincent mounted the stairs and placed the bag of groceries next to the door. He knocked loudly. Halfway down the stairs, he realized the first package was no longer there and smiled. Progress.

❆

The knock at the door sounded the next installment in Vincent's campaign of overwhelming generosity. So far, besides the charging cord, he'd brought her soup, ibuprofen, Gatorade, protein drinks, a paperback novel, and slippers in the second delivery. The third delivery contained bath bombs, a rubber duck, and another paperback.

She couldn't see the door from her position in the club chair and waited, expecting him to go away and leave the bag by the door. The knock sounded again, this time, a key was inserted, and the door opened. "Hilary, it's Iris. I know I said I'd never enter without your permission, but I want to know that you're alright."

Deflated, Hilary called out, "I'm here. Come on in."

She didn't bother to get up, just put her book down and sat up straight. Iris rounded the corner with a plate of cookies in hand. To her credit, her eyes didn't widen, her mouth didn't drop open, and she didn't collapse in a faint at Hilary's appearance.

"How are you feeling?" She placed the cookies on the coffee table and stepped back.

"Better than I look. How are *you* feeling?"

Iris wrapped her arms around herself. "Better than I thought I would. Fiona and I had a long conversation on our way to the police station. It seems Eddie led us both astray."

That's an understatement. Aloud, Hilary asked, "Do you want to talk about it?" She gestured toward the couch.

Iris sat and pulled a tissue out of her pocket. "I posted bail for my son today, and Fiona will file for divorce soon. She won't allow him back into the house and convinced me not to let him stay with me. I don't know what he's going to do." Her chin wobbled as she looked at Hilary.

Lips as flat as the tone of her voice, Hilary spoke, "You'll have to forgive me, I don't have much sympathy for him."

Iris bobbed her head and sniffed. "I can't figure out where we went wrong. I had two miscarriages before Eddie, and we were so thankful when he was born that perhaps we overindulged him."

Hilary had nothing to add, so remained silent.

"I can understand the drifting away from us, but I can't understand the lying. And not just if we questioned him about something. He'd lie about the oddest things. He told me the school cafeteria served only fish sticks on Friday because the principal was Catholic. He told Darryl that Fiona's father said KBS would go out of business soon. He also said that Fiona thought our house smelled." Iris stared into space, pieces of shredded tissue falling to the floor at her feet.

"He sounds like a pathological liar."

"Um-hum," Iris said with a sniff.

"Was there a scene at the police station?"

"Um-hum." Pulling out another tissue, Iris wiped her nose.

While she could muster up some sympathy for Iris, she had none for Eddie. "Do you want to tell me about it?"

"Nuh-uh."

Don't blame you. One of the romance novels Vincent had given her sat on the coffee table, the couple on the cover gazing soulfully into each other's eyes backlit by a glorious sunset. Why couldn't every story end with a happily ever after?

"Eddie never introduced us to any of the girls he dated, so we were surprised when he wanted us to meet Fiona. He told us he wanted to bring her to the house, but she was uncomfortable with white people."

Hilary covered her mouth to avoid saying anything, unsure whether Eddie was a master manipulator or Iris was incredibly naïve. It was probably a bit of both. She settled back into her chair to let Iris ramble on. It seemed important to her to get the story out.

"So we met them at a restaurant Fiona chose on the Kirkland waterfront. Darryl and I had been there for our anniversary once or twice. It was nice but kind of pricey. As we were parking the car, I got a text from Eddie with a list of topics not to bring up at dinner."

"Seriously?" Hilary straightened up. "I'm sorry, but that's just weird."

Iris turned big eyes her way and nodded. "That's what Darryl said. He was pretty annoyed. But like I said, this was the first girl Eddie wanted us to meet. I knew she was important to him, so I wanted the evening to go well."

"And did it?"

Staring at the shredded tissue in her hand, Iris shook her head. "Fiona would not look at Darryl, and seemed to hesitate and look to Eddie for approval before answering any questions. She was very quiet. Eddie did most of the talking. When we were finished and waiting for the car, I tried to hug Fiona, but Eddie waved me off."

Hilary debated with herself before speaking. "You may want to ask Fiona what she remembers about it." When Iris gave her a quizzical look, she continued, "I wouldn't be surprised if Eddie told Fiona things about you and your husband that made *her* uncomfortable."

"It's possible," Iris conceded.

The past twenty-four hours having sapped her energy, Hilary closed her eyes and left Iris to her own thoughts.

The door closing woke her. Iris was gone. The cookies were gone. The cushions on the sofa plumped, and the tissue pieces all picked up. Sniffing the air, Hilary rose to follow her nose. A box of pizza and a bottle of chardonnay sat on the table. The note beside it read, "For medicinal purposes." Stepping to the door, she saw Vincent descend the stairs and walk toward his home, shoulders slumped and feet dragging. She moved to the counter and disconnected her phone from the charger. Twelve texts and five voicemails waited for her. All from Vincent, all filled with remorse.

Her fingers hovered over the screen as she wondered how to respond. He seemed sincere, but could she trust him? Throughout her bout with cancer, David had treated her like precious cargo, at his best when she was at her weakest. That made his deceit and the divorce that followed all the more painful. She wouldn't allow herself to be treated that way again by someone who claimed to care for her.

Her eyes drifted over to the letter, and then she sat down and took her time crafting a reply. Two minutes after she pressed send, Vincent appeared at her door. At her nod, he entered, jaw tight, eyes solemn.

Sympathetic eyes roamed all over her. The outfit she'd put on in the morning was now wrinkled, and she hadn't bothered to comb her hair.

"Hi," he said. "How are you feeling?"

"Limp and worn out, but I'll survive. Thank you for the gifts. That was very thoughtful."

"Did they help?"

"They did. But this did more than anything," she said, tracing a fingertip across his handwriting before holding out her hand.

Heaving out a sigh, he took it and dropped to his knees before her. He wrapped his arms around her and rocked back and forth. "Does this mean you forgive me?" he whispered.

"I'm thinking about it," she whispered back.

He picked her up, carried her to the couch, sat down, and cradled her in his lap.

"I screwed up so badly," he said.

"No shit."

"I saw you in his arms and thought…" Vincent cleared his throat. "I thought Eddie McLeod was not going to take something that belonged to me this time."

Hilary pulled back to look at him. "I'm not a possession."

"I know that. It's just…all my life…we didn't have much. Eddie got every shiny thing he wanted, and he'd wave it in my face. I'd ignore him. Tell myself I didn't care, and I didn't. But, seeing his hands on you…" His grip tightened on her arm as he breathed deeply. "You mean the world to me, and I know you can do better than me—"

Hilary pressed her finger to his lips. "Not true. Don't even go there. I have something to say, and then we won't talk about this again." When he opened his mouth, she pressed her finger against it more firmly. "What you did last night was seriously uncool. Well, the punching Eddie in the nose was cool. But what you said to me, in front of a room full of strangers and not bothering to find out what was really happening, was not cool." She saw the pain in his eyes but didn't let up. "Walking through that bar, people thinking I'd been with Eddie…I was humiliated."

He tried to speak, but she shushed him. "Not finished yet. When you realized you screwed up, you apologized. Immedi-

ately and profusely. And I appreciate that. I know you understand how you hurt me, and I am positive you will never do
it again." She removed her hand and pressed her lips lightly
to his. "There. Done."

Vincent deepened the kiss, then twisted his body to plant
her in the corner of the couch. "Am I allowed to speak now?"

"If you must." She snuggled into his chest. "I was hoping
you'd kiss me some more."

He lay his big body next to her, crowding her against the
cushion, and holding her close. "I intend to do so. I want a
do-over. I want you to get dressed up, and I want to show
you off. I want everyone to know that this beautiful woman
belongs to me."

She frowned. "Did we not establish the fact I am not a
possession?"

"Yes." His gaze held hers as he moved a hand to stroke her
bottom lip. "However, you are *my woman*. Exclusively."

Butterflies took flight in her stomach at the deep rumble
of his voice. "And you're *mine* exclusively?"

"For as long as you want me."

Hilary drew his head down to kiss him. There was
nothing left to say.

❄

*V*incent ate the pizza while Hilary settled for soup
and ginger ale. The wine went into the fridge for
another day.

Lying in her bed with her head on his chest, he drew lazy
circles on the small of her back. Fear, guilt, and exhaustion
had dogged him all day, and he was thankful she'd accepted
his apology so quickly. He really didn't deserve her and
would make it up to her until his dying day, if she'd let him.

"Tell me about the Australian girls you met."

Vincent stiffened, then relaxed. "I haven't thought about

them in years. Why are you asking? Do you want details about who I've slept with?"

She shook her head. "No, I was just wondering about them."

"Okay, but why now?"

"No particular reason. Just curious," she said.

"Okay. I met and stayed with Ilsa when I went there to ski. We dated for a while, and when they came to Washington to ski, they stayed with me."

"Did you rekindle your romance?" Hilary lifted her head to glare at him.

Vincent squeezed her and smiled. "No, by then Ilsa had a boyfriend back in Canberra, and I wasn't interested in Nadia, she was way too much drama for me. They just stayed in my spare bedroom between partying and skiing."

"They partied a lot?"

He chuckled. "They're Australian. It's a national pastime. Ma and I were at Iris and Darryl's house for dinner one night when Ilsa called. They'd met up with some frat boys from UW, were partying in the U district, and didn't have a way home. Eddie volunteered to pick them up, and one of them threw up in his car."

Hilary raised a questioning eyebrow. "Why would Eddie volunteer?"

Vincent snorted. "He'd met them and probably expected to get laid. Anyway, Ilsa flew back home a couple of weeks before Nadia left. And you know the rest."

Hilary changed position to see his eyes. "What about Nadia?"

"She was already on her way to Vancouver when I was arrested, and flew home to Australia the next day. Again, my lawyer was a moron, so Nadia was never contacted for a statement. Mom refinanced her mortgage to hire a good lawyer who managed to reduce my sentence, and I got out after three years." Restless from reliving crappy memories, he folded his arms behind his head and stared at the ceiling.

"You never heard from Ilsa or Nadia?"

He glanced down at Hilary. "No. I didn't try, though."

"Why not? You could clear your name." She pulled back and propped her head on her hand. "Don't you want to?"

He blew out a frustrated breath. "It's behind me. That's all that matters."

She was silent for a moment. Then leaned forward to kiss his chest and asked, "Do you mind if I look for Ilsa and Nadia?"

Vincent gave her the side-eye. "How?"

"Hello?" She gave him a mocking smile. "There's this thing called the internet. Most young women have a presence on social media. Give me their names, and I'll see what I can find."

After a moment's consideration, he agreed. Nothing bad could come from her search. "Yeah, sure."

"Good!" Hilary hovered over him to kiss his nose before settling back down on his chest, and was asleep soon after.

He wrapped her in his arms, happy to put one of the worst days in his life behind him.

CHAPTER 22

"Where did you learn to do this?" Vincent asked, watching Tomas's fingers skim across the keys of the laptop.

"You don't know how to use PowerPoint? What rock have you been living under?"

The remains of their lunch had been pushed aside, and they sat at Marcia's kitchen table peering at a laptop. They were killing two birds with one stone. Vincent replacing a washer on the sink while Tomas worked on their presentation for Keeney Works. Neither one was thrilled about speaking to the board of directors. However, Hilary had told them that creating their own presentation would make it go smoother—they would be using their own words and experiences, not reading a script written by someone else.

"Dude, I do construction." Vincent sat back and crossed his arms.

"Dude, so do I, but eschewing technology won't help our business." Tomas didn't spare him a glance, focused solely on the computer.

"Eschew? Nice word choice." Vincent smirked in mock admiration.

"Thanks, it's got a minimum point value of fifteen." In their time together, Vincent and Tomas played many a Scrabble game. They memorized tile values, two and three-letter words, and were ruthless competitors. "I figure we can alternate speaking. I'll cover one slide, you do the next."

Vincent's leg jiggled as he glared at the computer screen. He hated speaking in public. In prison, he and Tomas discussed many aspects of their future business, but it never occurred to him that they would have to convince a group of people to invest in them. He took comfort in the fact he wouldn't be doing it alone. Ali, Tomas, and Hilary would be present. Although Hilary being there might be hard. She'd invested a lot of time and effort in the project, and it would suck to develop performance anxiety in front of her.

"Seriously, how did you learn to do that?" Vincent waved at the screen. "Since, you know…"

Tomas had been diagnosed with dyslexia in prison. Great with numbers, words got jumbled in his head, making reading and writing difficult. He compensated by memorizing instructions read aloud to him. Scrabble was a game to pass the time, and a tool to build his comprehension skills. "I found a tutorial on YouTube. Creating the slides is pretty easy, but someone will have to proofread my writing."

Marcia came in and cleared the table. "I can do that for you. Do you want to practice on me? I can give you feedback."

Tomas leaned back and exchanged looks with Vincent, who shrugged. "Sure, if you've got time. This is rough. So let us know if we're covering all the bases."

"Got it." Marcia left the dishes on the counter. Rummaging through a drawer, she returned to the table with a writing tablet and pen. "Angle the screen so I can see it as well."

The two men rearranged themselves, sitting on one side

of the table, Marcia on the end, and the computer screen close to Tomas, but angled so all three could see it.

Tomas said, "Hilary is starting us off. She'll state the roles of each organization—Keeney Community College, Keeney Building Supply, and Keeney Works, and how they benefit each other."

"Which is?" Marcia interrupted.

Vincent waved a hand in dismissal. "Ma, you know this."

"*I* do. But the more you practice saying it, the easier it will come. You need to hone your pitch." She tapped a finger on the table for emphasis.

"Fine." Vincent took a deep breath. "We see Keeney Builds as a joint project benefitting people with difficulty finding and keeping jobs. It would be a mix of classroom education, on-the-job training, and paid internships, as well as a support system for keeping students on track. KCC will provide facilities, accredited classes, and career counseling. KBS will provide job training at their location and paid internships with their building contractors, meaning Tomas and myself. Keeney Works has a proven track record for finding jobs for at-risk persons. It is the go-to place for those trying to re-enter the workforce. Keeney Works doesn't have an in with the building trades. *We* can provide that. This is an opportunity for people who want to work with their hands, and get trained for long-lasting and varied careers."

Marcia scribbled on the tablet. "Not bad. Tomas, can you change each of the logos into a puzzle piece and have them fly together to become one entity?"

Narrowing his eyes at Marcia, Tomas pulled the laptop toward him, and pounded away at the keyboard. He turned it back to her. "Like this?"

"Much better. It's a good visual for the board to focus on how each group can fit together. Do you mind if I use it for the website?"

He nodded slightly, but Vincent grinned, knowing what that meant for his friend.

Tomas picked up from where Vincent left off. They worked together seamlessly, feeding off each other, enthusiasm picking up as they went along.

"Excellent!" Marcia said when they finished. "Here are a few notes for you. But on the whole, I think you've covered everything."

Tomas took Marcia's notes and tucked them into his backpack with his laptop. "Thanks, that was useful."

Marcia stood and went to the fridge to pull out bottles of beer and pass them around. At Vincent's raised eyebrow, she shrugged, "The sun's over the yardarm somewhere."

Taking a drink, he watched his mother scribble on her notepad. "You're really into this, aren't you."

"I am. It's far more interesting than dealing with medical billing, and will positively impact the community if we succeed. Now, you may want to take Carl with you to the presentation. He can give a testimonial about what he has learned from working with you." She leaned back in her chair and thought some more. "I take it Ali is speaking on behalf of KBS?"

"Yeah," Vincent replied. "I know they're getting along better, but we thought it would be awkward for Iris to present to her daughter-in-law."

"She won't be *that* for much longer. Fiona is divorcing Eddie," Marcia announced with a satisfied smile.

"No shit? Good for her." Vincent raised his beer in salute. Tomas sipped his beer and didn't say anything.

"Yep. She kicked Eddie out of the house and demanded his key back."

"My heart bleeds for the guy," Vincent had no sympathy for him.

"Should she get the locks changed? Eddie may have more

than one key." Tomas's face was expressionless, but his jaw was tight.

Vincent shared a look with his mother before speaking. "Good idea. I'll have Hilary suggest it to her."

"Screw that. Text me her address, and I'll take care of it." Tomas rose from the table and gathered his things. "Thanks for the lunch and the beer, Mrs. Ortiz." He lifted his chin at Vincent and was gone.

❆

The phone rang three times before Hilary absently picked it up. "Hello."

"Ms. Banks, there's someone in reception waiting to see you."

"Really?" Hilary brought up her calendar but could not see any entries for the day.

"It's a woman named Marcia Ortiz."

"Really. Umm…I'll be right there." Her mind went blank before panic seized her. Something must have happened to Vincent because why else would his mother be there. Not bothering to put on her shoes, she raced out the door and down the hallway. Images of him lying beneath a stack of lumber or cut and bleeding from an errant saw blade flashed as she passed gaping faces, and careened around the corner to the brightly lit reception area.

Spotting Marcia, she blurted, "What happened? Is he okay? Is he in the hospital?"

Looking at Hilary like she'd lost her mind, Marcia came toward her. "What are you talking about?" Then her eyes widened, and she reached out to grab Hilary's trembling hand. "He's fine. Everything is fine. I am so sorry, I shouldn't have shown up without an appointment."

Hilary waved off her apology and sank into a chair to

wait for her heart to reattach itself in her chest. Giving Marcia a weak smile, she said, "Hi. Is there something I can help you with?"

"Yes and no. Do you have a few minutes?"

Hilary took in the white knuckles clutching the portfolio. "I could use a break. How about we go get a cup of tea?"

"That would be lovely," Marcia said on an audible exhale.

After retrieving her shoes, Hilary waved at the receptionist, then held the door open for Marcia to precede her. Not knowing why she was visiting her, Hilary started with a safe topic. "It's beautiful right now, I hope it stays this way for the evening."

Marcia agreed, mentioning the need to water her flower beds when she returned home. The conversation limped along as they headed outdoors. The campus of Keeney Community College was laid out in a quadrangle. Three buildings held classrooms and labs, while the fourth was the administration building where Hilary worked. Some summer classes were in session, but for the most part, the campus was quiet. Hilary led the way to an espresso cart under a tree with a few bistro tables and chairs around it.

"Please," Marcia pulled out her wallet, "let me treat you. What would you like?"

"An iced London Fog, please. Thank you. I'll find us a table." Hilary grabbed a table in the shade and sat, mentally listing the reasons for the visit. Each item started with Vincent. She squared her shoulders, prepared for Marcia to tell her to leave her son alone. By the time Marcia arrived with the drinks, she was ready to mount a defense and declare her love.

"I am—" said Hilary.

"I want—" said Marcia.

"What?" they said at the same time.

Hilary picked up her drink and motioned to Marcia. "You go first."

"First off, I'm glad you've forgiven Vincent. He treated you so badly I was afraid you wouldn't. It was all I could do not to break off his arm and beat him over the head with it. My son needs to learn his lessons the hard way." Her lips were so thin they almost disappeared.

Hilary hid her smile. Vincent had told her about the tongue-lashing he'd received. What would Eddie have been like if Iris were more like Marcia? Aloud, she said, "We're good. Your son is...very special to me." She held Marcia's gaze briefly before the older woman looked away.

Marcia blinked a couple of times, cleared her throat, and straightened her shoulders. "I want to work for Keeney Builds." At Hilary's bemused expression, she continued, "I have the time and energy to devote to the project. I know my way around spreadsheets, PowerPoint, and copy machines. I may not know much about marketing strategies but take direction well. I'm good at herding cats, I can corral Vincent and Tomas, and handle Iris." Her voice faltered on the last name.

She cleared her throat. "Iris is my best friend. She doesn't have the energy to give to the project right now. But I know she supports it. She believes in community. She believes in combining forces to accomplish a goal. She's given my son a purpose and an opportunity. Without Iris, Vincent might still be struggling to find work in construction.

"I want to support her. I want to take this vision you and she share and make it into a reality. I can subtly push her. I can get her out of her pity party, and help her find direction. Please let me help." Marcia picked up her drink and sat back. Her face looked composed, but her jiggling leg gave away her anxiety.

She was a good friend, and Iris was fortunate to have Marcia Ortiz in her corner. Keeney Builds would need her energy and drive to get off the ground and succeed. "I think you're right. Iris is wounded right now and unable to give much. I know she wants to be left alone, but we don't have time before the board meeting." Hilary sipped her drink and asked, "You heard Vincent and Tomas present yesterday? How was it?"

Marcia opened her portfolio and took out some papers. "I made notes. Here's a copy for you. They work well together. A bit stiff, but they loosened up after a while. There's a couple of places where they geeked out over power tools and CAD design, which was endearing. People like to see that kind of passion. I also think they should each talk about their release from prison and finding work."

Hilary flicked her gaze from the papers to Marcia. "I agree. Do you think they'll do it?"

Marcia blew out a gusty sigh. "Men don't like to admit weakness or need. We'll have to work on them. Let's meet for dinner at my house tomorrow. You call Vincent and Tomas, I'll call Iris, Ali, and Carl. You and I can tag team."

Hilary saluted her with a smile. "Yes, ma'am."

"Sorry about that," Marcia replied, pressing her lips together. "It's just that this project excites me."

"It's not a problem. I spend too much time in meetings where no one wants to take the lead, so I appreciate your determination."

They gathered their drinks and papers, and walked back to the admin building. "I'm going to find the Australian girl, Nadia," Hilary declared. At Marcia's raised eyebrow, she continued, "If we find her, there's a chance she can help us clear Vincent's name."

Rapidly blinking, Marcia looked away, sniffed, and nodded. "Good. Vincent didn't want me to. I'll go through my files from the lawyer and let you know if there is anything in there for you."

"Great. Thank you."

Marcia reached out and touched Hilary's sleeve. "Thank

you. You're good for my son." Her gaze went down to Hilary's shoes. "And I think he's good for you as well." She lightly patted Hilary's arm, and walked off.

Hilary looked down at her leopard-print shoes, smiled, and returned to work.

The kitchen table could not accommodate seven people. Vincent and Tomas rested against the counter with their plates while Iris, Hilary, Ali, Carl, and Marcia sat at the table. Vincent didn't mind. It meant he was closer to the food for seconds and thirds. It also allowed him to watch the people at the table, people he cared a lot about.

He'd surprised Marcia earlier when he was the first to arrive.

"Please tell me you're early," she said, her gaze darting to the clock. "No one is supposed to be here for another half hour."

"Relax, Ma, you're fine." He kissed her cheek and handed her an envelope.

"What's this?"

Shoving his hands in his pockets, he rocked back on his heels. "It's the first loan payment. I'll set up an automatic transfer for the rest, but I don't have your bank information so cash will have to do today."

Her eyes bugged out when she opened the envelope. "Vincent! You don't—"

"Yes, Ma, I do. I'd still be in prison if it weren't for you, so take it. Put it in the bank or go wild. Maybe buy yourself a new adding machine."

She stared at him with watery eyes, and hugged him fiercely. His eyes were just as watery when he hugged her back.

"Can I buy you a new toolbox?"

"No."

"A custom-made carpenter's belt?"

"Ma…"

She chuckled, sniffed, and went back to setting the table.

With the single-mindedness of a nineteen-year-old boy, Carl plowed his way through his food, oblivious to those around him. Hilary sparkled. She'd stripped off the white jacket she'd worn to work, revealing a sleeveless, close-fitting, turquoise top over a white skirt. Her hair piled on top of her head in a messy bun, she looked comfortable and relaxed as she engaged everyone in conversation. Lavishing praise on Marcia's food, inquiring about business at KBS, asking Carl about his studies, and Tomas about his family.

To this, Vincent paid close attention. Even when they were inside, Tomas rarely spoke about them. But to Hilary, he shared, however sparingly. His story was similar to Vincent's own. His father left when Tomas was nine, moved to California, and was rarely heard from. His mother remarried, and Tomas had two much younger sisters. His mother and stepfather had a thriving restaurant in Woodinville, where multiple family members worked. Hilary asked if he'd worked in the restaurant. Tomas replied with a firm no, which was the end of his sharing.

When Ali scraped the last evidence of his meal from his plate, Vincent said, "We'll take care of the dishes, head on into the living room."

Chairs shifted, cutlery clattered, and Carl had moved to follow Iris when he was nabbed from behind. "Not so fast, college boy." Tomas stopped him. "You've got kitchen duty, too."

Carl made a face but turned to the table and gathered up plates. It obviously was not his first twirl around the dance floor because he loaded the dishwasher like a pro, knowing enough to rinse the plates first. Vincent was elbow-deep in soapy water when Carl said, "Dinner was awesome. Your mom is a great cook. But umm, why am I here?"

"Because you're the centerpiece of the dog and pony show we'll be performing at the board meeting," Tomas said. His tone brooked no argument.

Carl's Adam's apple bobbed. His head bobbed as well. "Okay…"

Vincent rolled his eyes and nudged Carl with his elbow. "It'll be fine. We want you to be there. You can testify that Tomas and I haven't corrupted you and led you into a life of crime."

"Okay," Carl repeated, looking less like a deer in the headlights. He took instructions well but showed initiative often, suggesting design changes that worked well. The laugh was on Eddie for giving Vincent a babysitter.

"Did you pack up leftovers for everyone?" Marcia called, bustling into the kitchen. Clearly in her element, a pencil tucked behind one ear, she carried a sheaf of stapled papers. Stopping by the fridge, she surveyed the room; the table was clean, the dishwasher loaded, and the pots and pans were drying on the counter.

"Yes, Ma, I packed everything in plastic containers and put them in the fridge," Vincent replied, drying his hands and draping the towel over the edge of the sink.

"Good." Marcia nodded and headed to the coffee maker. "Tomas, can you serve up the pie? Carl, pull down the coffee mugs. Vincent, dig out two trays. I'll bring in the coffee."

"Yes, ma'am," all three replied in unison. Vincent glanced at Tomas to see how he reacted to being bossed around. The quirk of his lips indicated he was just fine with it. They filed into the living room, placing their loads on the coffee table per Marcia's instructions. Carl sat beside Ali and Iris on the couch, while Vincent sat beside Hilary on the loveseat. Tomas propped a shoulder on the wall by the entranceway, leaving the armchair for Marcia. He declined the offer of a kitchen chair and crossed his arms.

When everyone had pie and coffee, Marcia cleared her throat and began. "We have a week before the presentation, and I want to make sure everyone knows what's expected of them, that we all have the same materials, and that we know the timeline."

"Do I need to know all of this if I'm not going to be there?" Iris asked, looking wilted. She'd hemmed and hawed, coming up with a variety of excuses not to be at tonight's dinner, finally giving in when Hilary offered to drive her. She didn't talk much during the meal and had barely eaten. While not dressed differently from what she would normally wear, Iris did not have her usual spark. Since Eddie's arrest, her passion had all but disappeared.

"You won't be present, but you may receive questions. The program wouldn't exist without KBS, and *you* are KBS," Hilary told her, passing printouts to everyone, then sitting back down. Iris nodded absently.

"Whoa." Vincent shot a look at Tomas. "Take a look at page five."

Tomas put his empty plate on the coffee table and picked up a packet. Turning to the correct page, he read for a moment, then glared at Hilary. "Not happening," he stated in an uncompromising voice.

Carl and Ali flipped to page five as well. Carl's gaze bounced between Vincent and Tomas. Page five specified personal testimonials from them about leaving prison.

Ali's eyebrows went up. "Good idea." He took in Tomas and Vincent's matching scowls. "I get that you don't want to talk about it because you want to put your time in prison behind you. You two went through a good training program, but where would you be if it hadn't been for your connection to KBS?" The two men glowered but didn't respond. "Exactly. No references. You know what that's like and how difficult an obstacle it is to overcome. You two are precisely the ones to speak up for the program." Ali indicated Carl with his thumb. "This guy was a useless tool when you got him. Now, he's a craftsman. That's why he's gonna speak." Ali looked down at the paperwork. "Hilary, do you want me to testify as to what Carl learned from working with the guys?"

Hilary looked to Marcia for confirmation. "Yes. Also, would you recommend another company hire Carl?"

Ali took a bite of pie, chased it with a swig of coffee, and swallowed. "No, I would not."

Carl's fork clattered to the plate. His shoulders fell, and he stared at his shoes.

Ali smiled. "I won't write him a recommendation because I intend to offer him a full-time position as our third contractor."

Carl's head came up. His smile shone brightly against his dark skin. "Seriously?"

Hilary sighed.

Lips pursed, Marcia reached across the coffee table to smack Ali on the shoulder. "That was mean."

"I know, but damn fun." He nudged Carl with an elbow. "We'll talk about the details tomorrow."

Carl whipped out his cellphone. "I gotta post this."

Ali stilled him with his big hand. "Not yet. It's gonna happen, but don't jump the gun informing all your peeps."

"Peeps?" Vincent smirked.

Ali sat back and crossed his arms. "Yeah, I'm hip and with it. I'm down with the lingo."

"Sure, Grandpa," Vincent muttered.

Hilary looked between Vincent and Tomas. "So, are you two on board?"

Vincent ran a hand through his hair and exhaled loudly. "I'm in. Tomas?"

Arms crossed and still scowling, Tomas was definitely not thrilled with the idea.

"How about I write something as a starting point?" Hilary suggested. "You can alter it as you see fit."

The room was silent, waiting for Tomas's reply. Vincent understood his reluctance because he didn't want to share the humiliating experience of constant rejection, either. But he was far more vested in the program than Tomas was: it would be a big coup for Hilary, and he was willing to walk through fire for her.

The ping of a text broke the tension as Tomas nodded.

Marcia beamed. "Tomas, can we meet up tomorrow to review the PowerPoint? I want to add a few more slides." Again, he nodded.

"Right, I'm out of here." Having reached his limit for socializing, he lifted his chin at Vincent, then pulled open the front door.

"Oh!"

Everyone in the living room craned their heads to see who was there. Tomas shifted to the side, revealing Fiona Han. The two eyed each other as if no one else existed. Tomas frowned, stepping aside to let Fiona enter, and then was gone.

Fiona turned to the others, shaking her head like she was clearing her thoughts. "Umm…hi," she said, glancing around the room. "Iris asked me to come and get her." She stood in the entryway, dressed as if she were headed to a country club luncheon, her hair swept up in a complicated knot. Vincent wondered if she even owned jeans.

Hilary and Marcia rose at the same time that Iris announced, "I'm ready to go," and hustled to the door.

Marcia protested, "But we're not finished. We need to go over—"

Hilary interrupted Marcia with a hand over her arm. "Should we call you if we have any questions for KBS?"

Iris waved a hand in dismissal. "Ali can answer them. You don't need me. I'll see you later." And then *she* was gone.

Ali caught Vincent's gaze and shrugged, furrowing his brow, while Carl picked up Iris's untouched piece of pie to attack it with his fork.

"Mrs. Ortiz, I'm Fiona Han."

"Yes, we met at your wedding." Marcia smiled stiffly, taking her hand.

Fiona gave a slight laugh. "Of course. It's lovely to see you again." To Hilary, she said, "I'll make sure Iris gets home safely." She nodded to the others and left quietly.

Marcia closed the door behind her and walked back to her seat. "Obviously, they've bonded. Have I missed something?" She glanced around the room with a guilty look on her face. "I've been so caught up with this damn proposal I've barely talked with Iris."

Ali rubbed a hand over his bald head. "Fiona has been to the store twice to visit with Iris. Both times she left with red eyes. And Iris is leaving most of the decision-making to me. Which isn't a good idea because I could be pulling an Eddie, and she's not aware of it."

"They've been talking to a lawyer," Carl spoke around a mouthful of pie.

Four pairs of eyes swiveled his way. He looked directly at Vincent and shrugged one shoulder. "I hear things."

Vincent nodded. He could see it. Carl shuffled around the building, earbuds in place, bopping to whatever music he listened to. Vincent's shadow, he was a fixture at KBS, and for the most part, the staff ignored him.

Carl swallowed the last bite of pie, and put the plate on the coffee table. "They're fixing it so Eddie can't access anything at KBS. Fiona has filed for divorce, and she and Iris are trying to figure out where the money is going. Oh, and a new password system will be set up for the company computers." This last information he directed at Ali, who grunted in response.

Hilary settled next to Vincent on the loveseat. "I think I know where the money is going. I looked through social media and found a bunch of old photos with both Eddie and Nadia in them." She turned to Vincent. "Nadia left right before the police raided your place. I think Eddie planted the stuff, and Nadia is blackmailing him."

"That only happens in the movies," Ali scoffed.

Looking puzzled, Carl turned to him. "Who's Nadia?"

"I'll tell you later," Ali said, shooting him a glance.

Hilary held up a hand. "Hear me out. We know Eddie hates Vincent. What if Eddie broke Nadia's heart? What if, years later, she sees him boasting about his success all over social media, and figures she has a way to make him suffer?"

"A woman scorned can be very dangerous," Marcia muttered.

Hilary continued, "I'm going to do a bit more digging. Maybe reach out to Nadia and see if she will talk to me."

The room went quiet as everyone ruminated on the idea.

Tears glistened in Marcia's eyes as she stared at Vincent. "This could clear you."

"Yeah, but crush Iris," he replied.

No one looked happy.

CHAPTER 24

"What now?" Vincent asked, starting up the truck. He drank from his water bottle while Tomas flipped through his notebook, looking for the address of their next stop. Carl was taking his final exam at the college, so Tomas and Vincent were working together.

"Installing a garage door opener for a woman who lives in a gated community near the winery."

Vincent put the truck in drive and started down the street. They'd spent the morning installing bookshelves and wine racks in a shop downtown. The owner liked Vincent's design ideas, which made the work more satisfying. The light fixtures hadn't come yet so the afternoon would be spent doing smaller jobs. Vincent took the next right and headed out of Keeney. A familiar face caught his eye, and he turned sharply to pull over.

"What the hell!" Tomas complained, looking up from his notebook.

"That guy on the park bench over there. It's Eddie." Vincent pointed to where a man wearing dark glasses sat in the shade, looking at his phone and periodically glancing toward the parking lot of the small park on the side of the slough. He sat up straight when a woman approached, rising when she got closer. As she reached up to kiss him, he wrapped his arms around her and returned the kiss. They pulled apart, Eddie's hand settling on her lower back, and they walked to a car and got in, the woman in the driver's seat. "And that's Nadia."

Tomas snapped photos, a step ahead of Vincent. "I don't think she's blackmailing him."

"Nope," Vincent replied. Checking the mirrors, he let three cars pass before pulling out into the street. Ten minutes later, the car turned into an apartment complex. Vincent continued on; they were far too obvious in the KBS truck. "I bet that's where the money is going. Rental on an apartment for her."

"Yeah, but that doesn't mean Eddie didn't set you up. I think you should go to the cops."

Vincent gave Tomas the side-eye. Given his record, Tomas's suggestion was out of left field.

"The stolen property is probably still at the station, locked in a storage room. Ask for it to be dusted for prints or tested for DNA, or whatever the hell they do. Eddie and Nadia together is too much of a damn coincidence." Tomas waved his phone at Vincent, the photo of the couple kissing on the screen.

The thought of going to the police station gave him the shivers. He didn't have fond memories of the place or the people there. "That's not something I really want to do."

"I don't blame you, but is there an alternative? Or aren't you interested in clearing your name?"

"Of course I am," he snapped. If for no other reason than he owed it to his mother. No doubt she'd hire a skywriter to announce it to the world.

They drove in silence while Vincent mulled it over.

"Hah!" He smiled triumphantly, remembering something his mother mentioned in passing.

"What?" Tomas side-eyed him.

"Ma plays Scrabble with the new police chief on Thursday nights," Vincent said.

"Of course she does," Tomas muttered.

"Got it. Thanks, Ma." Disconnecting, Vincent placed his phone on the bedside table. Beside him, Hilary sat propped against a stack of pillows, computer in her lap, looking enticing in a lacy purple camisole he knew matched the panties she wore. He'd removed them once and intended to remove them again before the night ended.

"And?" Hilary asked around the pencil clamped between her teeth.

"Chief Reyes said she would have the evidence examined for prints."

Hilary removed the pencil and tucked it behind an ear. "Didn't they do that when you were arrested?"

He nodded. "At the time, they were only interested in *my* prints. They didn't find any, but that wasn't enough to *not* convict me."

"Where do you think Eddie got the stuff?"

Vincent shook his head. "Paying kids to shoplift for him, maybe. You can find brand new stuff without paying retail if you look hard enough."

"What's this going to do to Iris?" Heaving a great sigh, Hilary stared at her laptop.

He knew what she was feeling. If Eddie's prints were on the stolen items, Vincent would be exonerated, and Eddie would go to jail. The thought of Eddie in jail was satisfying. The thought of Iris having a son in jail was not.

Hilary twisted to look up at him. "I haven't known her long, but Iris seems like one of those people who feels responsible for everything."

"Yep."

"I bet she apologizes to both you and your mom."

"Yep."

She met his gaze with a determined expression. "But if Eddie *is* guilty, he needs to suffer the consequences."

"Yep."

Eyes narrowed, she continued, "When something good happens to someone you care about, but that means someone else you care about is going to be hurt, no one really wins. Do they?"

"Nope."

Turning back to the computer, Hilary gazed at the screen before closing the program. She moved the laptop to her nightstand and turned off her lamp before snuggling against him with a soft sigh.

He stroked her back, feeling the tension in her muscles. "I can make you feel better."

She peered up at him. "You can?"

Plucking the pencil from behind her ear, he tossed it to the nightstand before pulling her over to straddle him. He eased her back against his bent legs, and stroked her soft skin from hip to heel, and back up, keeping his eyes locked on hers.

She shivered and sighed again, the tension easing from her frame. He moved his hands up her thighs until his thumbs brushed against her panties, and her eyes closed to half-mast.

"That *is* better," she whispered.

Like a bright red beacon, the pimple on her chin couldn't be more prominent. Hilary scowled at her reflection. She had gray hair and wrinkles, how could she still get zits? And why did they insist on showing up on important days?

"Shit, shit, shit, shit, shit." Vincent stomped into the bedroom, removing his shirt and tossing it onto the bed.

"What's wrong?"

"I spilled my coffee. Do I have another—oh, thank you, Jesus."

"Actually, it was me," she said from the bathroom doorway. "Jesus wasn't with me when I bought those shirts for you."

"According to my Sunday school teacher, Jesus is always with us." He emerged from the closet, buttoning a light blue dress shirt and smiling at her. "You look amazing."

"Thank you." The navy linen sheath fit her well. Hopefully, she could keep it clean until after the presentation.

Their phones dinged simultaneously, and Vincent rolled his eyes. "I wonder who that could be?"

Hilary patted his arm and scooped up her phone on the

way to the kitchen, knowing it was Marcia confirming everyone had their marching orders. They'd met at her place again last night because Marcia insisted on a complete run-through. They did it twice, but Tomas balked at the third, and they all hustled out the door before Marcia could persuade him otherwise.

Fortified with coffee and peanut butter toast, and after ensuring they had Hilary's laptop as backup in case something went wrong with Tomas's, plus phones, charging cords, and printouts of the presentation, they took Vincent's truck to meet everyone in the parking lot of Keeney Works.

"Have you got the—"

"Yes, Ma," Vincent answered, kissing her on the cheek.

"You don't even know what I was going to say."

"Have you thought of something else since your last text message?"

"No."

"Then we've got everything." Vincent kissed her again, rolled his eyes at Hilary, and strolled away to join the men.

Seeing her freak out reduced Hilary's own nerves. Marcia seemed more invested in Keeney Builds than the four men and Hilary combined.

"Do you want to check that we *do* have everything?" Hilary asked, opening her tote bag.

"I trust you," Marcia replied but then stopped Hilary from closing the zipper. "On second thought, I *will* take a look."

Two hours later, the group filed out of the Keeney Works building into the bright sunshine, Vincent, Ali, and Carl removing their jackets and loosening their ties. Tomas wore neither; he rolled up the sleeves of his shirt.

Hilary high-fived all four of the men. "You guys rocked it! Nicely done."

The presentation went off without a hitch. Well, except

for Ali not having his reading glasses and needing to borrow a pair from one of the board members. Receptive to the presentation, the board had many questions. All of which the group answered easily. And then brainstorming happened. Ideas were bouncing around the room, and it became apparent it wasn't *if* Keeney Works would come on board but *when*.

"Who knew Carl could be so eloquent." Ali clapped Carl on the shoulder, sending him stumbling forward a few steps. "Proud of you, son. Proud of all three of you." The three younger men smiled. Ali walked to Hilary and wrapped an arm around her shoulders. "But *you* put this together. I'm not sure why you chose Keeney, but I'm glad you moved here. We need you." He kissed her on the forehead before releasing her. She blushed. Ali's validation meant the world to her. She beamed at Ali and the others.

"Thanks. I needed Keeney, too." Her gaze moved to Vincent, who stepped forward, wrapping her in a fierce hug.

The door opened, and Fiona walked through it with a broad smile. "Are you ready to celebrate? Because it's a go."

"Excellent!" said Hilary.

"Yes!" said Carl.

Ali clapped as Marcia whooped.

Vincent and Tomas grinned at each other.

Squealing tires drew their attention. Eddie leaped out of his car and stalked toward Fiona. "You stupid bitch. You sicced the cops on me."

Fiona's smile disappeared. "What are you talking about?"

"I got home to find the cops in the apartment questioning Nadia." Eddie's anger rolled off him in waves.

"Who's Nadia?" Fiona whispered.

"His girlfriend," Vincent responded, moving closer to Fiona.

Looking at Vincent, Eddie snarled, "Get the hell out of here. I'm talking to my wife."

"Eddie." Ali placed a hand on Eddie's arm. "Calm down, son. This is not the time and place for this conversation."

Eddie shook him off. "Fuck that. And fuck you, old man. I am not your son. You're just a lackey who sucks up to my mother." Vincent's hand was in his chest, pushing him back.

Turning his wrath on Vincent, Eddie went on. "What? Are you going to hit me again? You're worse than he is. Life was great when you were in jail. None of that *'Isn't Vincent wonderful'* shit from Mom. Now you're back, and she thinks the sun shines out of your ass." He swung back to Fiona. "And you, KBS was going to be mine. But you screwed everything up for me."

Hilary sidled closer to Fiona, taking her hand. Tomas stood behind Fiona, slightly to the side, big hands curled into fists. Realizing that Vincent and Ali were maneuvering Eddie away from the tiny woman, Hilary looked to the side and spotted Carl filming the scene, phone held low to be unobtrusive. She caught Vincent's eye and angled her chin toward Carl before saying, "You've been siphoning off money from KBS."

Eddie jerked. "It's not siphoning when the company belongs to you."

"But KBS *doesn't* belong to you. You paid wages to nonexistent employees and funneled the money to your own accounts. That's not siphoning. That's theft," Hilary said, thankful her voice didn't quaver.

Rounding on her, Eddie's voice rose. "You dried-up old bitch. *You* called the cops."

"I called the cops," a loud voice overrode him. Marcia stepped in front of Ali just as Iris approached from the parking lot. Looking shattered, lips trembling, focused on her son. Fiona darted past Hilary to take Iris's hand while Marcia confronted Eddie. "The cops questioned Nadia about the stolen goods found in Vincent's apartment. They've been in the evidence room for years. I think you hid those things in the apartment, and the cops are going to find your DNA on them."

Eddie reared back, the fading bruises standing out against his suddenly pale face. He looked around wildly before fixing his gaze on Iris and Fiona. His features hardened, and he strode toward them. "Now you're ganging up on me? You chose Vincent over me," he spat at his mother. "You moved him into your house, you set him up in business, and you parade him around Keeney like he's the second coming." Swinging his head toward Fiona, he continued, "My own wife knew how much damage that bastard did to me, now she's waving the banner in the All Hail Vincent Parade."

Releasing Iris's hand, Fiona stepped up to him. "You lied to me about your parents. You told me they were disappointed you married me. Why should I believe what you told me about Vincent?" She glared at him. "And now I find out you have a girlfriend."

Eddie gave a derisive laugh. "Of course, I have a girlfriend. I only married you for your family's money. But those cheap slant-eyes wouldn't let me near their business. And you were so cold and unresponsive, it was like fucking a—"

Thwack!

Standing over Eddie's now prone body, Marcia reared back to hit him with her purse again.

"Easy tiger," Ali said, restraining her with a firm hand.

"I've wanted to do that for years," Marcia muttered.

"Me too," Ali replied.

Vincent brushed past his mother and crouched beside Eddie, his thick thighs and work-scarred hands a stark contrast to Eddie's slim frame. "Did you set me up?"

Eddie nodded, not bothering to look at him.

"Why? What did I do to you?" Hands clenched in tight fists; it was obvious Vincent had thought about this for years.

"You're a nothing. Barely made it through high school. Worked just enough to pay for ski trips. *I* got a degree. *I* got an MBA. And they couldn't care less. Yet when you decided to go back to school, my parents were so impressed." Eddie met his gaze, venom in his eyes. "It was trade school, for fuck's sake!"

"You took away three years of my life." Vincent ground out. "I couldn't find work. Ma had to remortgage the house to get me out. All because your parents *liked* me?" He stood and flung his arms wide. It was all Hilary could do not to grab Marcia's purse and hit Eddie herself. She hoped Carl was recording everything and that his battery wouldn't die.

Eddie rose to his feet, smoothing back his hair. "They wanted to take you on at KBS. Like an annoying fly, you refused to go away. So I made it happen."

In a soft, tentative voice, Iris asked, "But why have you been stealing for the past year?"

Eddie leveled an angry look her way. "When Dad got sick and you asked me to come back, I was thrilled. This would be the time to show you what I could do. But I saw the corporate papers. I'm not an equal partner. I'm not the CEO. I'm a goddamn employee of my parents' business. It will be my business when you die." Eddie straightened his shirt and brushed off his hands. "So I decided to access the money now instead of waiting." He headed toward the parking lot.

The group gaped at each other and then at Eddie.

Carl held up his phone. "Should I call the cops?"

"Already done," Marcia said, tucking her phone in her purse.

Sirens approached, and Hilary and Marcia went to support Fiona, who was holding up a sobbing Iris. They watched Eddie's car disappear in traffic.

"Well, that certainly put a damper on the day," Carl muttered.

$\mathcal{H}$eads turned as Marcia climbed the stairs to Hilary's deck. "She took a sedative and went to bed. I'll check on her in half an hour, but I expect her to be out like a light."

Vincent, Ali, Tomas, Fiona, and Hilary sat at the patio table. Settling into a vacant chair, Marcia announced, "I don't know about anyone else, but I could use a drink."

"On it," Ali said, flipping open the cooler he'd brought up from his truck and set at his side. "I brought beer and a bottle of sparkling wine." He grinned at the faces around him and looked at Hilary. "I've got everything but the wineglasses."

"On it," said Vincent, rising from the table and going into the house.

Marcia looked at the assembled group. "Where's Carl?"

"He had some kind of family thing," Ali continued to root through the cooler, pulling out containers of food, which he set on the table. He called to Vincent, "Bring plates and stuff as well." Removing lids, he displayed the bounty; hummus and veggies, three kinds of cheese, crackers, salami, olives, artichoke dip, and pickles. He smiled at the oohs and ahhs. "I figured we'd have something to celebrate." He popped the cork, poured wine for everyone in the glasses provided, and raised his glass. "To Keeney Builds!"

Glasses clinked. Tomas poured his wine into Fiona's glass and dug a beer out of the cooler for himself.

"Are we being premature? Is Iris going to want to continue?" Vincent asked. Satisfaction and guilt warred inside him. Seeing Iris sobbing in Fiona's arms as Eddie was cuffed and frog-marched to the police car took some of the shine off the day's events.

Ali shifted in his chair, looking at Marcia before speaking. "Iris wants to step back from KBS. She thought when she returned to work, she, Eddie, and I would be a team. Now, she needs to regroup."

"Are you moving up the ladder?" Vincent asked Ali.

"Nope. I like it where I am. I'll step in until we settle on an executive, but just for the interim."

"How long will that take? It can't be easy to find someone to take over." Vincent didn't say it aloud, but would they be able to find someone supportive of Keeney Builds, someone comfortable working with ex-cons?

"We've found someone." Ali exchanged smiles with Marcia. "We just haven't asked her yet." They both looked toward Hilary.

She was busy layering salami and cheese on a cracker and didn't notice. When the table went silent, she looked up. Five pairs of eyes were turned her way. "What?"

Ali leaned forward, his hands clasped in front of him. "On behalf of KBS, Hilary Banks, would you accept our offer for the CEO position?"

"What?" she asked, frowning in confusion.

Ali grinned. "Wanna come work at KBS?"

"I don't...I didn't..." She looked around at the expectant smiling faces.

"The employees like you," Ali gestured at Vincent and Tomas. "You have excellent references," he gestured at Fiona. "And Iris wants you."

Vincent reached over and unclenched her hand from around the arm of the chair. "You can do this," he said in a soft voice meant just for her. The idea of working with her filled him with pleasure. She had vision and determination, and believed in him. KBS would thrive with her at the helm. "Please?"

Blinking rapidly, she nodded, then downed the contents of her glass in one gulp.

"Good," Ali said, looking smug.

Marcia smacked him on the arm. "Don't even think of taking credit for the idea."

Fiona rose from the table, holding her phone. "Thank you

for inviting me, this was nice. Hilary, congratulations, I'll talk to you soon." With a polite smile for everyone, she gathered up her purse and turned to the stairs. "I've called an Uber, so I'm going to wait in the driveway."

Tomas stood as well. "I'll drive you home."

"Oh." She craned her neck to meet his eyes. "That's not necessary."

With a fierce frown, he moved past her. "I'll drive you home." He jerked his chin at Hilary, "Bye, boss," and headed down the stairs.

Fiona looked at Hilary as well, her cheeks stained red. "I guess he's driving me home." Silently, she trailed behind him.

The table was quiet, listening to the slam of closing doors and the truck starting up. Then they exchanged glances and laughed. When it died down, Marcia said, "I'll go check on Iris."

"Are you going to press charges against Eddie?" Ali asked, reaching for the beer and passing one to Vincent.

Vincent shrugged. "I doubt that it's up to me. Besides, isn't he in enough trouble?"

Ali started counting things off on his fingers. "Sexual harassment charge. Theft—provided Iris presses charges, and framing you—provided you press charges."

Marcia returned at that moment, snagging an olive off Ali's plate and settling into a chair. "Iris *is* pressing charges. She's had some long conversations with Fiona, and Eddie tracked the transfers in his planner. It was sitting right on the coffee table when the police interviewed Nadia. Letting Eddie off the hook won't benefit anyone. And," reaching for her wine, she raised the glass, "Nadia made a statement. Apparently, she thought Eddie and Fiona were divorced." She took a sip and smirked. "Before she left for Australia, she'd been seeing Eddie and gave him her house key to return it to you." She nodded at Vincent. "They'd broken up because she was headed to a six-month spiritual retreat where she went off-line for the duration, and lost the habit of going on social media. She looked Eddie up when she returned to the States early last year. One thing led to another, and she moved into an apartment here in Keeney about a year ago."

"That's when the money started going missing," Hilary stated.

"Mm-hmm," said Marcia. "Feathering a love nest. He claimed Fiona had left him, get this, for a Latino man she had met through her non-profit." Marcia put air quotes around the last phrase. "Almost like he was conjuring up Tomas."

Ali shook his head. "The man just drove her home."

"Sure," said Vincent, nodding sagely. "Like I just needed to borrow Hilary's laptop to order a new cellphone."

"You didn't?" Hilary asked, twisting to look at him.

Vincent dragged her chair closer to his own. "Not really. It was an excuse to spend time with you."

Speechless, Hilary stared at him. Forgetting about the presence of Ali and Marcia, she leaned in and softly kissed his lips. "I'm glad you did that."

Vincent returned the kiss. "So am I." Climbing those stairs was the best decision he ever made. That and going to find her at the bar.

"Can we get back to the story?" Ali asked with mock disgruntlement.

Vincent wrapped an arm around Hilary, and smiled. "Sure."

"So when Nadia realized Eddie was stringing her along, she sang like a canary." Marcia rocked in her chair with glee. "Eddie told her he'd discovered the stolen goods in the back bedroom of your apartment and called the cops from a payphone. He didn't want to hurt Iris by being the one to inform on her best friend's son."

"How much does Iris know?" Hilary asked.

"Everything," Marcia stated flatly. "Chief Reyes called me while I was with her, and I put it on speaker."

"This must be killing her," Hilary glanced between Ali and Marcia.

"Hence the sedative. She's going to need some counseling. At some point, every parent realizes they are no longer responsible for the actions of their children." Marcia regarded Vincent. "That being said, I'm claiming responsibility for you and Hilary getting together."

"Whatever," Vincent muttered with a mock glare.

Marcia finished her wine, and rose from her chair. "You can drive me home," she turned to Ali.

"Umm…okay…" Tossing the containers into the cooler, he said goodnight and headed down the stairs.

Marcia winked at Hilary and Vincent, and sashayed after him.

Vincent gaped at his mother, then turned to find Hilary grinning at him. Slowly, he returned the smile and waggled his eyebrows. "It's about damn time for those two."

She nestled into him, and he kissed the top of her head. Life was good. The evening sun slanted over the yard, highlighting the contours of the tiny house. He was pleased with the work he'd done for Iris and where it had led.

"Who's going to move into the tiny house?" Her voice brought him out of his reverie.

"What do you mean?"

"Well," she said, moving to sit in his lap, "you're not going to need it because you're moving in with me."

"I am?" He circled his arms around her.

"You are." Sifting her hands through his hair, she nodded. "Boss's orders."

"Yes, ma'am," he said before kissing her.

EPILOGUE

our months later...

Vincent propelled Hilary up the stairs by her hips. She stumbled slightly in the pale, high-heeled shoes that matched her tight pale skirt setting off her blouse's peacock blue. Hands firmly clutching his, she muttered, "Fuck me" under her breath, all the way up. He wasn't sure what he thought about her vocabulary, but it made him smile. "Any time, any place," he said aloud. She stopped muttering.

Since moving in together, their attraction had strengthened. There wasn't a flat surface on which they had not had sex.

Working together made them a team. Keeney Builds was their baby, and a beautiful baby it was. The program was simple: Keeney Works funneled potential students to the college. Instructors from the college taught the construction classes. Students then rotated through six weeks at KBS, working both in the store and with the contractors: Vincent, Tomas, and Carl. Between building a tiny house at the college (which was then donated to the city) and on-the-job training at KBS, students graduated with skills and confidence and were placed in building jobs in and around the community.

Things had changed considerably. After Eddie's arrest, Iris needed a break from KBS, and Fiona found a place for her at Keeney Works, strengthening their bond. During Eddie's trial, she and Fiona held hands, supporting each other when, after his conviction, Eddie was escorted from the courtroom, hurling vitriol at them. In an interesting twist of fate, he entered prison the same day Vincent received word his sentence had been overturned and his record expunged.

Holding down the position of marketing manager for KBS and sitting on both the Keeney Works and Keeney Builds boards, Marcia oversaw the construction of a tiny house community. She gave up her medical billing business when Iris insisted on repaying the money Marcia spent on Vincent's defense. Rumor had it she and Ali were considering moving in together.

No one moved into the tiny house. Instead, it became an artist's studio for Hilary. It was Vincent's idea. He caught her painting one day, supplies spread out over the kitchen table, and approached Iris, who was more than willing to rent it to them. Hilary wasn't interested in selling her paintings but had been approached more than once.

Reaching the top of the stairs, Hilary stood motionless, leaning into Vincent's bulk, expecting him to lead her. He smiled. A woman on top of her game, a woman with multiple offers available, yet she chose *him*. He squeezed her hip, kissed her behind the ear, and steered her down the hall. When her feet went from linoleum to carpet, she halted, turning blindfolded eyes toward him, lips quirked up. "I know where we are, this is Iris's office," she stated with a confident smile. Too uncomfortable with Eddie's ostentatious furnishings, Hilary used the small bookkeeping room as her office, believing the bigger office was being converted to a conference room.

"Nope," he said.

Brow furrowed, lips pinched, she hummed.

He did not give anything away. In their time together, he'd learned he had far more patience than she did. Finally, she huffed out, "I give. Where are we?" Turning her body toward his, he pressed a kiss to her forehead, and removed the blindfold. "You're close. Not Iris's office, yours."

Blinking rapidly, she digested the information. "Are you serious?"

He grinned at her. "As a heart attack."

Frowning, she turned to take in the space that had a completely different vibe. The wall of windows was still there, but the dark wood paneling was gone. In its place was a light, creamy yellow paint. The heavy wooden desk the size of a football stadium was gone. In its place was a free-standing desk at the left of the door, angled toward the center of the room and the windows. To the right of the door was another free-standing desk, angled toward the center of the room and the windows. Directly in front of the door sat a conference table, the end of which bumped up against the window overlooking the floor of KBS, surrounded by six chairs, all anchored to the floor by a jute rug in shades of green and blue.

She moved into the room, turning in a complete circle. Then she stepped close to one wall, examining the photographs hanging there. An old photo of a much younger Iris, Darryl behind her, and Eddie in front, standing in front of KBS, broad smiles on everyone. A photo of Ali—with a complete head of hair—standing next to Darryl beside a display of circular saws. The photos moved through the history of KBS to the present— Vincent, Tomas, and Carl standing in front of a tiny house, surrounded by their first class of students. Hilary shot a smile at Vincent, and took a chair at the conference table. Stroking its surface, she said, "This wood is exquisite. And the table is enormous. Did you bring it in through the windows?"

He grinned and seated himself across from her. "Eddie's desk was too big to move. So I busted it up and repurposed it. Including the huge-ass coffee table he had, there was enough wood to build this table and the two desks."

"One desk is for me, is the other one yours?"

He spun his chair to the side. "Me, Tomas, Carl, Ma—whoever needs the space."

She nodded. "Good idea, which one is—" She glanced at him before rising to her feet and approaching the desk to the left side of the door. Picking up an engraved nameplate, she ran her fingers over the lettering, and raised big eyes to him. "It says Hilary Ortiz. Are you trying to tell me something?"

He came to her, cupped her head with his big hands, stroking a thumb along her cheekbone. "Is that too subtle?"

Her breath hitched on a shaky laugh. "Maybe. I'm not terribly bright, you know."

He touched his lips to her forehead before stepping back, and tilting her head up. "Will you marry me?"

Wrapping her arms around his waist, she met his gaze. "I guess I'll have to. It would be a shame to replace that nameplate."

Growling, he removed her smirk by kissing her deeply.

Perfectly Polished
(a sneak peek)

*F*orty-five minutes.

Fiona Han discreetly turned off the alarm on her smart watch. It wasn't that she was having a bad time, these were nice people. But they were people who knew far too much about her, and she was ready for this day to be over. With a small smile, she said, "I called an Uber. Hilary, thanks for inviting me. I'll talk to you tomorrow."

"I'll drive you home."

Fiona blinked and stared at Tomas Alvarado. "Umm… Thanks, but I'm fine." She waved her phone at him and put it into her purse.

He stood and looked down at her. "I'll drive you home."

Eep!

She did not want to make a scene. He didn't give off the axe-murderer vibe, and her friends were grinning at her like he was perfectly safe, but the man unnerved her.

Marcia Ortiz, a woman in her mid-fifties, and best friend to Fiona's mother-in-law Iris, touched her hand. "You'll be fine," she murmured.

Fiona rose, tucked her purse under her arm and followed Tomas to the stairs leading from Hilary's deck to the driveway. She glanced back at Marcia, who winked at her.

Eep!

Descending the stairs, she was aware of the man behind her. It seemed that for the past two weeks, Tomas had been at her back, without saying a word. Reaching the driveway, she faced three white pick-up trucks bearing the logo for Keeney Building Supplies, the company Iris owned. With a hand to her elbow, Tomas guided her to the one in the middle, distinguishable from the others by the rosary hanging from the rearview mirror, and opened the passenger door. Fiona eyed the distance up to the seat of the truck, then down at her pencil skirt and heels. Then she was up Tomas placed her gently on the seat and reached around to buckle the seat belt.

"I'm not a child!" She glared up at him.

He met her eyes fully for the very first time. "I know you're not." He closed the door and walked around the hood of the truck.

Walk was the wrong word. Tomas prowled like a predator. Did that make her his prey?

He climbed behind the wheel, his presence taking up all the air in the truck. Fiona wanted to open the window, to breathe, perhaps to crawl out.

Placing a large hand on the back of her seat, he ignored her as he turned to back out of the driveway. She could smell him. If she turned her head, ever so slightly, she could brush up against his hand and rub his scent all over her. Where had that thought come from? Fiona shook her head and stared forward.

"I live on Dunlop Street," she told him.

"I know." Tomas met her eyes in the rearview mirror. "I changed the locks on your doors last week."

"Right," she said in a small voice. To keep the douche canoe of her soon to be ex-husband out. Her eyes got big. "I haven't paid you yet! I'm so sorry, I forgot all about it. I can write you a cheque when we get to the house. It's just—"

"It's taken care of."

"Oh." Tomas worked for her mother-in-law. Iris must have had him do it. "Thank you."

He drove in silence.

Not knowing how to converse with someone who clearly didn't like to talk, she leaned her head back, and closed her eyes.

She awoke to see Tomas scouring the word 'cunt' off her garage door.

Fiona threw herself from the truck, stumbling as she hit the ground. She righted herself and flew around the hood of the truck. Tomas whirled and grimaced.

"Ohmygod. Ohmygod. Ohmygod," she chanted, pacing back and forth in front of the garage. Scrawled in dripping red paint, each capital letter was at least two feet high.

Eddie.

He'd chosen a public and humiliating way to get back at her.

Tomas dropped a scrub brush and moved closer to Fiona, stepping between her and the offensive word. He pulled her hands away from her face and squeezed them. "Go into the house. I'm going to get some paint and take care of this."

The setting sun full in his face highlighted the ticking muscle in his jaw. The angry slash of his eyebrows mirrored the angry slash of his mouth, but his eyes were full of concern.

"You can't… Where will you…" she was unable to form a coherent thought, let alone a complete sentence.

He squeezed her hands again, bringing her attention back to him. "I've got this." He released one hand, led her around the truck to retrieve her clutch and fished out her keys. Still holding her hand, he guided her to the front door, unlocked it and led her inside. Closing the door, he pressed her back against it and said, "Stay here."

He waited for her to nod before moving quickly through the house. When he returned and said, "All clear," Fiona released the breath she didn't know she was holding. Once again Tomas took her hand. He led her to the living room and gently pushed her down onto the couch, then sank onto the coffee table facing her. His gaze roamed her face and Fiona took in a deep breath and squared her shoulders, feeling slightly less wobbly.

"I'll be back as soon as I can. Lock the doors behind me and try to relax." He gently unclenched her hands from around her purse, opened it up and pulled out her phone. "Add me to your contacts. I don't think you'll need to, but call me—don't text—call me if you get scared."

Tears welled in her eyes. She tried to blink them away, but one escaped and he wiped it away with a calloused thumb. His eyebrows rose in a silent question which she answered with a quick nod then he got up and moved to the door. She locked the door behind him then headed to the kitchen to find the wine.

For more about this and other upcoming stories, go to www.lynnehancockpearson.com to join her newsletter. You can unsubscribe at any time.

Reviews are like a warm hug, consider leaving one to let others know you enjoyed *#HotAndHandy* and guide readers to my books.

Grand Gestures

Jane will grit her teeth and smile at the snobby and suspicious CFO if it means landing the contract. But she won't put on a dress and definitely not heels.

Fraudulent Trust

How was Delia supposed to know she needed to support herself? That's what trust funds are for.

Holiday Headaches

Sid and Connie are practically strangers but they could be roommates. What could possibly go wrong?

ABOUT THE AUTHOR

Lynne Hancock Pearson writes fun, flirty, feel-good fiction that simmers at a low heat. Stories of people finding their way, even if it takes a while to get there. She lives near Seattle with three finicky felines, two towering offspring, and one long-suffering husband. She is a left-handed middle child who grew up in the Great White North and is a proud member of the Métis Nation of Canada.

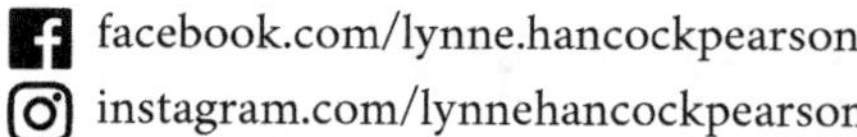

facebook.com/lynne.hancockpearson
instagram.com/lynnehancockpearson

www.ingramcontent.com/pod-product-compliance
Lightning Source LLC
Chambersburg PA
CBHW060304310726
48976CB00007B/2201